The Marauders, the Daughter, and the Dragon

The Azure Archipelago, Volume 1

K.R.R. Lockhaven

Published by Shadow Spark Publishing, 2022.

This is a work of fiction. Similarities to real people, places, or events are entirely coincidental.

THE MARAUDERS, THE DAUGHTER, AND THE DRAGON

First edition. August 20, 2022.

For Alicia.

When the dark clouds are persistent, you are my bright blue sky.

THE MARAUDERS, THE DAUGHTER, AND THE DRAGON

THE AZURE ARCHIPELAGO
BOOK 1

K.R.R. LOCKHAVEN

10% of all proceeds will be donated to the Washington State Council of Firefighters Burn Foundation. They sponsor Camp Eyabsut, a free summer camp for burn survivors ages seven to seventeen. For more information, or to donate directly, go to campeyabsut.org[1]

---

1.   *http://campeyabsut.org/*

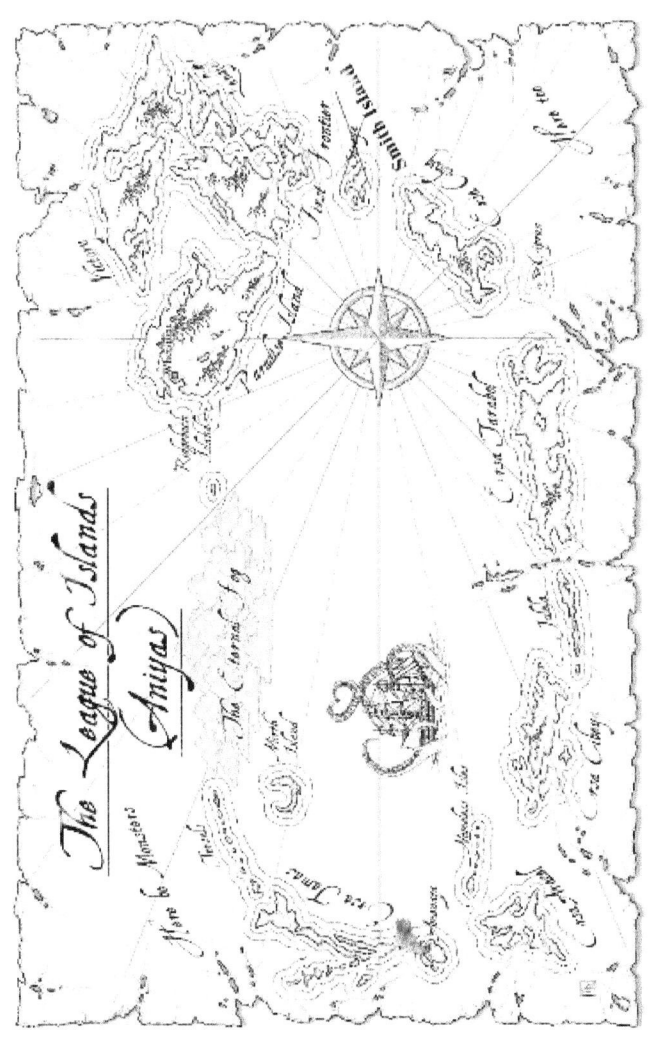

Chapter 1 The Governor's Ship

From a small window on the seaside of the Red Dragon Inn, Azure Brine watched as the massive galleon slowed to a stop near her town's only dock, the flag of the capitol fluttering in the breeze from its stern. Aboard, a methodical crew numbering in the dozens prepared the ship for its landing. Men moved about the rigging like spiders in an intricate web, furling sails and securing innumerable lines, while others along the port rail heaved thick ropes to workers on the dock, who helped pull the ship in to rest.

Azure stared at the scene, spellbound. Nothing like this had ever happened in Barren, and the chaotic crowd circling the calm bay affirmed its strangeness. Both cheers and curses could be heard from Azure's vantage point—about fifty feet above the water, atop sheer white cliffs. Many people waved the light-blue flag of the capitol, several shot pistols in the air, whooping and hollering, while a smaller contingent of protestors held signs over their heads, only one of which Azure could make out. It read, "We Stand With Non-Humans!" Several ciguapa women, and at least one faun, stood with the mostly human dissenters. This, too, was far from normal. She hadn't seen a single ciguapa person in at least five years.

Azure took in the commotion with bittersweet anxiety. On one hand, it was exhilarating to see a spectacle like this in her sleepy hometown. Azure couldn't help but picture herself at the helm of the giant ship, barking orders to her loyal crew. On the other hand, this meant the thing she had been dreading for months had finally come to pass. Reginald Pratt had likely just been elected Governor of the League of Islands.

She tried to push the thought away, letting her eyes wander over the view. The sun had begun its descent into the western sea, and the sky along the horizon was awash in vivid oranges and pinks. The Ring rose out from these brilliant splashes of color and continued in its constant arc across the heavens, upward and northward until the frame of the window cut it off from sight. Further west, the ever-present column of smoke poured from the volcano on Amenaza Island.

A breeze wafted the salty sea air up to where it mingled with the aromatic blooms in the window-side planter, creating the perfect, familiar scent. A little, red-breasted bird hopped along the windowsill, taking in the scene as well.

As Azure leaned out the window to get a better view of the maelstrom below, the door of the inn crashed open, causing her to start and nearly fall from her perch to certain death. She caught herself and turned to see a man with a curled white mustache enter the premises. His white hair, probably a wig, was coiled into rolls along his temples. He wore the red silk cape of the particularly pious—or at least those who wanted to be seen that way—over his expensive-looking white waistcoat and breeches. He had heavy golden chains around his neck, and a golden wand tucked into his red silk belt. Azure hated to judge people based on looks alone, but this was too damned much. This guy was obviously wealthy, biased, and a "Humans First" Pratt follower.

Reginald Pratt had whipped up a religious fervor amongst the devout in the islands, even though Azure doubted he could name all thirty-seven gods.

The man scanned the empty inn, disappointment written on his well-creased face.

"Get me a beer," he said without a hint of warmth.

The little, red-breasted bird flew from the windowsill and alighted on Azure's shoulder. "Do you want me to peck his fucking eyes out?" the bird said as the man sat down.

A smile tugged at the corner of Azure's lips. "No, Robin, that's alright."

"Well... can I?" Robin said as Azure meandered to the taps in the back room.

"We can't attack customers, no matter how much they may deserve it." Azure kept her voice low while pouring the beer.

"But he—"

"Here you go, sir," Azure said in her most monotonous voice, setting the thick-headed beer down just hard enough to slosh some onto the table.

The man looked her up and down without a hint of shame. He seemed unimpressed, not that she cared what he thought.

Azure was short—just over five feet—and, by her own estimation, a little overweight. She wore a home-spun white jacket, with sleeves a touch past her elbows, over her stay and gray skirts, and a dirty white apron tied askew around her waist. Her long black hair was weaved into a simple braid.

She turned away from the man, head held high.

A gunshot followed by a cheering crowd sounded from the street.

Azure was heading back to the window when the man asked, "Why do they call this the Red Dragon Inn?"

After sighing, Azure turned around. "A red dragon was seen flying over our town years ago. Many people saw it, and for a while, this area was a tourist destination. We still have souvenir spyglasses for sale if you want to search the skies."

"Interesting." It was clear the man had barely heard a word she had said. "Well, since there isn't anyone else in here, would you like to hear a proposition?"

"Not really."

Again, the man seemed to not hear her, because he launched right into a spiel. "My name is Paul Sancti, and I am here on behalf of the newly elected Governor Pratt."

So, her guess was right.

"He has authorized me to invite you aboard his magnificent galleon to sail to Whetstone for his inauguration festival."

"Not int—"

"For agreeing to go on this voyage, you will receive a free golden wand."

Azure's knees wobbled beneath her, her breath caught in her throat.

A golden wand cost what she made in an entire year. She had always assumed that she would never be able to afford one, that using magic would always be just beyond her reach. Of course, that wasn't exactly true. She and her parents had scraped enough money together to buy a conjuring wand when she was little, but those were smaller, much cheaper, and made of silver. A golden wand was needed to do any magic beyond basic conjurings.

"Seriously?"

"Yes. If you promise to use it as directed in the inaugural festivities."

"What do you mean by *use it as directed?*" Robin asked the man.

"Not that I owe an explanation to a talking bird, but the young lady will find out all the details once we are underway."

"I... uh... I'll get right back to you." Azure bolted for the back room.

"A golden wand!" Robin said as she landed on a tap. "It's what you've always wanted. Well, that *and* to sail on a real ship."

"I know..." Azure stared out at the galleon, her mind a tangled knot. She watched as workmen with golden wands used magic to detach the figurehead on the front of the ship—a beautifully carved, topless mermaid—while another man on a ladder painted over the ship's name, the *L.O.I. Valorous.*

"So, what are you going to do?" Robin hopped about from tap to tap.

"Well, you're right; I *have* dreamed of going to sea and of practicing real magic. But I'm not sure I could live with myself getting it all... this way." She pointed to the main room.

"That guy out there is a prick, and I know Pratt is even worse. And that thing about using the wand as directed bothers me a bit. But can't you just, like, smile and endure until the crap is over with? I mean, it's kind of a small price to pay to have an actual golden wand, and get to see the Capitol Isles."

"But my dad needs me at the inn. I can't just run off, or I would have a long time ago."

"I'll say what I always say about that sentiment: bullshit. He can hire anyone off the street to do the half-ass job you do around here, and you know I mean that with love. Your heart's just not in it, Az. You were meant for different things."

Outside, through the small window facing the town, a capybara strolled by with a squirrel monkey napping on its back. Azure couldn't keep the corner of her mouth from quirking up, again. This kind of thing was what she loved about this place. There was a lot to love about this place, just not the people.

Nearly everyone on the island was a fervent Pratt follower these days, making interaction with them difficult. Azure tried her best to look past this, to avoid the topic with them, to talk about sailing, or magic, or capybaras, but it always came back around to Pratt, no matter how hard she tried to steer it away.

Azure's mom had died years ago during an anti-faun protest, and ever since, Azure's relationship with her dad had been deteriorating, their once-strong connection all but lost. If she was being honest, she could barely stand to be around him anymore.

Her two best friends had gotten married to each other and weren't coming around as much these days. And as far as romance in Azure's life, there wasn't much to speak of. She was much too busy fantasizing about getting out of The Red Dragon Inn, out of Barren, and off of the Nameless Isles altogether. Unfortunately, her fantasies, like her, lacked direction. Azure felt lost in a place she had known since birth, and the worst part, she didn't truly have her father there for her anymore.

Another gunshot startled her from her reverie.

"Sorry, Robin. I'm thinking. This is a huge decision, out of the deep."

"Yeah, I know," Robin said in a comforting tone as she hopped to the sea-facing window. "What... the unholy fuck... is that?"

Azure peered out to see the workmen who had taken down the mermaid figurehead installing a new carving on the front of the ship. This one was a somewhat realistic depiction of Governor Pratt holding a sword out in front of him in a ridiculous—but apparently meant to be triumphant—pose. The man painting over the old ship's name was just finishing up, too. The new name of the galleon, which made Azure snort with derisive laughter, was *The Savior*.

"He didn't even let them leave the L.O.I. on there. That's him in a coconut shell. It's all about him, always. It's not about the League of Islands at all." Azure turned away from the window. "Okay, forget it. I'm not setting foot on that thing, now."

"I get it." Robin shook her tiny head in disappointment.

Azure stepped back out into the seating area where the man sipped his beer while waiting for her. "I can't go on the trip," she said, hanging her head. "I've got to stay and work at the inn." She didn't know why she avoided telling the man her real reasons, but it was probably rooted in her usual desire to avoid conflict. Speaking her mind was difficult, especially, and seemingly paradoxically, when the topic inflamed her passion, like her hatred of Pratt.

"Well, that's unfortunate. To pass up an opportunity like this is..." Paul finished his beer. "I see the decision has not come easy for you."

"No. It didn't." She felt like she should say more, but also that she didn't owe this guy anything.

"Do you really want something like this low-paying job to keep you from getting something you want?"

"My father and I are co-owners of this inn, so it's not just a job, if that's any of your business."

"Oh, I see. I don't intend to be intrusive, but I still don't understand how you could let your co-ownership of this small inn hold you back from giving the proper respect to the savior of our islands. He—"

"The savior of our islands?" Azure didn't hide the sarcasm or anger in her voice.

"Absolutely. I believe he has been chosen by the gods to lift our race up where we belong."

A near growling noise came from Robin, who bounced irritably on Azure's shoulder.

Azure glared at the man, almost pitying him for the unequivocal stupidity of what he had just said.

"You're not one of those Harm-Phonies, are you?" Paul said, smirking.

Azure rolled her eyes at the toddler-level wordplay. "I don't belong to any political group, but yeah, I tend to agree with the Harmony Faction more than the Cocks." She was, after all, not above using juvenile wordplay herself.

"The Hawks are the only ones keeping the League of Islands together." His level of calm enraged her. "And Governor Pratt is putting humans first to make us stronger."

"Give me a fucking break." Her reluctance to engage in conflict had been buried by her righteous indignation. "He thinks strength can only be gained at the expense of others."

"Others? Like who? The ciguapa, who have been hoarding magic and keeping it from us? Or the fauns, swarming over our islands, taking more than their share? And now there are tales of orcs trickling in, invading our islands, too. And they almost certainly bring dark magics with them. Do we not deserve access to magic, too?"

"We have access to magic! But it's rich assholes like— You know what? I don't know why I'm having this conversation with you. The beer will be half-a-copper."

"His eyes are looking awfully soft and vulnerable," Robin said, not bothering to keep her voice down.

"That's okay, Robin. He'll be on his way, now."

The man chuckled as he stood and fished a copper from his pouch. "The scales have tipped, little lady. Don't let your weak ideas keep you from claiming what every human deserves. Good day." He flipped the copper to Azure, who let it clatter against the stone floor, not taking her eyes off of him.

"What a prick," said Robin as the door shut behind the man.

Azure picked up the coin, then marched to the taps and poured herself a beer. She slumped onto a chair at one of the tables and splashed some beer into a little saucer for Robin, who flew down to the table and began drinking.

"Cheers," Azure said, holding her cup in the air. "To being trapped on this tiny island forever."

Before she could take her first drink the door swung open again. Her father rushed in, an excited grin on his tanned and lined face. A majestic tiger strolled lazily behind him.

"I've got big news," her father said, his movements manic. "I have been selected to go with our newly-elected governor to the Capitol Isles to participate in his inauguration! We're leaving in a few hours!"

Azure chugged her entire beer. "Who's we?"

"Well, of course Thunder Paws is going." He glanced down at the tiger, who was gracefully licking his own privates. "I was hoping that you would go with me, too." He looked at her with a very cautious optimism while holding two golden wands out in front of him.

"Gods damnit." Azure buried her face in her hands.

Chapter 2 The Secret Teacher

"**Y**ou can't be serious," Azure said, her heart pounding.
"Why not?"

"What about the inn?"

"We can afford to close up shop for a month or so. It'll be fine." He glided to the back room and returned with a board, a brush, and a jar of paint. "I was already thinking about the sign I'll post while we're gone." He began painting letters on the board.

"What about..." Azure racked her brain for a mundane excuse, trying her best to hide her disgust with him.

"You see?" her dad said, looking up from his work. "You can't even think of a good excuse not to go. I mean, you've always wanted to take a voyage across the sea and see the Capitol Isles." He began painting again.

"But not like this." Azure's face felt hot.

"Like what?"

Was he truly this oblivious? He knew how she felt about Pratt and his followers, but he acted like all that didn't matter now. "I..." she glanced down at Robin, wanting to focus on anything other than the coming confrontation.

Robin's features took on a knowing determination, with eyes narrowed and head tilted to the side. She took another gulp of beer from her saucer and fluttered down to the ground next to the wall.

"I think I had too much to drink," Robin said with an eye toward the tiger, who was now watching her intently. "I... think I'm... so drunk I prolly couldn't even... fly."

Thunder Paws crouched low to the ground, noiselessly. His whiskers twitched as he stared down his prey.

"I know... what I need," Robin continued. "More bee—"

The tiger pounced with impressive speed and strength.

Robin took wing, zipping up just beyond its reach.

The tiger's momentum carried it forcefully into the wall, rattling the ornamental sconces above every table. It stood on wobbly legs and glared at the gloating bird. "One of these days I'm gonna getcha," Thunder Paws said, his voice a low rumble. "You ain't gonna be nothin' more than a snack, but I'll enjoy the shit out of every chew." The tiger's accent was strange and foreign on the Undering. Azure often wondered where he'd come from.

"You ain't gonna catch shit," Robin said, mocking his drawl. "Yer too fat to catch me."

Robin looked at Azure as she hovered near the ceiling, as if the bird's shenanigans were supposed to have cheered her up. Azure tried to force a smile, but she knew it wasn't convincing. Robin shook her tiny head and landed on the table.

"Done!" her dad said, holding up the sign he had painted.

It read: The Red Dragon Inn Will Be Closed Until Further Notice. May the Gods Bless Our Great New Governor.

"Our great new governor?"

"Yes, Azure, and don't even start right now. He won, so the best thing, the patriotic thing for everyone to do is to get on board."

"To fall in line, you mean."

"Don't be so dramatic. You don't have to associate everything about him with negativity. I know you think he's this horrible person, but that's just not true."

"I don't know him personally, but his ideas are horrible. I'm sure I'd find him horrible if I ever met him." Azure was nearly yelling, now.

"What has he done to make you hate him so much?"

"Well, for one thing, he organized the fucking protest where mom died!" Azure almost never cussed at her dad, but rage had clouded her filter.

"It wasn't his fault the dock collapsed!" her dad shouted.

"But he drove her there. It was his bullshit about invading races that convinced her to go out and protest against people who just needed a little godsdamned empathy."

"Fauns."

"Fucking living beings!" Azure hurled her glass across the inn, smashing it against the front door.

Azure's dad looked at the broken shards of glass. He started to say something but stopped himself.

"You wouldn't have stood for this before." Her voice had lost all fervor.

"Stood for this? What does that even mean?"

"You wouldn't have been such a follower. So ready to forget...everything and buy into someone's bullshit." She shook her head. "You used to be so...I don't know, noble." Was this true, or just the gullible beliefs of a little girl looking up to her infallible father?

"That's the thing, Azure. You act like I'm the one who has changed, but it's you." His eyes were pleading. "You mean well, but you're naïve to the way things are."

"And you, or Pratt, are the final authority on *the way things are*?" Her voice was getting loud, again. "You suddenly have this infuriating inability to empathize with anyone. You know, you used to—" Azure cut herself off. She had almost told him that he used to be her hero, but she found him pathetic now. She could feel a knife running through the threads that tied them together, but she wasn't ready to sever them all.

"I used to what?"

"Nothing." Azure stood and breathed, feeling as if she were looking across the inn at a stranger.

He seemed as if he wanted to press the issue, but turned away, staring at the broken glass strewn across the floor. After a sigh, he turned his gaze back to Azure, a deep sadness in his eyes, and held out one of the golden wands to her.

"I'm not taking that." Azure clenched her jaw, trying not to betray any weakness.

"Come on, Az. The ship's leaving soon. We gotta get on boar—we gotta go." He had pushed his sorrow away, replacing it with a cold resolve.

"So you're choosing Pratt over me, then?"

"It's not like that. Not—"

"Enjoy your little cruise. Leave me out of it. I'll stay back and run the inn for you." Her delivery was monotone.

"I don't—"

"Fuck off!" Rage permeated her entire being. Nothing else mattered aside from her anger. Her eyes tried to well up, but she blinked the tears away, jaw still clenched tight.

Her dad hung his head. For several seconds there was silence as Robin and the tiger looked to him with anxious expectancy. Azure felt like flipping a table over but remained motionless.

"Come on," Azure's dad said to Thunder Paws. He turned and left the inn without another word.

As soon as he was gone, Azure hurried to the back and poured herself another beer, which she chugged before filling up the cup again.

"I'm sorry, Az," Robin said.

"It's fine. It was always going to end up like this between us, anyway." Azure didn't exactly believe what she was saying, but despair had taken hold of her.

When the glass emptied, Azure refilled it. "I'm going to get some air," she told Robin, her voice flat.

"I'll give you a little time." Robin flew away through the sea-facing window.

Outside, the night was still. The faint scent of petrichor, a remnant from a midday cloudburst, filled the twilit air. The clouds had all drifted away, and the darkening sky was a theater of stars on either side of the pale blue glow of the Ring. Frogs chanted a rhythmic hymn in the forest as sounds of celebration made their way up from the dock.

Another gunshot.

Azure leaned against the side of the inn and slid down to the ground. She took a gulp of beer and rested her head against the siding. From the corner of her eye, she spotted markings along the white door frame—her height tracked from the time her parents had bought the inn until she had reached her full height of about five foot two inches. Her eyes were in line with a marking that read: *Azure: 7 years old!*

Memories flooded her half-drunk mind. She could almost feel the block of wood on top of her head. She could hear her dad saying, "Are you standing on your tippy toes? No? Are you sure? Or did you get a golden wand? Are you making yourself float an extra inch with magic?"

Azure's face pinched into a grimace, tears spilled down her cheeks. She dropped her glass, its contents pouring out on the ground where she used to stand and be measured. She let out loud, ugly sobs, not caring if anyone walked by. She hadn't cried in a long time—ever since her mom had died—and the years of buildup were now gushing out.

"Why are you crying?" a small voice said.

Azure looked up to see a little girl standing sideways in the road. Although blurry through tears, the kid looked a lot like Azure's younger self with light brown skin, dark brown eyes, and shiny black hair, pulled back into a ponytail. Azure found herself answering the child's question honestly. "I just had a big fight with my dad. He's leaving on that big ship in the bay."

"Oh." The girl giggled and tilted her head away from Azure. "So why are you sitting there crying?"

"Because, kid, I feel like this may be the end of our relationship, which used to be really good." Azure wiped her eyes with the backs of her hands.

The kid paused, seeming to concentrate. "Well, how is sitting there crying going to help?"

Azure focused on the little girl, who had a streak of purple berry juice smeared across her cheek. When the girl flashed her a smile as bright as a sunbeam, the *Epiphany* flashed in Azure's mind; the part in which Saga, the King of Gods, said, "Everyone you meet in life is a secret teacher, sent to give you a message, a clue, an idea, inspiration, a warning, direction. The gift they have for you will appear when you make yourself aware of their value."

The *Epiphany* was what people called the speech given to humankind by the King of Gods, Saga, over a century ago. Azure, although not particularly devout herself, had memorized the entire thing, both because she believed in its message, and, maybe more importantly, because she often used it to counter so-called religious people when they spouted off bullshit about non-humans, or gay people, or whoever else they targeted with their venom.

"Bye. Hope you feel better." The girl skipped off into the night.

"Bye." Azure rubbed her temples and burped.

"Nice one!" Robin said as she flew in for a landing on the dirt.

"Hey, Robin. Where were you?"

"Just...taking a lap around the bay. It's pandemonium down there."

"Yeah." Azure looked up at the Ring. It was always shockingly beautiful on a clear night, no matter how much time she had spent staring at it. "I don't want to lose my dad to the same shit I lost my mom to."

"I understand." Robin hopped onto Azure's knee.

"I mean, it could be a really long time before I ever see him again. He could die, or just decide to never come back. My last words to him could be, 'Fuck off.'"

Robin nodded. "So...?"

Azure stood and brushed the dirt off her butt. Robin flew up to her shoulder.

"I'm glad you decided to go before the boat left," Robin said. "I don't think you'd have ever forgiven yourself if you hadn't."

"Did I decide to go?"

"Didn't you?"

Azure took a deep breath. "Screw it."

She swung open the door of the inn, hurried to collect her coin purse from a hidden drawer, locked up, and took off down the road to the dock.

She didn't know what she was going to do or say, but she knew she had to do something.

Upon arrival, Azure found that the bay really was in pandemonium. Raucous crowds had swarmed in and covered the beach. Several people stood on the statue of Fobos, hanging onto his massive arms, both of which held swords meant to sow fear in would-be invaders. But the dock was completely clear, save for a muscular, rather Fobos-looking man barring access to it.

A bell sounded from the deck of the ship and a cheer rose from the large crowd of people on board. Azure sprinted to the dock and came to a panting stop in front of the muscular man.

"None shall pass," he said, holding out a meaty hand and glaring down at her.

Chapter 3 The Dock Guard

"I have to get on that ship."

"That sounds like something that is firmly not my problem." The man straightened his spine, becoming even taller.

Azure looked the guard up and down, assessing him for weaknesses. Unfortunately, he didn't seem to have any. He was at least six feet tall and rippled with muscle—he looked like a drawing out of a history book of a warrior back on the Continent. He had a conjuring wand, a pistol, and a sharp-looking cutlass tucked into his belt.

"This guy...a rich, religious guy...uh...Paul, Paul Sancti invited me on the voyage."

"Well, where's your wand, then?"

"Oh, he said he ran out and had to get another one from the ship."

"He didn't mention anything like that to me."

"Well, he might have had one too many beers up at my inn." Azure pointed up the cliffs to the Red Dragon Inn, barely visible in the Ringlight. "See that inn up there? That's where Paul recruited me."

"I think the real owner of that inn is already on the ship."

"Yeah, exactly. I'm his daughter and I co-own the inn with him."

"I don't know." The guard glanced back at the ship. Crew members were hoisting ropes from the dock to the deck with magic. "Sounds kind of fishy. They weren't just inviting anyone along. I don't remember seeing any women as young as you get on board. Are you really a follower of Governor Pratt?"

"Why else would I want on this ship?"

"That's awfully suspicious, answering a question with a question." Again he looked back at the ship. "Oh! I know. If you're really the devout type that Paul would have recruited, who is the God of... revenge?"

"Rinye, the Crusher of Dreams."

"How about the other God of revenge?"

"Neme, the Spiteful."

The God of... sea warfare?"

"Zriton, the Collector of Wreckage."

"The God of land warfare?"

"Zares, the Collector of Bones."

"The God of murder?"

"Also Zares, when known as the Silent Blade."

"Damn. I thought I'd get you with that one." He scratched his chin. "How about the God of violence?"

"Zia."

"The God of violent anger?"

"Otios."

"The God of violent death?"

"Xeres. The boat is moving now. Can I please just get by?"

"Well, I guess you passed my little test, but the ship is full and setting sail as we speak. I was told to not let anyone else on board."

"Eyes?" Robin said from Azure's shoulder.

"Not quite yet," she whispered back.

Azure surveyed the dock, looking for a way around the guard. The ship began separating from the dock. Soon it would be out in the bay, beyond reach.

"Look behind you! A three-headed monkey!" Azure pointed with an expression of genuine shock.

"Yeah, that's just my conjured companion, Milton." The three-headed monkey climbed up the man's frame and sat on his shoulder.

Azure was getting desperate. "Can you swim?" she asked the guard.

"Yeah, why?"

"Can Milton swim?"

"Of course."

Azure turned her head. "Don't hurt his eyes but get him."

"Huh?" the guard said.

Robin leaped from Azure's shoulder and darted for the man's face. He threw both his arms up in an attempt to guard his eyes. The monkey screeched in triplicate and mimicked its conjurer.

Azure charged forward and pushed the guard with all her strength. At first he didn't budge, and Azure felt as if she were pushing against a brick wall. But as Robin continued her relentless attack, Azure picked up one of the man's legs and drove him backward into the water. She nearly fell in on top of him, teetering on the edge of the dock, arms windmilling, but was able to right herself before she tipped into the bay.

Robin let out a sadistic, victorious laugh as she hovered above the swimming man and monkey.

The crowd along the beach jeered and swarmed onto the dock. Azure couldn't tell if they were coming to get her or trying to board the ship. Either way, she was not in a great position.

"Let's go!" Azure took off toward the moving ship.

As she approached, she tried to gauge the distance from ship to dock. It seemed about nine or ten feet away, maybe more. She scanned the hull, looking for anything to grab onto. With a grunt of maximum effort, Azure jumped from the edge of the dock and latched her hands around a hanging rope ladder. She barreled into the side of the ship, barely able to keep her grip, then glanced behind at the advancing crowd. A few of the faster members were almost at the end of the dock. Azure scurried up the rope ladder, willing the ship to move faster.

The young man in the lead made a leap for the ladder but fell woefully short and plummeted into the cool water. A woman tried to keep herself from jumping at the last second but fell into the bay between the dock and the man.

Azure continued up the ladder. Her foot slipped on the wet rope and she just caught herself by hooking an elbow over a woven rung. Hanging by her elbow, she closed her eyes, took a deep breath through her nose, rededicated herself to carefully climbing the ladder, and blew the air out through pursed lips. On the way up, she wondered if anyone on the ship had seen any of the commotion below. She hoped they'd all been too busy celebrating to notice.

As she neared the top of the hull, Azure slowed down and peeked one eye over the rail. The vacant eyes of a human skull stared back at her.

"Hello," the skull said, its jaw articulating in surreal, unnatural movements.

Azure shrieked and inadvertently pushed herself back. Before she could correct her mistake, she had fallen beyond the reach of the rope ladder. She threw out her arms, grasping nothing but warm night air. Her foot became tangled in the ladder, and her fall into the dark water below cut short as she slammed into the hull of the ship, upside down. All air was forced from her lungs. She hung gasping for breath, dangling from one painful, twisted ankle.

With difficulty, Azure craned her neck to look up to the rail. The skull—apparently affixed to the top of some sort of horrible re-animated skeleton—hung over the side of the ship.

"Yeah, that's the response I'm all-too familiar with these days," the skeleton said, its voice glum and dejected. "I don't blame you. I'm a hideous creature and should probably be at the bottom of the sea as opposed to the deck of this beautiful galleon."

It reached out the bony fingers of a skeletal hand toward her. "But if you're not too terribly disgusted by me, let me help you up from there."

Chapter 4 On Board

A zure felt her foot begin to slip. After a heartbeat of hesitation, she engaged her core and pulled herself up, lunging for the skeleton's hand. Its grip was cold, but strong. In one fluid motion, it pulled her over the rail and onto the ship's deck.

Azure looked up at her savior in anxious awe. It was a fully formed skeleton wearing a green vest and knee-high leather boots.

"Thank you," Azure said in a whisper, finding it hard to speak.

"You're welcome." The skeleton's voice was decidedly male, and consistently gloomy. "My name is Elijah. But you probably don't care what my name is. You'd probably rather run away screaming than talk to me for one more second. I get it."

"I'm Azure." She found herself instantly taken with Elijah, disarmed by his constant self-deprecation. "Thanks again for helping me."

"No problem. Glad I could be of use to someone."

Azure didn't know what to say, still shaken from everything that had just happened and the fact that she was talking to a skeleton.

"Awkward silence is pretty standard in conversations with me." Elijah sighed. "Hey, you haven't seen a golden medallion about the size of a saucer with a capybara etched on the front, have you?"

"No, sorry."

"Yeah, I fig—"

"Get away from that young woman!" A group of people, led by Paul Sancti, hurried across the deck to Azure. Paul pushed Elijah to the side. The skeleton hung his head and skulked away. "It's you, from the inn," Paul said. "I guess you've decided I was right after all?"

"No, I—"

"Do you know this stowaway?" The plump figure of Governor Pratt pushed to the front, a sardonic grin between chubby cheeks. A white wig curled into rolls at the temples sat atop his head. He looked like what Azure's dad used to refer to as a dandy. Frills and lace seemed to have been forced onto his clothing wherever it could fit.

"Yes, sir," Paul Sancti said. "I had tried to recruit her earlier, but she... spurned me."

"Well, everyone deserves the chance to have a change of heart, do they not?" The small crowd that had gathered around all nodded their assent. Pratt turned to Azure. "You must have really wanted to be a part of this, didn't you? And I completely understand."

"I—"

"You know what?" Governor Pratt now addressed the crowd. "I say, let her stay. She's pretty. I mean, she's too short and could probably stand to lose a few pounds, but she's pretty enough. Plus, we are running a few short of what we'd hoped for on this island. So, why not?"

"Running short?" Azure said, curious about his comment despite herself. "The beach is packed with people who were dying to get on this ship."

Governor Pratt chuckled as if at some inside joke. "Those unwashed masses? I don't think so, little lady. Only civilized people are allowed on this voyage. We need people who are going to be able to use powerful magic. But I'm getting ahead of myself. Welcome aboard, uh... What's your name?"

"Azure Brine."

"Azure!" Her dad pushed through the crowd. He didn't look like he knew whether he was excited or embarrassed.

"Oh, you know our little stowaway?" Governor Pratt said, still playing to the crowd.

"Yes, sir. She's my daughter."

"And they say that I don't bring families together." The crowd laughed, half-heartedly, as one. "What's your name?"

"John. John Brine, sir." His nervous smile vanished as he turned to Azure. "What are you doing, Az? Why are—"

"You know what?" the Governor interrupted. "You two should join me in the captain's quarters for dinner. Let's say, tomorrow night. Deal?"

"Of course, sir," Azure's dad said. "It would be an honor."

"Well, it's set. But for now, we've guests to welcome." Governor Pratt put an arm around Azure's dad and led him toward a small stage that had been erected on the deck.

They didn't get more than ten yards, though, before Pratt tripped over a terrified capybara and almost fell on his face. The capybara squealed as it scurried away.

"Get that filthy fucking thing off this ship!" the governor roared to Paul.

"But, sir..." Paul lowered his eyes. "It's considered bad luck to not have a capybara on board throughout a voyage."

"I don't buy into idiotic superstitions. I want that thing overboard." Pratt turned to Azure's dad, who was still under the governor's arm. "Didn't I see you boarding with some sort of horrible, conjured tiger?"

"Yes, sir." John seemed embarrassed by the fact.

"Feed the filthy thing to this guy's tiger if you have to. I just want it gone."

"Right away, sir." Paul barked orders to catch and dispose of the animal to Elijah, who nodded and took off after it.

The small crowd following the governor mixed into the larger crowd assembled around the stage. There must have been hundreds of people on board. Azure didn't budge, trying to take in everything that was happening.

On the stage, the governor took a seat while Paul Sancti approached a podium.

"Honored guests," Paul said, his voice amplified by some kind of magic, "as you can see, we are about to leave the safety of the bay and enter into the Mirror Sea. So we must pray to the gods for a safe journey." He bowed his head for several seconds of silence while fidgeting with the heavy gold chains around his neck. "We must never forget that the gods upon the Ring are always watching. It is said that Narkis, the great God of Pride, uses the calm waters inside our ring of isles as a looking glass. These are the very waters we now sail upon. And as we sail, let us fear and praise all of the gods, not just Saga. Let us remember the gods of strength and power and war, the gods who have given these islands to us. Let us never forget their ancient wisdom and great deeds.

"And now, speaking of wisdom and great deeds, it is my absolute pleasure to introduce for the first time, Governor Reginald Pratt!"

The crowd roared.

Someone stepped out from what Azure assumed were the captain's quarters. A ciguapa woman, her indigo skin radiant in the combination of Ring and torchlight. She wore a green vest, similar to the one Elijah wore, over a white, V-necked blouse and shorts cut off at the top of her muscular thighs. Deep blue hair framed her stunning features. It curled around her graceful body, down to her knees. Like most, if not all ciguapa women, she was absolutely gorgeous, but more than that, she was brilliant, vibrant—she gave off an aura, an ambience.

The woman closed her eyes, drew a deep breath, then strode back inside.

"Hello from the new Governor of the League of Islands!" Pratt shouted, his voice also magnified. "I won! When so many thought it couldn't be done. I won!" He paused for applause, playing to the crowd for what felt to Azure like several minutes. "So, we all know what I'm going to do now that I am governor: I'm going to save these islands, and I'm going to do it by putting humans first. We...will...once...more...be...strong!" More applause. "But first things first, I want to talk to you lucky few about the voyage we are embarking upon. This will be unlike anything that has ever been done before. With your help, my inauguration will be the stuff of history books. I'll save the best for later, though. For now, let me tell you how this is going to go.

"We are going to pick up even more loyal followers from several other islands on our way to Whetstone. We'll stop at Smith Island!"

The crowd cheered.

"First Frontier!"

Another cheer.

"And Paradise Island, to our capital of Whetstone, where my inauguration will be held!"

The cheering grew louder.

"Then comes the most exciting part." He paused, a sinister grin covering his face. "We will continue on to a very special, secret location where my hold over the islands will be solidified."

An excited murmur swept through the crowd.

Azure wondered what he could possibly mean by this statement.

"On our way, we will veer north to avoid the kraken that has strayed from the open ocean beyond our ring of islands and lurks in the south. This will take us to within sight of Mirth Island. Well, I call it the lost island because it's full of lonely, lost souls." He made a gesture of disgust. "I say they can have it. I, for one, am heading for greater, godlier things."

Most of the heads in the crowd bobbed in approval.

"Our bearing increases the possibility of encountering pirates, but I assure you, this galleon has enough fire power to repel even Captain Roberts. Seventy-four heavy cannon, and, as you'll soon see, a governor with powerful magic at his disposal."

The crowd response was half cheers, half murmurs.

"Another sight you will get to see due to our northernly course is the Eternal Fog."

A stronger murmur.

"I heard there's a rumor going around that I penetrated the Eternal Fog and actually found Dragon Island."

The crowd wasn't sure whether to laugh or cheer. Governor Pratt rubbed a gaudy ring on the middle finger of his right hand.

"You might have also heard a rumor that I had a fierce red dragon by my side at the time. Are those rumors true?" He shrugged, waiting an awkward length of time before speaking again. "Anyway, this voyage will give us two weeks to practice magic with your new wands!"

The loudest cheer yet.

"Now, we all know that wand magic is limited. It's limited because of, well, let's not get into all of that just yet. Let's just say that things are going to change now that I'm here. But for the time being, you can only do so much with those beautiful golden wands I gave you."

"You'll be able to shoot bolts, like lightning, lift things without touching them, and create wonderful illusions!"

The crowd was giddy with excitement..

"But I don't want to give away everything we're going to do with them, yet."

Another murmur.

"For now, let me leave you with a demonstration."

The governor pulled a wand from his belt and raised it in the air.

"What the?" Robin said, twitching, on Azure's shoulder.

"What is it?" Azure asked.

"I..." Robin's winged flapped, unnaturally. "I can't stop..."

Robin jumped from Azure's shoulder and flew to a spot over the top of the stage. There she was joined by hundreds of other birds coming from every direction.

They began to fly in a giant circular pattern over the ship. Then, the circle morphed into several smaller shapes. Words began to take form in the Ringlight. The birds spelled out *Governor Pratt* in fancy script over the enrapt crowd.

Azure glanced at Pratt, whose gaudy ring gave off a faint green glow.

When the demonstration was over, Robin darted back to land on Azure's hand as the other birds scattered. Governor Pratt continued to play to the crowd, but Azure focused on her friend.

"What in the thirty-seven hells just happened to me?" Robin said in a daze.

"Do you not remember?"

"No, I remember. I just couldn't control myself. I *had* to fly up there and move around like I did. It was the strangest thing I've ever felt in my life."

"Are you okay?"

"Yeah. I'm fine, now." She stared out at the horizon. "The only thing that makes me feel even slightly better is that I dropped a little treat down on one of their gaping faces while I was up there. Whatever was controlling me wasn't in control of everything, if you know what I mean."

Azure didn't know what to say.

"I mean I shit on one of those assholes."

"I know, Robin. I just..." Azure was struck silent. Her mind went back to the glowing ring on Pratt's finger.

"You know," Robin said, "I always bite my tongue and keep my beak shut because I know that keeping the custom you had at the inn is important, but now that we're going out into the great wide world, I'm not gonna hold back anymore. This guy can go fuck himself as far as I'm concerned."

Azure burst into laughter, then covered her mouth.

"Do you remember when you first conjured me?" Robin asked.

"Yeah. I was six, right?"

"Yes. And what did you ask me after the first fun day we spent together?"

"I asked you if you wanted me to return you to your world."

"And I said, 'No, thank you, but I'm good right here. I lived in a shithole before. I was constantly facing starvation and murder by hawks. I'll stay right here with you forever if that's okay? I like you, and I'll rain down hell on anyone who ever messes with you.'"

Azure laughed again. "Yeah, of course I remember that, but—"

"All I'm saying is, that still stands. Whatever we just got ourselves into, I've got your back."

"Thanks, Robin. I've got yours, too."

"On to adventure," Robin said, raising a wing.

"On to adventure." Azure smiled down at her friend.

Chapter 5 Murder on the Galleon

With her senses overloaded, Azure didn't really feel like talking to her dad just yet, so she hurried across the deck to the port side of the galleon as the crowd began to disperse. There she noticed the re-animated skeleton, sitting on a barrel and resting his bony elbows on the rail.

"Hello, Elijah." She tried to lean into his peripheral vision and wave.

Elijah startled and spun to face her.

"Sorry for scaring you," Azure said. "I just wanted to say hello, again."

"I should be the one apologizing to you. My presence alone is scary."

"I don't think so." Azure playfully rolled her eyes in an attempt to confirm her words. "And I wanted to thank you again for helping me."

"Oh."

"This is my friend, Robin."

"Hello, Robin. Ever seen a cursed human skeleton before?"

"Hello, Elijah. Can't say that I have."

"I'm sorry you had to dispose of that poor capybara." Azure hung her head.

Elijah looked around the immediate vicinity. "I didn't dispose of anything," he said in a low voice. "It's hidden in my room. Only my co-worker Roger and I know. Well, now you, too."

"That's great! I'm so glad to hear it."

"I know enough about curses and bad luck to know not to mess with them. Plus, I don't have the heart—" he looked down at his empty ribcage, "—literally and figuratively, to kill an innocent creature, anyway."

"If I'm not being too forward," Azure said, "what *are* you doing here on this voyage?" She immediately felt like a jerk for asking.

"Pretty stupid, right? For a not-exactly-human to be on the same ship with this crowd." He grabbed and lifted both sides of his vest. "But I'm working. Well, kind of. The captain is a friend of mine, and he's allowing me to work as an able-bodied sailor, ironically enough."

Azure wasn't sure if that was supposed to be a joke or not.

"To answer your question more truthfully, I had a strong inkling that I should be aboard this ship. I can't really explain it, but my intuition told me this was the place to be. My intuition is usually wrong, of course. I've been following bogus inklings for damn near a hundred years, now."

"Really?"

"Yeah."

"So you were cursed? How did that happen?"

"You want to hear my story? I wouldn't blame you if you didn't. I can make even the most thrilling stories sound boring, and it's probably not all that interesting anyway."

"Of course I want to hear it. And I seriously doubt it will be boring."

"Alright. I warned you." He took a deep breath, even though he had no lungs. "I see that confused look. So, no, I don't actually breathe, but old habits die really hard. Anyway, my story starts about a hundred years ago...

"I was a sailor on a merchant ship when we were attacked by pirates. The pirates captured me and gave me a choice between dying and joining their crew. So, being young and opposed to death, I joined them and became a pirate myself.

"Now, I have to backtrack a bit and tell you about something else. See? I'm no good at stories. I never know where to start, and I have no idea how to seamlessly add in backstory.

"Anyway, there was this pirate in the very early days of the human colonization of the islands, before they were even renamed the League of Islands. This pirate *loved* capybaras. Like, really loved them. He had many as pets on board his ship, and he treated them better than he treated his crew. He even printed pictures of them on the gold he would steal. It became his trademark.

"Well, eventually the newly-formed government caught up to him. They chased him and his crew to a small island in the northwest of the ring of islands. He had just enough time to offload his treasure and put a curse upon it. Those were the days when the Old Magic was still barely clinging to life.

"The pirate was caught on the island. He and his crew were all hanged. But the government couldn't reclaim any of the treasure due to the curse, so they left it there, uncharted.

"Now, we are back to the part where I was forced to join this other pirate crew. Another brilliant transition....

"They had stolen a map to the small island where the treasure was hidden from a government office or something. And, disregarding the curse, we went and found the treasure.

"So, needless to say, the curse turned every one of us into these horrible skeletal beings.

"Oh yeah, I forgot to say that when we took the treasure from the island, a terrifying wraith appeared and said, 'Any man who dare take this gold shall become an accursed monster until every last piece of the treasure sits on the bottom of the sea.' I know that's a pretty cliché curse, but that's what happened." He shrugged his skeletal shoulders.

"Seeing ourselves as skeletal monsters, our crew took a quick vote and decided to dump the treasure directly into the sea. But one greedy guy snatched this big medallion and escaped. We've been trying to track him down ever since. I've lost contact with all of my accursed crewmates, but they're out there somewhere. Most are still searching, I think, but many have given up. I'm near giving up too, but I thought I'd follow one last stupid inkling."

Elijah shrugged. "Well, that's my story. I really ended with a bang, didn't I? You'd think after living for over a hundred years I'd be better at telling it."

"That was a very interesting story, and you told it really well," Azure said. "I'm so sorry that you've been cursed. If there's anything I can do to help, just let me know."

"Yeah." Robin nodded in agreement.

"Thanks, but I'm pretty much doomed to an eternity as a bony abomination."

Azure struggled for something to say in the awkward silence that followed.

"Oh." Elijah pointed a finger skyward. "The whole lucky capybara superstition started with that captain way back then, if you didn't already know that."

"Really? I always wondered where that came from."

"Yeah." Elijah nodded.

Another silence.

"What were things like back then? On the islands, before the war?" Azure asked.

Elijah rubbed the back of his head. "We humans had been fighting wars back on the Continent for as far back as anyone could remember. It was in our blood. We saw ourselves as sharpened weapons, ready to take on any threat. But when you're an arrow, everything starts to look like a target. The ciguapa here on the islands were relatively peaceful, but humans saw another enemy." He shook his head.

"At first, things were great, but..." Elijah looked across the deck to an imposing man in a long red coat and tricorn hat who manned the ship's wheel. "Well, I'm sure you know your history. I'm sorry, but I'd better get going. I should probably be working on the guest cabins."

"Alright. I'll talk to you later, Elijah."

The skeletal figure trudged to a staircase and disappeared belowdecks. About a minute later, the beautiful ciguapa woman followed him down, carrying a large tray of food.

Azure scanned the crowd for her dad and found him searching for her on the other side of the ship. She called to him, and when he heard her, he ran over to greet her, wearing a cautious smile.

"I am so glad you decided to come, Az." He handed her one of the golden wands.

Azure stared at it in her hand. She could hardly believe she was holding an actual, magical wand.

Through force of will she pulled her eyes away from the wand. "Well, I couldn't let you leave after yelling at you like I did. I just... I don't even know why I'm here, really." She considered apologizing to him, giving the wand back, and going home, but it was too late for that now. It wasn't like she could jump overboard and swim back to Barren. And if she was being honest, giving the wand back was something she wanted to avoid, preferably forever.

"This is great. I think you're finally going to see why the laws that Governor Pratt is going to enact are going to be so good for us."

Anger made Azure's heart bound and muscles tighten, but she tried not to show it. "I don't think laws always set the distinction between right and wrong, and I don't think that I am better, or more deserving of happiness, than any other being on the islands."

"But you will grow out of these kinds of thoughts. You will see, someday soon, I hope, that these laws are being put in to place for a reason, and we can't let everyone walk all over us, or we'll lose everything we've worked to attain. It may not be what you want to hear, but the world is harsh. We have to fight for what is ours or lose it all."

"Not at the expense of others. I'll never believe that bullshit."

Azure's dad sighed. "Sometimes I wish we'd never read you so many stories when you were younger. They fill your head with unrealistic images of harmony and love and adventure. They soften your heart, which is fine for a child. A child needs a soft heart until she has grown up and is ready to see the world for what it is."

"Life *is* about harmony and love and adventure, you—" Azure cut herself off before calling him a name. "You know, when I was a child, you always discouraged my dreams of being a ship's captain. I've never understood why you'd want to crush your kid's dreams like that."

"I just—"

"And by the way, the world is the way it is because people like Governor Pratt make it this way."

"There you go, blaming everything on him. Our new governor is what is right with the world. He is unafraid to say what needs to be said, and do what needs to be done. He wants nothing more than to secure a good life for you, for us. How can that be a bad thing?"

"I don't think he cares about us at all. I think he's only out for himself. To make himself more powerful, and richer."

"What evidence do you have?"

"Literally everything he does and says." Azure was losing her temper, again, and really regretting her decision to catch the ship. "You know, I can't believe you. We have this awful fight and you just storm off. Then I risk my damned life to get on this ship and you immediately start in on me with your political bullshit."

"I'm sorry, Az." He looked sincere. "I didn't mean to, and I was heartbroken about our fight. I didn't want to leave you that way. But you're a grown woman, now, and I—"

A scream issued from belowdecks.

A man rushed out, fought his way through the crowd to Governor Pratt, and whispered something in his ear. The governor looked surprised as he followed the man across the deck and down the stairs.

The crowd was abuzz with excited conversation.

"What do you think that was about?" Azure's dad said.

"I don't know." Azure hoped it didn't have anything to do with poor Elijah.

Several minutes later, Governor Pratt reappeared and made his way back up to the podium.

"There has been a murder on board," he announced.

The crowd gave a collective gasp.

"Rest assured our best people are looking into it. As of now there are no suspects, but I assure you, justice will be done." He stopped and seemed to consider what else he was going to say. The decision didn't appear to come easy. He narrowed his eyes down to slits and rubbed both temples with one hand. "There are nefarious forces here that clearly don't want me...or us, to succeed. We must remain vigilant against any conspirators who want to stop the glorious things I'm going to do before I have the chance to begin them."

He sighed, in what Azure took to be a poor bit of acting. His body language tried to tell the story of someone who was very upset, but his eyes remained untroubled.

"This makes what we're doing even more important. But I must warn you, when we get to the Capitol Isles, I shall ask you to do something for our cause. This will be difficult and possibly a little dangerous. I wouldn't ask you if I didn't think you were completely capable, and our cause wasn't absolutely crucial to our continued existence as humans on these islands. Are you with me?"

The crowd roared in approval.

Chapter 6 Wand Class

The next morning, Azure awoke feeling seasick. She rushed upstairs and burst into the fresh air of the deck before leaning against the rail, trying not to puke. As she stared out at the horizon to the north, she thought she could just make out the mirage-like image of another island. Maybe it was Mirth Island. She'd heard lots of stories that made it seem like an impossibly fun fantasy land, and wished she could see it for herself someday.

With visions of mirth in her mind, Azure took several deep breaths and spit a mouthful of thick saliva overboard, already starting to feel better.

Absentmindedly, she pulled out her coin purse from a pocket sewed into her skirts and counted her money. Seven and a half coppers. Not an amount that would get her very far. She wished she would have grabbed the silver she had hidden under the taps.

"You alright?" Robin said, yawning, as she landed on the rail.

"Yeah. I guess the water was a little rough last night. And being cramped up inside..."

"I hear you. I spent the night out under the Ring, perched on the mizzen-mast."

"You just wanted to say mizzenmast."

"Ha! You know me too well."

Azure spit over the rail, again. She thought back to the night before, and the panic that had ensued after Pratt announced there'd been a murder. People immediately began speculating that the non-humans on board were to blame. Not wanting to hear a word of this rhetoric from her dad's lips, Azure had gone belowdecks to find an unused room. A cute, but giddy, crew member named Roger helped her find a room that would have been more appropriately dubbed a closet. But, as tired as she was, Azure curled up and drifted off to sleep to the gentle rocking of the sea.

"Beautiful morning," Robin said, bringing Azure back to the present.

"Yeah." The sun reflected across the rippling water, creating sparkles of dancing light for as far as Azure could see. Puffs of pure white clouds made striking contrasts against a cerulean sky that was a deeper blue than she had ever known. As she took in the scene, the movement of the boat became soothing again rather than puke-inducing.

"I wonder what kinds of birds we're going to see," Robin said, breaking Azure's reverie.

"I don't know. There were an awful lot of them that flew in last night."

"Yeah, but I didn't get a chance to check any of them out, being hypnotized and all."

"Check them out?"

"Yeah, you know, a bird's got her needs, right? I was thinking, a little fling while we're out of town wouldn't be such a bad thing."

Azure chuckled. "I'll keep an eye out for you."

Turning away from the rail, Azure searched the deck for Elijah, but he was nowhere to be found.

"Hey... it's Azure, right?" Roger approached, wearing his green crew member vest.

"You nailed it, Roger."

"Is this your first time on a big ship?"

"Yeah." Azure felt her face get warm, embarrassed about her motion sickness.

"I remember my first time. We sailed up along the Torsals, where they disappear into the Eternal Fog."

"Where orcs have settled?" Azure asked, both frightened and thrilled at the idea.

"Oh, you know about that?" Roger seemed to be trying his absolute best to appear laid-back. "Yeah, we saw orcs up that way."

"You saw orcs?" Azure blurted.

"Yeah. They're huge, and they've got these big tusks sticking up out of their mouths. They have gray skin and carry these giant scimitars, and their arms look like gorillas' arms."

"Have you seen a gorilla, too?"

"Well, just in old drawings from the Continent. But I have seen orcs." Roger's chin reached for the sky.

"Did you talk to any of them?"

"Uh, no. And if you saw one, you wouldn't want to talk to it either. I mean, I've been a lot of places and seen a lot of things. I'm a pretty tough guy, but those orcs were terrifying."

"Oh." Even though his bragging was a bit much, Azure was jealous of Roger's life.

"Did I hear you two talking about orcs?" a tall man in fancy clothes said.

"Yeah," Roger replied.

"Can you believe they're trying to give orcs the right to vote in our elections, now?" the man said, incredulous. "Seriously, it's bad enough that ciguapas and fauns get to vote, but orcs? What's next, capybaras?"

Azure hated this man as fast as she'd ever hated anything, but she didn't respond.

"Oh, I don't know anything about all of that," Roger said. "I was just telling her I saw some orcs, like, in real life."

"And can you believe they're still trying to figure out this supposed mystery about who murdered that guy?" the man said as if he didn't hear Roger's response.

"Uhh," said Roger.

Azure remained tight-lipped.

"It's obvious; the ciguapa or that skeleton monster did it. The only mystery is figuring out which one of them it was, unless they were working together, which is also very likely."

"Exactly," said a passerby.

"I gotta go, Roger," Azure said, seeing her dad coming up from belowdecks, and wanting to get away from the asshole who had taken over the conversation. "I'll chat with you later."

"Oh." Roger seemed surprised. "Okay. We'll chat later, then."

Azure caught up to her dad, who was heading toward the stage.

"Hey, Dad."

"Good morning, Az." He stopped, looking down and rubbing the back of his neck, seemingly searching for something to say. "How did you sleep?"

"Not bad. I woke up a little seasick, but it's going away."

"That's good. Are you ready for this magic wand class?"

"What magic wand class?"

"There's a class starting any time now, on the stage. They announced it last night."

"Gods' blood!" Azure turned and sprinted for the stairs. "I'll be right back," she called as she dodged through a throng of people coming up from below.

Azure lifted her thin mattress and snatched her wand from where she had hidden it, cursing herself for not keeping it with her at all times. She zipped back up the stairs and found her dad near the stage.

"That was fast as lightning," he said with a smile. Nostalgia swept through Azure as she remembered hearing those same words when she had beat all the neighborhood kids—boys and girls—in a footrace at age twelve.

A man in relatively plain dress approached the podium.

"Good morning, and welcome to session one of your magic wand training. My name is Samuel, and I'll be your instructor." He drew his wand from a sheath on his belt. "Let's get right to it! I think you'll find that wand magic is fairly easy. Well, the basics, anyway. What we'll start with today is something we call a *bolt*."

An excited buzz swept through the crowd as people drew their shiny new wands.

"I will need a volunteer," Samuel said, scanning the audience.

Azure's hand shot up before she was aware of it happening.

"You." Samuel pointed near her. "The short young girl."

Azure's heart began to thump, now that so many eyes were on her. After pointing to her own chest and getting a nod from the instructor, she made her way up onto the stage. An assistant rolled some kind of sword training dummy next to the podium.

"What is your name, little lady?"

She hated being called that, but said, "Azure," anyway.

"Azure, I'd like you to aim your wand at this dummy."

She aimed her wand, her hand tremulous.

"No, not me! The other dummy!" He grabbed her arm and pretended to change its position. The crowd found his joke quite funny.

"Now, I want you to focus. Let everything fall away; the crowd, the stage, the ship, everything. Put every bit of your concentration into one thing. Picture a lightning bolt shooting from the tip of your wand." He paused. "What does it look like? What does it sound like? What does it feel like?" Azure focused on his words. "See the bright flash! Hear the crack of thunder! Feel the magic coursing through your body, trying to find a way out. All you have to do is give it direction! Direct its fury at your target! Now!"

Azure could feel the magic pulsing throughout her entire body—it was pure exhilaration. With an unintentional roar, she visualized the bolt striking the target and ripping it into tattered shreds. She looked down at her wand, expecting her vision to manifest in the world.

A yellow spark, barely visible, seemed to dribble out of her wand and fall to the stage.

The crowd erupted in laughter.

Azure lowered her wand.

"You laugh," Samuel said to the crowd, "and indeed that *was* funny, but magic is often elusive early on." He turned to Azure. "If you'd like to try it again, let me give you some advice that may help you achieve a better result. Sometimes magic needs an emotion to manifest itself, at least it does when we, as humans, are trying to direct it. The easiest, and many would say best, emotion to use is anger. Tap into your anger and see how it works. Pretend this dummy is someone or something you can't stand, or something that is standing in the way of what you want or deserve."

Azure hesitated. This made magic seem dirtier, in a way; less magical. Was this really how it worked?

"Go ahead," said Samuel.

Azure raised her wand. She visualized the same lightning, the same sounds, but this time she tried to imagine Pratt's smug face on the dummy. She thought about every reason she had to hate the man, the most immediate of which was his apparent control over her dad's mind. She felt power within her surging, tingling, thrumming, longing to be sent into the world. As she directed this power, the face of Pratt contorted and morphed into something that more resembled her dad's face.

A yellow bolt blasted from the end of her wand, smashing into the dummy and tearing its head clean off.

The crowd gasped.

Azure's arm dropped. She felt seasick, again, like she might collapse right there on the stage.

"Whoa, little lady!" Samuel said. He addressed the audience with his mouth hanging open. "Looks like someone has a bit of an anger problem."

As the crowd broke out in laughter, Azure took a seat on the floor of the stage.

Samuel waited for the laughter to die down. "As you can see, magic has a cost." He pointed at Azure, who was trying to catch her breath and looked as if she might throw up. "This will get better with practice, but it's important to remember that the bigger the magic you're trying, the bigger the cost will be. This isn't true with the ciguapa and their tattoo runes, but that's a topic for another time. Most of you, with steady practice, will be firing bolts with minimal discomfort in no time at all."

Samuel helped Azure to her feet. "Get some water and take a rest, little lady. You'll be back to feeling normal soon, I promise you."

Azure descended the stairs from the stage while Samuel instructed the crowd to form two lines, and another dummy was brought out.

"Are you okay?" Azure's dad said, hurrying to her side.

"Yeah. Just a little woozy."

"That was great, Az!"

"Thanks. I... I just need to take a little rest. You go ahead and get in line. It's quite the experience."

"You sure?"

"Yes, Dad, I'm sure."

As she headed to her cabin, Robin perched on her shoulder. "You're really fine?"

"Yeah. I really am. I just need to lay down for a few minutes." If Azure was being honest, she was pretty much back to normal already, physically. She just didn't want to be around anyone at the moment. She wanted a chance to process the blasting of her own father's head off.

"I think that Roger guy likes you." Robin tilted her head in her version of a smile.

Azure shrugged. She wasn't sure if she could possibly care less about that at the moment. "Thanks, Robin. I'll see you in a little bit."

Chapter 7 Dinner in the Captain's Quarters

Soft pecking at her fingers awoke Azure from accidental sleep. "What time is it?" she asked, sitting up and stretching her arms over her head.

"You've only got an hour or so until that dinner with Pratt in the captain's quarters," Robin said.

"Really?"

"Yeah. That magic really did a number on you, didn't it?"

"It wasn't that, not totally, anyway. I think it's just the whole thing; the seasickness, the magic, fighting with my dad, being around this many Pratt followers. It's a bit draining."

"Well, shake it off, it's time to get up and get ready."

"Do I have to go?"

"No, but your dad would be pretty upset if you didn't. He's out there dressed in his best clothes already."

"Gods' asses." Azure looked down at her tattered skirts. "I'm not dressing up. I couldn't if I wanted to, anyway. I'm here with nothing but the clothes on my back and my best friend."

Robin made a happy little hop. "Actually, someone, probably that Roger guy, procured a beautiful new dress for you. It's hanging up outside."

Azure stuck her head out into the hall and retrieved the dress from a hook outside the door. It was silk, a vibrant sky blue, with ornate white lace at the sleeves. She usually wasn't all that into dressing up and trying to look fancy, but she had never had an opportunity to wear something quite like that.

"Why not?" she told Robin as she brought it back in the room. "I gotta admit, I like it."

"I do, too," Robin said. "I'll go fetch someone to help you get it on."

In minutes, Robin came back with a young girl in a green vest. The girl was more than happy to help Azure get dressed, even though it was a complicated process. When the job was done, Azure gave the girl a copper. She thanked Azure, squealed with delight, and hurried away.

"So, how do I look?" Azure asked.

"Gorgeous!" Robin said. "Absolutely stunning!"

"Thanks, Robin." Azure felt herself blushing.

In the hall, Roger was heading toward the stairs. "Thank you for the dress," she called to him.

Roger spun around, the confused look on his face turned to wide-eyed shock when he saw her.

"This dress. Didn't you find it for me?"

"Uh... no, but it looks great."

"Hmm." Azure looked down the long hall behind her.

"We'll have to solve this mystery later," Robin said. "Let's get going."

As Azure ascended the stairs to the deck, she was surprised to see that the sun had already set. It wasn't quite dark yet, as the faintest band of fading sunlight still lit the sky to the west.

Off to port, Azure noticed the blue glow of a ciguapa ship. She hurried to the rail to get a closer look. The only place she had seen them before was the far-off view from atop the cliffs in Barren, and she had always been fascinated by them.

"Fantastic," she mouthed, as she watched the smaller ship cut silently through the hyaline. Its sails gave off a silvery blue glow, like the Ring above, and each one had a black symbol stitched into it. She had heard that the ciguapa were able to propel their ships with rune magic. She wondered if that was true, and if so, how it worked.

"Az!" Robin sounded like an exasperated mother.

Azure pulled herself away from the rail, blue lights still dancing in her eyes, and headed for her dinner.

The captain's quarters were impressive. A crystal chandelier threw sparkling light all around the room from above a huge oak table, set for four. The walls were adorned with framed charts and maps of every island in the League. Four large windows along the back wall allowed a view of the galleon's wake as it carved through the tranquil waters.

The ciguapa woman Azure had seen earlier greeted them at the door. She was impossibly glamorous, without an ounce of visible effort. Just being in her presence made Azure's mouth dry. Her indigo skin was decorated with five silver tattoos, each a different rune.

"Welcome," the ciguapa woman said. "My name is Brisa. I have the great honor of serving your dinner tonight." Her accent and the timbre of her voice made every word achingly beautiful. "Please, follow me."

She led Azure and her father to the table, where she pulled out a chair for Azure to sit.

"Thank you." Azure's voice came out as a whisper.

As they sat, Governor Pratt and another man approached the table. The man wore a long red coat and tricorn hat, which he took off as he entered the room, revealing frizzled, shoulder-length gray hair that was tied in the back with a string. "May I present Captain Hornigold," Pratt said. "Captain, this is Mr. John Brine and his daughter, Azure, wasn't it?"

"Yes." Azure took the captain's hand, which he had extended out to her. His smile was warm and fatherly.

"We are well met," the captain said as he shook Azure's dad's hand. "I hope the ride hasn't been too rough for you."

"It's been great," Azure said. "You don't mind if my friend eats with us, do you?" She tilted her head toward Robin on her shoulder.

"Of course not." Another warm smile. "And speaking of that, who's ready to eat?"

Everyone took their seats, and Brisa brought out a colorful plate of assorted fresh fruit. She then took a decanter from a tray against the wall and poured a rich red wine for the guests. "Would you like some?" she asked Robin.

"Oh, yeah. Thank you."

Brisa poured a splash of wine into a saucer. For the first time, Azure noticed that her dad hadn't brought Thunder Paws to dinner.

Captain Hornigold raised his glass. "To Ms. Azure, enhancing our otherwise beauty-challenged table with her elegance and grace."

Azure's ears flashed hot. "Thanks," she said as the guests clinked their glasses together. "But compared to Brisa, I feel pretty graceless."

The captain gave Azure a nod.

"But, young Ms. Azure, you're comparing mangoes and dragon fruit. You should never be made to feel inferior to any being on Undering." Pratt's tone and timing screamed bigotry, but Azure remained silent, not wanting to ruin dinner before it started. Her pulse, however, began to speed up.

"Captain Hornigold," Pratt said. "Are you perfectly comfortable having a ciguapa working on this ship? Or has your hand been forced in the matter?"

"Not at all." The captain narrowed his eyes. "I have had a great many ciguapa work on my ship over the years. Fauns and accursed skeletons as well. They've proved to be more than capable of earning my esteem, and frankly, I'm shocked you would ask such a question in polite company, sir."

"Far be it from my intention to shock a man such as you on your own ship," Pratt said. His expression betrayed no emotion. "I think, unfortunately, I am often mistaken for a—what do they call me—a bigot, when that couldn't be further from the truth. I simply want humans to get their due in our League, nothing more."

"Well, how do you explain the forcible removal of fauns from the Nameless Isles to Ersa Aracel, or wherever you had them sent when you were finished exploiting them in your mines?" Azure said, pulse really racing, now.

Pratt's eyes flashed, but his countenance remained stoic. Azure's question had clearly exposed and embarrassed the governor. There was the slightest noticeable tension in his jaw.

"You state this as if it's a fact."

"And you imply it's not?"

"Azure," her dad said with a nervous chuckle. He turned to the captain, obviously desperate to change the subject. "So, Captain Hornigold, exactly how many people can fit on this massive ship?"

"Well," the captain replied, also excited to steer the conversation away from the confrontation, "if we're really packing on the passengers, like we're doing on this voyage, we can fit more than five hundred people on board, although not very comfortably."

Brisa brought out a tray with four steaming bowls of soup. It smelled delicious and almost made Azure forget about her argument with the most powerful man on the islands. Cilantro and lime and slow-roasted—

The ship shuddered, the table screeched across the polished wood floor, and the chandelier threatened to crash down on top of the dinner party.

"What was that?" Robin said as she perched on Azure's shoulder. The ship rocked again, nearly knocking Azure from her chair.

Both the captain and the governor rushed out of the room. Azure, her dad, and Robin followed.

As Azure stepped out into the open air, a giant black tentacle thumped the deck in front of her. She cried out and backed away, stepping on the hem of her dress and toppling backward to the hard floor. The tentacle writhed in front of her, searching for something to grab hold of. Eventually, it found the mizzenmast, creeping up and snapping off a ten-foot section like it was a matchstick before dropping it to the deck.

Another tentacle found a man as he sprinted away. It lifted him into the air and brought him down onto the deck with a sickening thud. Azure looked away as the man's head lost all sense of form, but not fast enough to avoid seeing blood and brain smeared across the timbers.

Azure's eyes were drawn to the starboard side of the ship, to something surreal. The massive, vacant eye of some sort of unthinkable monster looked back at her. Its head rose high above the rail of the ship. Its mouth—lined with rows of jagged teeth—opened wide in a silent scream. The creature's slimy tentacles, covered in countless squelching suckers, undulated all around her, groping for something to wrap themselves around.

Something wet enveloped Azure's ankle, the tip of a searching tentacle took hold with an otherworldly strength. She shrieked and kicked at it with her other foot as it dragged her across the deck. Robin dove down and began tearing at the monster's slick flesh with her beak.

Then, as suddenly as it had grabbed her, the tentacle let go and moved slowly away.

Governor Pratt had drawn his wand and raised both hands in the air. He moved his arms together as if dancing. The gaudy ring on his finger shone with a bright green light.

The creature's eye focused on him in a blank stare. The tentacle that had seized Azure squirmed its way toward the mizzenmast, finding the ten-foot section it had torn off. The wood had splintered, creating a rough, sharp point on one end.

The tentacle lifted the broken mast, and with an unsettling ferocity, the creature drove the sharp end into its own eye. It pulled the mast, now covered in an almost black substance, back out, then thrust it into its eye at a different angle. Again and again it speared itself. Thick, black blood splattered the sails and poured out onto the deck.

The creature sank into the sea. Its tentacles slid limply behind it across the deck, pulling debris and the body of the dead man up over the rail and into the dark water.

"Azure!" Her dad fell to his knees beside her and wrapped her in an embrace. "Are you okay?"

"Yeah. Are you?"

He nodded.

Azure watched as the light from the ring on Pratt's finger faded to dark.

Chapter 8 Mock Trial

The next morning, Azure woke up in her dinner dress, as her other clothes had apparently been taken away to be washed. It still had kraken slime along the hem. She rubbed the sleep from her eyes and meandered to the deck, where Robin greeted her.

After pleasantries with her bird friend, Azure made her way to her father, who was standing with a group of passengers. As she approached, she could hear them discussing the kraken attack. The creature's blood had been scrubbed away, but still left a dark stain on the deck.

"Hey, Dad," she called out.

He turned and came over to her, his face serious. For a moment, no one talked, then her dad said, "You know what, Azure? I'm really happy that you weren't hurt last night, but I don't think we should talk right now."

"Why?"

"You really embarrassed me at our dinner with Governor Pratt. I'm pretty disappointed that you chose to act like that." His face had reddened, his eyes unable to meet hers.

"Seriously? We watched an actual kraken kill someone last night, and you're still worried about being embarrassed in front of your little hero?"

Azure resisted the urge to throw him overboard and walked away without another word. She headed toward the bow of the ship, where an audible commotion was gathering.

"What's going on?" she said aloud to no one in particular.

"I'll go see." Robin sped out ahead.

Azure pushed her way into a growing crowd, congregating on the port side and near the bow.

Robin zipped back with a report. "There's been another murder."

"Really?" A wave of dread washed over Azure.

"Yeah. It was a woman this time."

"Do they know who did it?"

"No, but I bet you can guess what the speculation is."

Behind her, Pratt and his entourage took the stage at the center of the ship. The crowd surged around the stage for a better view, sweeping Azure along with it. In the chaos, she somehow found her dad, again. They made eye contact, but neither spoke. They stayed together, finding a spot within view of Pratt on the port side.

"There has been yet another murder," Pratt stated, with what Azure took to be a hint of triumph in his voice. "A beautiful, innocent woman was taken far before her time." He tried to look upset, but it wasn't very convincing. "This voyage is supposed to be a celebration of my victory, and someone is trying to spoil it for me." In this, he seemed sincere.

A man rushed up the stairs to the stage and whispered in Pratt's ear. Pratt nodded, and the man rushed away.

"But there is good news; a silver lining around the storm cloud that has formed over this ship. It seems we have witnesses to the murder this time."

A clamorous hubbub erupted amongst the crowd. Pratt waited for it to subside before continuing. "The witnesses are being brought to this very stage as we speak. I shall say no more until they arrive, lest I sway the hearts and minds here without the entirety of the available evidence."

Azure turned to her dad. "What are they going to do, have a trial right there on the stage?"

"What should they do, let some murderer pick us off one by one?"

"Obviously not, but..." Azure had so many competing thoughts, she didn't know which one to voice.

"We are being attacked on all sides," her dad said. "How can you not see that?"

"Who is we? And who's attacking us?"

"Humans." He gave her a pleading look. "There are powerful forces at work trying to ensure that we, as humans, don't keep what we have bled and fought for. They see Governor Pratt's rise to power as a threat, and they're willing to do anything to eliminate him."

"Who are these powerful forces?"

"The Harmony Faction, or ciguapa sympathizers, or orcs." He looked at her as if this was the most obvious thing in the world. "I mean, I could go on and on, but you choose not to see what is so clearly in front of your face. I've been praying to the gods that you will open your eyes, but it's not working, Azure."

"Shit, you don't follow the gods, you practice the religion of Pratt." Azure had been waiting to use that line on him, and now let it sit in the tumultuous air. "But if you followed any of the gods, it'd be Zomus, the God of Blame, because that's all Pratt and his followers are good at: blaming others for their problems. What's happening on this ship is a convenient gods-damned microcosm of what's happening to our League."

Everyone around Azure and her dad had stopped to listen to their intensifying argument.

"I have tried to teach you about the gods since you were little."

"You taught me a few nuggets from the early writings, when it suited you. I had to learn about The Epiphany on my own."

As he looked around at the attentive faces surrounding them, his face became redder. "You need to stop this little outburst, right now!"

"You can't shut me up just because your fellow Pratt worshipers are watching. I'm so sorry I embarrass you."

He looked hurt and angry and ashamed all at once. He opened his mouth to respond, but Pratt's voice interrupted him.

"The witnesses have been gathered."

An older man and a young woman were escorted up to the stage by Paul Sancti. He motioned for the man to step forward to Pratt at the podium.

"What is your name, sir?"

"Edward. Edward Thomas." His voice was frail and hard to hear.

"Mr. Thomas, may I ask what you saw?"

The crowd seemed to hold their collective breath as the man composed his thoughts.

"I saw that cursed skeleton, wearing a green vest, coming out from the room where the murder happened."

"And what room was that?'"

"Well, I heard a commotion in the room next to mine, so I stuck my head out of the door to see what was the matter. After a particularly loud thud,

I saw that skeleton coming out of the room. Now, I was worried because I knew the room was occupied by a pretty little thing I had just met the night before, name of Jenny. So I went and knocked on her door but got no response."

"Did you then enter the room?"

"No, sir. I wasn't about to enter a lady's room uninvited. I called up and down the hall, and eventually, a crewmember found me. I told him what had happened, and he was the one who entered the room."

"And what did the two of you find there?"

"That pretty little Jenny, laying in a pool of her own blood."

The crowd gasped.

"Thank you, Mr. Thomas, for your brave testimony." Pratt looked to Paul Sancti. "And now we'd like to hear from the second witness."

The young woman took a tentative step forward.

"What is your name?"

"Darlene Bennett."

"And can you corroborate Mr. Thomas's story?"

"Well, no sir, I don't know anything about all of that."

"Then what do you have to add?"

"Last night, about midnight, long after you saved us from that monster, I left my room to get some air, as I was feeling awfully peaked due to the ocean swells."

"Yes?" Pratt said after a short pause.

"Well, I saw Elijah, that skeleton guy, huddled up all secretly with that ciguapa woman on board. They were carrying on about something in a hushed excitement."

"Is that all?"

"No. I felt a bit suspicious, so I tried to get closer, to hear what it was they were talking about."

"And could you hear them?"

"No, not exactly, but I did see her slip him a small key before they parted ways, looking back over their shoulders as they went."

"Is that all, Ms. Bennett?"

"Yes, sir. Sorry I couldn't be of more help."

Paul Sancti guided the two witnesses from the stage, golden chains clanking as he walked.

Azure had a sick feeling that she was watching a theater play, a farce meant to fool an entire boatload of people. Looking around her, it was clearly working.

The din of the crowd suddenly increased tenfold.

Paul Sancti had just escorted Elijah and Brisa onto the stage.

Sensing that it was the right thing to do, Azure began to push through the crowd toward the stairs.

"Your name is Elijah, is it not?" Pratt said.

"Yes, sir."

"And you are called Brisa?"

Brisa nodded, her head high and proud.

"Do you deny, Elijah, that you murdered a woman in cold blood?"

"I do deny it."

"You have no heart." He pointed into Elijah's empty ribcage. "But if you have an ounce of decency inside that obscene body of yours, I urge you to come clean."

"I didn't do anything," Elijah pleaded.

"And you, Brisa," he practically spat the name, "do you deny giving Elijah a small room key?"

"I never had anyone's room key in my possession to give."

"So it would be fine with you if we checked his vest pockets?"

"You'd have to ask him," Brisa said, staring Pratt down.

"Elijah, can we check your pockets, before men and gods?"

"Absolutely."

Paul Sancti slipped a hand into Elijah's left pocket and withdrew a small silver key.

The crowd, if not already unpleasant, turned ugly.

Chapter 9 Cast Out

"What shall be their punishment?" Pratt called over the noise. A glut of grisly suggestions were barked in from every direction.

"In years past, murderers at sea were forced to walk the plank." He looked very pleased with himself at this suggestion. "Or we could simply bind them, take them to Whetstone, and hope they get a fair trial there."

"Plank!" came shouts from all around.

Azure eyed her dad, who was tight-lipped.

"I hear you!" Pratt roared. "And I agree. We must not let our enemies continue to gain ground against us. This is our time, and nothing they can do will stop that. We must not stand idly by while good people are murdered. We demand justice!"

Captain Hornigold forced his way through the raucous crowd and onto the stage. The noise died down as he faced Governor Pratt.

"These two are crewmembers aboard *my* ship! I will not have your mob justice meted out to them today. As captain of this vessel, I claim the final authority on what is to be done with suspects, and I demand nothing short of a full trial for these two."

Pratt didn't even look at Captain Hornigold, instead facing the crowd. "Do you think *he* has the final authority on this ship?"

The response was overwhelmingly negative.

"Would you go so far as to say that a new authority now graces our League and everything in it?"

The crowd overwhelmingly agreed.

Captain Hornigold bowed his head, defeated.

"That's what I thought," Pratt said, gloating.

Azure had made her way to the stage. Without thinking, she rushed up the stairs.

"Ms. Brine," Pratt said, amused. "To what do we owe the pleasure of your appearance?"

"The captain is right. This was not a proper trial. You cannot put these people to death."

"People?" The crowd laughed along with Pratt.

"Yes, you fucking asshole! People!" Azure felt as if she were watching herself say these words from somewhere outside her body.

"Watch how you address your betters, little lady!"

No phrase in the Undering could have enraged her more. People who self-described as anyone's "betters" deserved to be punched in the nose. She balled up her fist, legs shaking.

"Who thinks this traitorous Ms. Brine should follow the murderers onto the plank?"

The crowd's cheer was the most enthusiastic, yet.

"Azure!" Her dad climbed up to the stage beside her.

"Oh, yes. The proud father. This just keeps getting better." Pratt's tone was sardonic. "Do you stand with your traitorous daughter?"

He paused.

It may have only been a fraction of a second, but the pause seemed a miserable eternity. In that space between heartbeats, Azure had never felt further away from her father.

"I demand a trial at sea!" she heard herself shout. "For all three of us."

"Ha!" Pratt chuckled. "Now here's an interesting twist. You wish to let the gods decide your fates?"

"I do." Azure tried to stand tall, despite her shaking knees. "I'm no legal expert, but I can see the Ring on a clear night. I think it's obvious this whole thing is a sham. A trial at sea is the only way to know for sure."

"Well," Pratt said to the crowd, "let's weigh our options, then." He scratched his chin with forefinger and thumb. "On one hand, watching them walk the plank would be extremely satisfying. It would put a clean, quick end to this unholy business. On the other hand, a trial at sea *was* outlawed by the previous governor of our isles." he stopped to spit on the stage. "It *would* be a perfect way to usher in my new regime." He seemed to be in earnest contemplation.

"Set out into open ocean, in nothing but a jolly boat," Pratt said. "It sounds pretty miserable to me. It sounds like a fate befitting two murderers and a name-calling traitor, do you agree?"

Of course, the crowd agreed, although many seemed disappointed they wouldn't get to see anyone walk the plank.

"Trial at sea it is!"

Paul Sancti approached Azure with his arm outstretched. "Give me your wand."

For a moment, Azure considered blasting a bolt into his face. But her mind played out the consequences, which would likely end in her being torn limb from limb by a bloodthirsty throng. Azure pulled the wand from a pocket tied around her waist and handed it over.

Paul seized Azure by the arm and led her toward the stairs.

"Az!" cried her dad as he threw himself at her.

Azure turned her head as she was led away. "I'll be fine, Dad. I don't want to be on this ship one minute longer, anyway. Just enjoy being a sycophant."

The part of Azure that had been dying for a long while died completely as she spoke those words. It joined the other dead, decaying pieces that had passed the day her mom sunk into the bay.

Numb, she allowed herself to be steered away as the crowd parted in front of her.

Paul Sancti brought her to where other men were holding Elijah and Brisa. Elijah was hard to read, but Brisa stood tall and proud, possibly more beautiful than she had ever been.

All three of them were shoved into the small boat.

Azure's dad pushed forward through the line of laughing people. "Can I at least give her a flask of water?" he asked Paul.

Paul looked to Governor Pratt, who shrugged and said, "Sure, why not?"

He rushed to the boat and handed Azure his flask. "I'm sorry, Az. I love you."

His words had no effect on Azure's numbness. It was way too late for declarations of love or regret. It was his choosing of a politician over her that was killing her. This banishment was simply the final twisting of the knife. He was right, images of harmony and love and adventure *were* unrealistic.

Two large men grabbed Azure's dad around the arms and pulled him away. He fought against them, bellowing curses, but eventually vanished into the feverish crowd.

Roger ran forward and thrust his coat and tricorn hat into Azure's arms. She took them, half expecting Paul to take them away, but he only said, "Enough," and had more men pull Roger away before he could speak.

Paul grasped Azure's arm and brought his mouth to her ear. His breath smelled like week-old fish.

"If you're ever seen anywhere near this ship, again, you'll be killed on sight. Do you understand?"

Azure didn't respond.

"Do you understand?" He violently shook her by the arm.

Robin dove from the sky, aiming her claws at his face. Paul raised his wand with an unexpected quickness and knocked Robin from the air. She fell to the bottom of the jolly boat with a tiny thud, completely unconscious.

Paul tilted his head back and cackled. The people who had seen him strike the bird joined in the laughter.

Azure yanked her arm from Paul's grasp and scooped up her little companion. Robin was out, but there was still a rapid movement in her breast.

"Of course, I don't know why I'm wasting my breath with warnings, when the gods are clearly not going to allow you to survive." A depraved grin spread across Paul's face. "You see, this jolly boat has been touched by the gods. You might say, it's holy."

Azure could barely be bothered to pay attention to his words as she watched Robin's chest.

"Lower the boat!" Paul commanded.

Men began to drop it into the sea with thick ropes wrapped around pulleys.

"Gods," Paul shouted, face to the Ring. "These three have been given over to your will. They will face the world you have created in a trial at sea. Their fate is in your hands. May justice be served, whether they be guilty and face your wrath, or whether they be innocent and receive your mercy."

The jolly boat touched down into choppy water. Although the sea seemed calm from the galleon, the waves tossed the small boat like it was a toy.

Robin stirred in Azure's palms. Her eyes fluttered open. Wordlessly, she looked at Azure, then Brisa, then Elijah, then the towering hull of the galleon.

"What the fuck just happened to us?" she said before closing her eyes again.

Chapter 10 The Mirror Sea

They sat, adrift in the rocking boat, watching the galleon melt into the horizon where the Ring touched down in silence.

When the ship was nothing more than a black dot against the blue Ring, Brisa said, "Thank you, Azure, for standing up for us."

"Yeah," Elijah said. "Thank you."

"You're welcome." Azure felt as if their appreciation was misguided, like she usually did when anyone thanked her for anything. "But it didn't do you much good."

"I'm sorry that standing up for others left you stranded along with us."

"Oh, that's—" Azure felt something wet on her foot. She gathered up her billowing dress to find that the small boat was taking on water, fast.

They began searching for the source of the leak. As if on cue, a shark fin crested the ocean's rough surface.

Panicked, Azure ran her hand along the floor, desperate to find the hole. As she groped around, she felt something solid. She wrapped her fingers around an object and pulled it from the deepening water.

"My dad's wand." She stared at it, forgetting about the leak for a moment. "He snuck me his wand." She looked to where the ship had gone, but not even a dot remained.

"I found it," Elijah exclaimed, shoving his boot into a jagged gap on the bottom of the hull. "There's a hole, here."

Azure realized the cruel and stupid joke that Paul had made just before lowering them and shook her head in disgust.

Thankfully, the rising of the water in the boat slowed. Brisa and Azure began scooping out water with cupped hands, but it was slow going. They could barely keep up with the trickle of water that was still pushing past Elijah's heel.

Brisa stopped bailing water and closed her eyes. She traced the rune tattoo on her left shoulder with her forefinger while saying, "Muay." She opened her eyes and looked down at the water in the boat. All at once, the water rose up from the floor. In a quivering mass, it floated over the side of the boat before splashing back into the sea.

Azure's mouth dropped open.

"That was amazing!" Robin said.

Brisa nodded, seeming slightly winded. "We'd better get going. I don't know how many times I'll be able to do that."

"And I don't know how long the bottom of this boat is going to hold," Elijah added.

"I think I see a small island to the north," Brisa said, squinting her eyes. "Can we sail that way?"

"Yeah. It will be slow going, but we can do it." Elijah turned to Azure. "Can you set the sail?"

"Uh." Azure looked over the tangle of ropes coming from the mast. "I hate to admit this, but no."

"Okay, just unwrap that rope right there and pull up the sail, then tie it down the best you can. I would do it, but I have to keep my foot in this breach. I wasn't thinking when I shoved my stupid bony foot in this hole. Big surprise, there."

Azure followed his instructions, feeling a warm sense of accomplishment as the ragged sail rose and fluttered in the wind.

"Now pull on that rope until the yard is pointing roughly toward Brisa."

Again, Azure did as she was told. The boat lurched forward as the sail swelled.

"Perfect." Elijah gave her a bony thimbs-up. "Now you can use that rudder to steer us toward the island."

Azure pushed a small wooden handle away from herself and the boat veered the wrong way. "Oh," she said as she pulled it back and corrected their course.

"You'll make a sailor, yet" Elijah said, with—although Azure couldn't explain how she knew—a smile.

"I hope so."

"You're a natural." Robin alighted on the top of the mast.

For a while, no one spoke as Azure experimented with the sail and rudder. Brisa regained her normal breathing and seemed to enjoy the wind on her face. Elijah concentrated on keeping the leak to a minimum.

"So," Elijah said, "is there no doubt in your mind that I didn't kill those people?"

"Absolutely none." Azure tried her best to look him in the eyes. "First off, I don't think you would do something like that, and second, I could tell that Pratt staged the whole thing."

"Why would he do that?" Elijah asked.

"Because he wanted me, or us, off of that ship," said Brisa. "And because he needs those people riled up so he can use them once they get to the Capitol Isles."

Everyone turned to her.

"Use them for what?" Robin hopped down to Azure's shoulder.

"I don't know, exactly, but he needs them so he can gain some sort of power at their expense."

"How do you know this?" Azure's mind raced.

"I was chosen by my people to gather information on Governor Pratt. I was working on Captain Hornigold's ship as a server but was also spying on behalf of the Ciguapa Matriarchs." Brisa gave Azure an empathetic look. "I discovered he intends to obtain a magical power, possibly some sort of Old Magic, and that he needs hundreds of followers to help him. I don't know for sure what he hopes to gain, or what will become of the followers, but I know he has gone to great lengths to keep these things hidden. I believe they are in danger."

A thought flashed through Azure's mind; they, including her father, deserved whatever they had coming to them. She tried not to think that way, but it was persistent.

She took her dad's wand from her pocket. He had risked a lot to slip it to her. And even though she couldn't stand the political movement he had gotten himself into, he was still her dad. If he was in danger, she would do everything in her power to save him.

"Governor Pratt has this ring," Brisa continued, "that can control the mind of any living being. He used it against the kraken the other night."

"I saw that," Azure said. A big part of her wanted to believe that Pratt was using the ring to control her father's mind, but deep down, she knew that wasn't true.

"I believe he got the ring from Ersa Trago, or Dragon Island. I also believe there is something there, still, that he really doesn't want anyone to know about. I heard him tell Paul Sancti that the only thing that could possibly stop him is on Dragon Island, but I'm not sure what that could be."

"A dragon?" Azure's pulse rate increased.

"I doubt it. The island earned that name long, long ago by my people, and not because it had an actual dragon on it."

"Well how did it earn the name?"

Brisa looked ahead, apparently gauging how much time she had for stories. The tiny island grew on the horizon but was still fairly far off.

"Let me go way back and tell you about the religion of my people, first. We believe in the Goddess, Teus. In the beginning, Teus blessed her people with the Old Magic, and riches beyond belief. But in time, the people became spoiled and yearned for more and more power. Using the Old Magic, they created a leviathan, a monster so great that it had the ability to swallow islands, hoping to use it to gain even more power over the world. But they could not control it.

"For years, there had been a prophecy of a messiah who would come down to Cimuno, what you call the Undering, to show my people the folly of their ways. When the leviathan was created, the messiah finally appeared.

"Teus herself came to the world in ciguapa form. She taught my people to shun the ideas of power and wealth. She took away the Old Magic and gave them a new magic that was less tempting. She brought with her a ring that could control the mind of any creature and used it to force the leviathan into a deep sleep. It is said that the leviathan lies dreaming under the sea to this day. Many believe this is the reason that other monsters usually stay out of the Mirror Sea.

"Teus left the Ciguapa Matriarchs with great knowledge, and the choice to do what they would with her teachings. She also left them the ring of power.

"After much deliberation, the matriarchs took Teus's words to heart. They decided to hide the ring away because it was too powerful and whispered to them about ways to control the people and gain power. They say the ring had taken on a will of its own. The matriarchs also decided to banish all things that had made people greedy, like gold and jewels, although they now look back on this decision as folly. The problem isn't the gold and jewels themselves, but our entanglement with them. Anyway, they took all of this to an island in the north, an island called Ersa Trago because it had the shape of a great sea dragon of old.

"Here, they left everything, and in order to hide the island from all future seekers of the ring, or the treasure, they cursed the island and enshrouded the entire area in what you call the Eternal Fog.

"This is what young ciguapa are taught. We are told that riches and power are not a true path to happiness—the only true path is love. Teus has given us a fire in our chests, a way for us to understand when we are acting true, or when we are straying from the path. When our fires are burning bright, we know we are headed in the right direction. When our fires dim and smolder, we know we have acted counter to our true natures."

Azure waited to make sure Brisa was finished, then said, "Thank you for sharing all of that. I feel like I should know it already, but most of that was new to me."

Brisa nodded.

"So, what do you think we should do?" Azure asked. "I mean, what should I do? I have to try and save my dad. I don't expect you to go with me, but I could sure use some advice on where to go from here."

"It sounds to me like we should go to Dragon Island," Elijah said. "But I wouldn't listen to me if I were you."

"I think he's right," Brisa agreed. She traced a rune tattoo on her left arm and whispered a word. A thin chain necklace materialized around her neck. Hanging from the chain was a golden key. "I stole this key from Pratt's quarters when I began to have a feeling that he was planning something against us. I believe it will unlock something on Dragon Island." She traced the rune backwards, said another word, and the key and chain vanished. "I don't think we stand a chance against Pratt without help, without the thing he is afraid of on that island."

"We?" A strong hope stirred in Azure's chest.

"You stood up for us at great peril to yourself. I am honor bound to help you in your quest, whatever it may be."

"Well, I release you from your honor binding. I only did what I thought was right at the time."

"And I am only doing what I think is right."

"Me too." Elijah nodded.

Azure felt as if she had a crackling fire warming *her* chest. "I can't tell you how much I appreciate that."

"We've got ourselves a nice little party, and a noble quest!" Robin said. "This is going to—"

A particularly big swell rocked the boat. Elijah's foot jarred loose from the breach. Water, again, began pouring into the boat. Elijah tried to fit his heel back in, but he accidentally made the hole bigger, knocking through another piece of the boat's brittle bottom.

"Zidon's ass!" he said, trying to clog the hole with both feet, now. "I ruined everything, again."

Azure looked ahead. The island was close, but still at least ten minutes away.

"I don't know if I can swim in this dress," she said to Brisa. "Can you help me take it off?"

"What if I cut the bottom off, instead?"

"Sure."

Brisa pulled a knife from a hidden sheath at the small of her back and began cutting into the silk of Azure's dress. She sliced through all the layers, being careful to not cut Azure's legs. When she was done, the dress covered Azure's left knee, but only about half of her right thigh. Elijah grabbed the extra material and tried to stuff it into the widening hole, with little success.

Azure threw on the coat and tricorn hat that Roger had given her, rolled up the sleeves, and stashed her dad's wand in the breast pocket. Brisa magically lifted the water from the boat, again, but it filled back up within a minute.

Seawater began spilling over the right side. Azure scanned the surrounding surface for fins, thankfully seeing none.

"I'll walk along the bottom," Elijah said. "Don't worry about me. But can you both swim?"

Both women nodded as they sunk into the sea, the mast and sail now the only parts of the boat still visible. Robin flew above, shouting encouragement.

With her legs now free, Azure found swimming fairly easy. If not for the rough water and her fear of sharks, she'd have enjoyed a leisurely swim into shore. As it was, she swam as fast as she could, not stopping until her hands dug into the soft white sand of the island. Brisa was just behind her and Elijah came trudging up from the deep to take up the rear.

Panting, Azure flipped around to her back.

"I'm sorry you had to ruin that dress," Elijah said, as if they hadn't just escaped death.

"Did you give this dress to me?" Azure asked between breaths.

"Well, I know your name means sky blue, and when I heard it, I thought of this dress that was left in the lost and found by some rich lady on the ship's last voyage. I thought it would look... Well, I thought you might like it."

"Thanks, Elijah. I did, er, I do like it."

"Did you know there's a place called Azure Bay on the Continent?"

"Yeah. That's what I'm named after. I guess my great-great grandmother lived there."

"Oh."

Azure picked herself up and looked over their new residence. The island was much smaller than the deck of the galleon. It had three wind-whipped palm trees, and, as far as she could see, not a drop of fresh water. The skeletal remains of two humans lay hand in hand under the closest tree. Crabs crawled over both skeletons, picking at their bones.

"Shit," both Azure and Robin said at the same time.

AS THE SUN SANK IN the west, the darkening sky brought fresh worries to the castaways. Help seemed impossibly far away. The miniature island they had found was most likely uncharted, and no ships could be seen on the horizon. The ocean stretched on for as far as anyone could see in any direction, excepting the vague gray blur of the Eternal Fog in the distant north.

"We should start a fire," Brisa said, gathering dead palm fronds from underneath one of the trees.

After arranging them, she traced the rune on her right shoulder, closed her eyes and whispered, "Fuay." The air around them immediately chilled. Tendrils of wispy smoke began to rise from under the fronds. An orange glow followed a flickering flame, and before long, a proper fire was burning.

"There should be enough dead stuff to keep this going through the night. Maybe someone will see it."

Azure sidled up to the fire, hoping to dry her newly modified dress.

"We should name this island," Elijah said. "Maybe something like New Friendship Island?" His head dropped. "Gods that was lame. Anyone else have an idea?"

"Mylaro?" Brisa said. "It means miracle. Because without this island being here, I think we'd be shark food by now."

"That's definitely better than mine. Azure, do you have an idea?"

"Uh... Three Tree Island?"

"How about We're Fucked Island," Robin said, exasperated. "I don't think naming it is a real priority right now. We're out in the middle of nowhere, with no way to leave!"

"You're right." Elijah looked as dejected as a skeleton could. "But maybe I could walk down to the sea floor and see if I could salvage our boat?"

"That'd be a great start," Azure said. "Robin, could you possibly try to fly somewhere and find help? Maybe Mirth Island or something?"

"Alright. Those are good ideas. Sorry, I lost it there for a minute." Robin shook her head.

The night was completely dark, now, except for the faint blue glow of Ringlight through the gathering clouds above. The castaways huddled around the small fire, the temperature drop being much more noticeable in wet clothes.

"Do you hear that?" Brisa held up a hand.

Azure cocked her head and listened. At first she heard nothing, save the crackling of the fire and a gentle breeze through the palm trees, but then she heard it. Was that the sound of... singing? After focusing her attention, she could tell that it was indeed the sound of a group of people singing from somewhere behind them. As far as Azure could tell, the singers must have been on a ship coming in from the other side of the island.

Azure held her breath, straining to listen.

"...as for me?" the song went, "I'll be true to the song I sing, and live and die a Marauder King..."

"Hide!" Azure said to her companions. "The climate in the League isn't great, right now. Let me figure out if whoever this is has any non-human bias. If they do, I'll..." She wasn't sure what she would do.

Without a word, Elijah lay down near the other two skeletons and pretended to be un-reanimated. Brisa ducked behind a tree.

Azure crept to the other side of the island, where she saw a ship approach. The song had been cut short in the middle, leaving nothing but the steady lap of water against the hull. Candlelight shone from the rails, but Azure could make out no life aboard. A black flag with a white skeleton holding up a mug of ale fluttered in the breeze.

The ship, about a sixty-foot sloop as far as Azure could tell, came to a rest in the shallow waters, it's keel must have driven straight into the sandy beach. Its figurehead—a carved dolphin—loomed above.

Azure's heart pounded as she waited for someone to appear. She had never been this far from home and had no idea what to expect. From the bit of song she heard, the ship was apparently full of marauders, pirates, of which she had heard disturbing things. But hiding on such a small island wasn't feasible. She'd have to greet them and hope for the best.

The sounds of a working crew came from the ship. The indistinct shapes of figures moved about in the candlelight.

Azure's heart leaped as two huge shadows vaulted from the bow and landed with beach-shaking thuds in the sand. Her knees weakened as her eyes processed what she was seeing.

Standing just thirty yards in front of her, were two scowling orcs.

Chapter 11 The Governor's Quarters

G overnor Pratt watched the jolly boat shrink into nothingness from the captain's quarters, which he had now taken for himself.

With a grin, he glided to the doors, opened them, and summoned Paul Sancti.

"Get me that girl's father, John Brine."

As he waited, he sat at the table, picked up a knife, and sliced into a fresh mango.

Before he was done eating the first slice, Paul had returned with a dejected-looking Mr. Brine.

"Come in," the governor said, smiling. "Sit down."

John trudged in and slumped into a chair.

"I'll get right to it," Pratt said, slicing slowly into the mango's flesh while staring into John's eyes. "Can I see your wand?"

"I don't have it." His voice was monotone.

"I figured as much." Governor Pratt ate the slice of mango right off of the knife's blade. "And let me tell you, I understand that you wanted to help your daughter, even though she was a traitor to our cause. You're her father, you absolutely must do what you can to help her." Pratt put his knife down, pulled a golden wand from his coat pocket, and handed it to John. "This is her wand. I think you should have it."

John made eye contact with the governor, who tried to give him a look of compulsion, sprinkled with just a bit of compassion. John reluctantly took the wand and dropped his gaze to the table. Pratt was happy to see that John was a defeated man.

"You'll have a chance to make everything right with her," Pratt said. "When she sees what we're going to do, and how great it makes our League of Islands, she'll have no choice but to see things our way, the right way."

"If she makes it long enough to see all of that." John's voice wasn't much more than a whisper.

"That boat was in great shape," Pratt lied, "and Mirth Island isn't too far away. That accursed skeleton was a capable sailor, and we know how powerful ciguapa magic is, right? They'll be fine. I wouldn't have been compelled to put on such theatrics, but the people on this ship demanded justice, and rightly so. I had to show them that those who support non-human murderers will be punished. I have no doubt in my mind that she'll be alive and well when you return home. So, try to cheer up, and keep practicing." He pointed to the wand. "We've got very big things in our future."

After being dismissed, John Brine plodded away and Paul Sancti came into the captain's quarters.

"We have to change the sign above the door to read: *Governor's Quarters.*"

"Yes, sir."

"Everything is going better than we had planned."

"The gods smile upon you, Governor. Truly."

"You know, they really must. I just got rid of all three dissenters on this ship in one swoop. I've still got the captain to deal with, but I'm not worried about him." He leaned back, put his feet on the desk, and interlaced his fingers behind his head. "A man from the Nameless Isles is about to be the most powerful person the Undering has ever known. I will be greater than Henry Whetstone when this is over. I will rival Griffin the Unrivaled." He looked to his own portrait, which hung in the spot where the captain's used to be.

Paul nodded. But not enthusiastically enough for Pratt.

"What? Does my talk of being the greatest man the Undering has ever known bore you?"

"No, sir." Paul fidgeted with his gold chains. "It's just..."

"It's just what?"

"Well, you're already the governor of the entire League of Islands. You're already an historic, great man. Maybe we could build upon that throughout your term? Maybe this...whole... business isn't exactly necessary?" At no time did he make eye contact with Pratt.

"If you don't understand me by now, you never will." Pratt grinned. Instead of anger, he felt an amused pity for a man with such meager ambitions. "There have been dozens of governors before me, and there will be dozens after me, *if* I were to play the game how it's meant to be played. But I'm not just another ineffectual governor in a long line of ineffectual governors. That isn't good enough for me. I am worth more than that."

"Yes, sir."

It was satisfying to watch Paul squirm, but Pratt decided to be merciful and change the subject. "Do you know why they're called the Nameless Isles?" he asked.

"No, sir."

Pratt couldn't tell if his religious advisor was just humoring him or not, but he continued on.

"It was a mistranslation from the primitive ciguapa language."

"Oh?"

"Yes. I believe the translation should have been something along the lines of soil-less isles, or the less commonly accepted, soul-less isles." His chuckle was both malicious and amused. "The ciguapa were very few on those islands because of the poor soil quality, which made it a perfect place for me to take root." He chuckled again at his own cleverness. "And I'm sure you know the rest of the story. I located the League's largest gold mine, and the rest is literal history."

"Yes, sir. I remember reading about—"

"How long until we reach our second stop at Smith Island?" Pratt said as if Paul hadn't been speaking.

"Four days, sir."

"Excellent."

Chapter 12 The Marauders

The orcs must have stood seven feet tall, their gray-skinned bodies rippled with muscle. Each had two white tusks protruding up from their lower jaws. The orc on the left had long black hair and held a menacing curved scimitar, glinting in the dull Ringlight. Both of them wore black bandanas tied over their heads, and they seemed to sway a little on their feet.

Azure was frozen. Her mind screamed for her body to turn and run, but her legs wouldn't cooperate. Robin hopped nervously on her shoulder, whispering curses.

The orcs' black, sunken eyes met Azure's across the sand.

Again, she tried to move to no avail.

Then, the orcs' scowls slowly morphed into something resembling... smiles.

"Hello," said the orc holding the scimitar. Its voice was deep and gravelly. "I'm Nargol, and this is Orok. How are you doing?"

Azure continued to stare.

"We understand," said Nargol. "We're intimidating. That's why they always send us down first, just in case. But you seem friendly enough. I don't think intimidation is called for any longer." The orc looked up at the ship and called, "It's all clear. Just a lone harmless cast-away."

"She's not alone." Brisa stepped out from her hiding place, followed by Elijah.

"Oh, hello to you, too," Orok said, waving. "You all don't mean us any harm, right?"

"No. Not unless you mean us harm." Brisa had stopped next to Azure on the beach.

"Well, then you've got to come up and have drinks with us."

"Drinks?" Azure had finally regained control of herself.

"Yeah, we were in the midst of a party when we saw your fire," Nargol said. "Thought we'd check it out real quick, thinking maybe it was someone in need of help. Are you in need of help?"

"Absolutely. Our boat sunk and we're marooned here."

"Good thing we stopped, then. But I'm losing my buzz down here in the dark. Why don't we continue this conversation once we've got drinks in our hands?"

"I think I like these guys already," Robin said.

"Oh, how rude of us." Orok slapped his forehead. "What are your names?"

After brief introductions and handshakes, the crew from above threw down rope ladders, which Azure, Brisa, and Elijah all climbed. The orcs pushed the boat back into the water, then followed them up. Once aboard, they were greeted by a shipful of smiling faces. Most of the crew was human, but besides the two orcs, there was also a faun on board. Many of the crew were sitting at a massive, half-circle bar that encompassed the starboard side of the main mast. Some others were sitting around a card table playing what appeared to be Dragon's Hoard. Everyone held a drink in their hand.

"Marauders," said Nargol to the group, "meet Azure, Brisa, Elijah, and Robin."

"WELCOME," they all sang together.

A tall man in a vivid purple coat stepped forward. He had a long, well-manicured mustache and what appeared to be a burn scar covering his right cheek and continuing down the right side of his neck. At first, the facial scar was slightly off-putting, but it only took a moment for the feeling to pass. The initial shock was only that of seeing something unexpected and unfamiliar. On second glance, the somewhat waxy skin of the scar shone in the ring-light and somehow complimented his kind eyes.

The man's round black hat had a large red feather protruding to the back. He wore a white silk scarf tied around his neck and a red silk sash around his waist. His white pants were spotless and baggy and tucked into high black boots. On his shoulder was a small bird, jet black with a bright red head and yellow legs. The man held a bottle of something in one hand and three glasses in the other.

"Yes, welcome aboard the *Adventure Ship*." He handed out the glasses and began filling them. "I am the Marauder King, elected by my wonderful crew. 'Tis a pleasure to meet you all. Apparently, we may have drank a bit much and strayed from our course to Mirth Island." He took a swig from the bottle. "Then we saw your fire and thought, 'Oy, it could be someone in need, or some such adventure, so we pulled up on the sandy shore. And I'm so glad we did! Our purpose is to help those in need, and we don't get many opportunities to do so." A finger shot into the air. "Hey, how would ya all like to be honorary Marauders until we're able to take you where ya need to go?" His pace was frantic, his face lit up with a constant warm smile.

"Sure." Azure tipped back her drink, finding it quite tasty, whatever it was. She had been tense for a few days now and relished the idea of relaxing with a few drinks.

She instantly warmed to these people. They were cheerful and kind and didn't even bat an eye at Elijah's skeletal form or the presence of a ciguapa.

"That's great to hear!" The Marauder King took a big gulp of his own. "Ya know, the world wants us to act like adults, as if that's in direct opposition to acting like children. Well, we don't feel that way. We feel that longing for adventure is the most natural thing in the world. What do ya think about that?"

"I like it." She did.

"You can learn more about life in a week on the open ocean than ya can in years of schooling, ya know?" He hiccupped.

"Well, I'd better get learning." Azure took another drink.

The Marauder King turned to the bird on his shoulder. "Nova, would you be so kind as to show Ms. Robin around, and get her a drink, too?"

"Of course," the bird said, its voice vaguely masculine. "It would be my honor to show the beautiful Ms. Robin around."

Robin giggled on Azure's shoulder, then followed the other bird across the ship.

"Well," said the Marauder King after taking another swig from the bottle, "if yer to be honorary marauders, I suppose you should peruse our code first." He led them to a wooden sign posted to the main mast. It read:

MARAUDER'S CODE:

I. Every Marauder shall have a vote in the affairs of the ship; has equal title to fresh provisions, or strong liquors, and may use them at their pleasure.

II. Every Marauder shall have an equal share of all treasure.

III. The lights and candles to be put out at eight o'clock at night: if any Marauder after that hour still remains inclined to drinking, they shall do it on the open deck.

IV. Marauders must keep their pistols and cutlass clean and fit for service.

V. Don't be shitty to fellow Marauders, or anyone for that matter. Forget not the Golden Rule.

VI. When using the plank as a diving board, each Marauder shall wait for his proper turn.

VII. Marauders shall always strive to not take themselves too seriously.

VIII. Deserting the ship, striking a fellow Marauder, dereliction of one's duties, robbery betwixt one another, or any other general shitiness shall be punished by exclusion from the next marauding expedition and/or extra duties for less serious offenses.

IX. If a Marauder sees Captain Roberts' flag, that Marauder shall call out, "Roberts!" thrice and ring the bell vigorously. If a Marauder spies a monster, the call is, "Monster!" with a likewise vigorous ringing of the bell.

X. Do not ring the bell as a prank. It's not funny. See Rule VIII for punishment.

XI. We must help people when we can, regardless of race, creed, or sexual orientation.

XII. Marauders will adhere to the Chivalric Code of the Continent.

XIII. What happens on Mirth Island stays on Mirth Island.

XIV. Have fun! Be kind!

"Who's Captain Roberts?" Azure asked. She had heard the name before, but didn't know much, if anything, about him.

"Let's not talk about him right now," the Marauder King said, his brow creasing for a moment. "We're drunk! And in a mood for merriment. Instead, why don't ya join us in a round of our favorite drinking song?" He faced the crew. "Whattaya say? Let's show them our drinking song! One, two, three!"

"IT'S OUR DRINKING SONG, SO DRINK ALONG AND SING ALONG WITH US. TELL US ABOUT A TIME IN WHICH YOU

DRANK TOO DANG MUCH!" the whole crew sang together as they quickly formed a large circle around the mast and bar while clapping an energetic beat.

Once the circle was formed, the crewmembers looked to each other, seemingly waiting for something to happen. Eventually, one of them stepped forward into the circle and sang, "I once got so dang drunk, that I snuck up and caught a skunk."

Collectively, the crew giggled.

Another crewmember came forward. "I once got so dang plastered, that I called a big orc a dumb bastard."

Orok shrugged and said, "That's true, he did."

Time after time, another crew member would step up and sing a rhyme. After every one, the crew would laugh, cheer, boo, or sometimes repeat the last words of the rhyme.

"I once got so dang blitzed, that I woke up with pants full of shit."

Then.

"I once drank so much grog, that I found my way through the Eternal Fog."

Then.

"I once was so far in my cups, I migrated south with some ducks."

This one elicited headshakes and polite smiles from the crew, but Azure found herself cracking up at its absurdity. She missed a few rhymes while trying to control her giggling.

"I once drank so much dang beer, that I got lost in the woods for a year." The faun sang.

"Well, I once drank so much dang beer, that I wet-willied my friend in the ear." A human jumped up and stuck his finger in Orok's ear, eliciting guffaws from the crew.

"I once drank so much dang beer, that... what happened is still quite unclear."

This one sparked off good-natured boos and ribbing.

A man who looked particularly drunk waddled forward and tried to sing. "I once got so dang hammered... that I married someone I met on Mirth Island after only courting her for a month... and she... controlled every... facet of my life from that moment on... She berated me in public... and she wouldn't let me go out marauding with my crew... that was the worst part... It was a loveless marriage, kept alive only by my inability to stand up for myself and leave her..."

"STAND UP FOR YOURSELF AND LEAVE HER," the crew sang as several people hurried out to retrieve him from the circle and pat him on the back.

For a while, the crew seemed to be done. They kept clapping in time, and looking around at each other, but no one stepped forward. Then, they turned their attention to the newcomers, encouraging them to try.

"Come on," said the Marauder King, who had taken a place next to Azure. "Give it try. There's no judgement here."

Azure finished her drink and noticed she was starting to get that light feeling which usually accompanied her second or third. She was glad there wasn't a mirror around, as she was certain her face was stamped with a permanent goofy grin. Concentrating, she racked her brain for something clever, unable to think of anything. The Marauder King refilled her glass.

Then, inspiration hit. And although she didn't think it'd be that funny, she found herself stepping forward and singing, "I once drank so much dang booze, that I joined a bigoted Governor's cruise?"

The crew cheered her effort, smiling and laughing as she shrunk away back into the circle. Azure nodded at Brisa and Elijah to try, but they shook their heads back at her while clapping to the beat.

Most people in the circle started looking toward a short man with a wild white beard standing near the starboard rail. Eventually, he limped forward and belted out, "I once got so dang gassed, that I went and shot off my own ass!"

"HE SHOT OFF HIS OWN ASS!" A roaring cheer filled the air, and the song was apparently over.

"Did he really do that?" Azure asked the Marauder King as the crew laughed around her.

"Would ya like to hear about it?" he asked.

"Sure." Azure took another drink.

"We've got a request!" the Marauder King shouted. "Blunderbuss!"

The crew cheered and rolled right into another song.

"OH! BLUNDERBUSS, OH, BLUNDERBUSS,

"WHEN WE WERE A MUCHER YOUNGER US,
"AND WE WERE CAUGHT UP IN THE PLUNDER LUST,
"HE SHOT OFF HIS CHEEK WITH A BLUNDERBUSS,
The short man with the white beard climbed onto a barrel and began to sing.

Once upon the sea, we spied a merchant ship,
Sailing upwind, Hey! We had it in our grip.
We pictured various riches, like silk and jewels and gold,
So we pulled alongside her, like pirates brave and bold.
I had my trusty blunderbuss, everything was feeling right,
Then I climbed up over the gunwale and had an awful fright.
Seven loaded pistols, were cocked and aimed at me,
I jumped and slipped and backed away and fell down on one knee.
I threw my weapon down, my eyes were filled with fear,
But when the gun struck the ground, it shot me in the rear!

The man rubbed his butt, shaking his head in mock dismay.

The merchants they had quite a laugh, and showed mercy for our sin,
We promised we learned our lesson…we'd never plunder again!
AND OUR FLAGS WERE HUNG, HUNG DOWN LOW AT HALF-MAST, AND WE DUBBED HIM BLUNDERBUSS…BECAUSE WE WERE TOO NICE TO NAME HIM HALF-ASS!

Again, the crew cheered themselves, then dispersed into lively conversations and drinking.

"Is that story true?" Azure asked the man as he approached them.

Blunderbuss turned around, threatening to pull his pants down. "Would you like to see?"

"Uh no, that's alright."

He turned back around, grinning. "Yes, it's true. And it was a formative experience, too. We realized then that it wasn't the stealing and plundering that we craved, it was more about spending time with each other and having adventures. We held a meeting and came up with a list of core values we all shared. We decided then to become what we are today. Marauders in name alone, having fun and helping others whenever the chance arises. Fighting only for justice, and only when completely necessary."

"That's great," Azure said, really feeling the drink now. "But aren't you embarrassed about that song? Like, everyone singing about a big mistake you made?"

"No. Not anymore. It's part of our code to not take ourselves too seriously. And the song tells of our origins, so I like it." Blunderbuss threw his hands out to his sides and shrugged.

"Blunderbuss is our cook," the Marauder King said. "And a damn fine one at that."

"Thank you, sir."

Elijah approached the small group that had formed around Blunderbuss. "Excuse me for asking, but I've never seen anything quite like this before, and I've been around a long time. What exactly are you guys?"

"We're pirates errant, I suppose ya could say. We sail the seas in search of wrongs to right, adventures to prove our chivalry, and of course, treasure."

"Chivalric pirates? Isn't that a contradiction? I've never known pirates like that before."

"Life is a contradiction." The Marauder King shrugged.

"How so?"

"The more I fail, the more likely I am to succeed. The more I try to impress someone, the less impressed they will often be. The more I know, the more I realize that I don't know shit."

"Oh." Now Elijah shrugged his bony shoulders.

"And that's kind of why we chose to call ourselves marauders instead of pirates, but really we just like the sound of it."

"I think it's great," Brisa said.

"Thank you." The Marauder King seemed genuinely touched. "Now, I'm kind of embarrassed about this, but we have created a really good system for warm baths. Don't tell anyone, but we marauders like to stay relatively clean. There's a nice big bathtub in my quarters if anyone would like to use it. I'll make sure ya have yer privacy."

Azure's hand shot up.

NARGOL, THE ONLY FEMALE marauder, took Azure into the captain's quarters to help her get situated.

The Marauder King's quarters was the strangest room Azure had ever been in. The walls were decorated from ceiling to floor with a wide array of paintings, bookshelves, nautical instruments, and bric-a-brac. A giant, ancient-looking tapestry depicting a man bending over with an elongated trumpet sticking out of his butt, accompanied by an anthropomorphic cat in a bright blue doublet and lacy ruff collar playing a lute caught and held Azure's eye.

A copper tub with an intricate network of piping sat in a room within the room at the far corner, surrounded by hanging lanterns that gave off a warm golden luminescence.

"This is the hot water," Nargol said, turning a metal knob. Water spilled out into the tub, and a blue glow began to emanate from the copper piping. "Don't touch that," she said, pointing.

"What is it?"

"I don't really know. Some faun magic that Syl put on the piping with sigaldry or something. I can't fit in this damn tub, so I don't pay that much attention to it."

Azure inspected the glowing pipe closer, noticing small, strange writing etched into it.

"The other knob does cold water, I guess." Again, Nargol pointed. "And there's some kind of magic to keep it from sloshing, so don't worry about that."

"Th—"

"One more thing." Nargol pointed to the other corner of the little room within a room where a strange white chair stood. "That's what they call a toilet. Not sure if you've seen one before. I know I hadn't before I boarded this ship. It's a place where you can... do your business." She shrugged her muscular shoulders. "It's the one thing I won't argue about when they talk about chivalry. Everyone else has to use the shit lines near the stern, but we women get to use this."

"Oh, well, thank you," Azure said.

"You're welcome. It's nice to have more women on board. I've been the only one for a while, now." She nodded, then turned away. "Enjoy!"

"Thanks, again!" Azure called to her as she left.

Azure took a deep breath of steam as it wafted up from the near-boiling water. She hadn't had a proper bath in way too long. She usually loved freshening up in her favorite creek, but a nice hot bath was the perfect thing sometimes, and this was one of those times.

After fine-tuning the water to the right temperature—just a touch cooler than scalding—Azure locked the door and slid rapturously into the tub.

Chapter 13 Helping Those In Need

Azure awoke the next morning clean and dry and slightly hungover. When she opened the door to the small cabin they'd given her, she found some knee-high boots outside with a note attached. The note read:

I thought you might like these
They'll give you a real Marauder look
I hope they fit!
MK

She slipped off her sandals and pulled on the boots, happy to find that they fit perfectly.

As she stepped out in her new boots, Blunderbuss shoved a plate of steaming food in her hands.

"Wakey wakey, eggs and bakey," he said.

The bacon smelled delicious and tasted even better. As she ate, Azure scanned the deck for her friends. Elijah was talking with a group of humans toward the bow, and Brisa was chatting with the faun near the mast.

Absentmindedly, she wandered over to the rail. Still chewing, she closed her eyes and took in the sounds of the sea—the gentle creaking of cordage and timbers, the crash and spray of seawater against the hull, the fluttering of the sails above. A sense of belonging, of being where she should truly be, washed over her as a fine, invigorating mist wet her face. In this moment, the feeling of relief was palpable. The muscles in her shoulders and back began to relax for the first time in a long while.

"Azure," the Marauder King said, startling her. "Good morning." He looked down and his eyes widened. "The boots fit!"

"Yes, thank you," Azure said.

"Oh, you're welcome. I—" He brought his fingertips to his forehead and temples and began massaging his head. "I always forget; is it liquor before beer makes a headache severe? Or liquor before beer, to this you must adhere? Or liquor before beer, next day shed a tear?"

"I thought it was liquor before beer, you're in the clear," Azure said, unsure of herself.

"Hmm. Well, I can't remember the order I drank anyway." He puffed his cheeks out and exhaled a noisy breath. "We should probably drink less, we marauders. I mean, it's fun, but we could really stand to cut it back to once a week or something." He looked up at the sails, pondering the idea as if it was a timber-shuddering revelation. "Anyway, I need to introduce you to some people ya didn't get a chance to meet last night. They're up on the poop deck." Both he and a nearby crew member tried and failed to suppress giggles.

As he began to lead Azure away, he suddenly stopped and made a deep bow to a pair of capybaras near the main mast. One of them was dressed in a luxurious green gown, the other in a smart black suit. "First, it is my pleasure to introduce you to the distinguished Mrs. Eleanor Covington and her husband Alistair. It is customary on this ship to show them the proper respect whenever crossing their paths. They also appreciate fresh fruit, if you ever find yourself in the possession of any." He lowered his voice. "And if you notice them make a mess on the deck, they prefer that you discreetly clean it up without making a fuss."

Azure made a respectful curtsey, liking this ship more and more.

The Marauder King led her aft, up a steep incline to the ship's steering wheel. "This is our sailing master, Mr. Cordingly."

"Happy to meet you," the man said, shaking her hand. He was the most serious man Azure had seen on board so far, but that wasn't saying much. He wore plain clothes that looked to be made out of the same canvas as the sails.

"This, unfortunately for us, is Mr. Cordingly's last expedition with us," the Marauder King said.

"I'm going to be a father in less than three months." He beamed. "My wife, may the gods bless her, is a special one. She's allowed me one last adventure before I settle down with our family."

"To start a new adventure," the Marauder King added, gripping Mr. Cordingly's shoulder.

"Congratulations," Azure said. "And it was nice to meet you."

"And this," the Marauder King said, whisking her to another man, "is Mr. Threepbrush, our Quartermaster." Azure shook his hand, as well. He had golden hair, which was an unusual sight, and his skin was a bit paler than most humans. He wore a fancy blue coat over a white collared shirt that was unbuttoned halfway down, nice leather boots over blue breeches, and a gold hoop earring in his left ear. He seemed to be the only person in the crew who had a golden wand.

"I'm Mr. Threepbrush, mighty marauder," he said with a grin.

"Nice to meet you." Azure smiled back.

"Mr. Threepbrush is second in command on this ship," the Marauder King said.

"So, Azure, where would you like to go?" Mr. Threepbrush asked, gripping the ship's wheel.

Azure told them about the governor's ship, and about her dad, and everything that had happened. She told them about Dragon Island, and their previous decision to go there.

"I have to save my dad," she said. "I just don't know how."

"Well," said Mr. Cordingly, "their galleon is faster than our ship, but if they're making a few stops, we should be able to catch up to it." He looked up at the sails. "But, if they chose to open fire on us, we wouldn't stand a chance."

"The Dragon Island thing sounds promising," Mr. Threepbrush said. "But getting there is close to impossible."

"Ah, but ya forgot about Old Jonas." The Marauder King wagged a finger in the air. "He found the door and apparently still knows the way to it."

"The door?" Azure said.

"There is a door somewhere in the Eternal Fog. If you find it, you can face a trial, and if you pass, the way to Dragon Island will be revealed to you. Or so Old Jonas says."

"Do you really think it would be worth it to go through all of this and find Dragon Island," Azure asked. "I mean, couldn't it be too late by the time we find it, if we ever do?"

Mr. Cordingly looked to the horizon, deep in thought. "I think we have two days before we would need to head to the Capitol Isles. If we haven't found Dragon Island in those two days, we'll set sail toward the Capitol Isles and still beat the galleon there."

"You're sure?"

"Yes. And that's a conservative estimate, allowing for the usual hurdles along the way. We just careened the ship last week and we're very fast in the water right now."

"So Dragon Island it is then?" The Marauder King had a gleam in his eye.

"Well yeah, if you all are willing to go through all this trouble for me," Azure said.

"Are ya kidding? This is what we live for. This could be our greatest adventure yet!"

"Thank you so much."

"Where is Old Jonas?" Mr. Threepbrush asked.

"I know exactly where he is," said the Marauder King. "Same place he always is. Mirth Island."

"To Mirth Island, then." Mr. Threepbrush gripped the wheel but didn't turn it. Apparently they were already headed in that direction.

Elijah and a few of the crew approached.

"Hey, sir, we were just talking with Elijah here, and guess what?" one of the crew said.

"What?"

"He's a real pirate. An impressive one at that. He needs to find this golden medallion to break his curse, so we kind of told him we'd help him find it, sir."

"Of course we'll help him find it, but we've got another pressing quest, too. We're on to Mirth Island."

The crew began discussing possible locations of the golden medallion, so Azure slipped away to talk to Brisa, who was in a deep conversation with the faun.

"Sorry to interrupt," she said, "but my name is Azure." She held out her hand.

"I'm Syl." The faun shook her hand. He had horns that curved down, then out to either side of his head, and there was a small but prominent scar just above his sincere, warm smile. "And don't worry about interrupting, we were just talking about the pervasive discrimination in the League of Islands." His accent was thick, but Azure could understand him perfectly.

"What do you think we can do about it?" Azure asked.

"Well, electing people like this Governor Pratt is definitely a step in the wrong direction."

"I know. I prayed to the gods that he wouldn't be elected, but it didn't work, obviously."

"Ah, the gods," Syl said, a mischievous grin across his face. "Their will is eternally hard to pin down."

"Do you believe in our gods?"

"I believe in whatever truths or untruths help me live a better life."

"So you're saying the gods are untruths, then?" Azure had no idea how this had so quickly diverged into a religious conversation.

"No, I'm saying our understanding of their purpose for us often comes from untruths."

"And you know what their true purpose for us is?"

"No! Absolutely not. I'm not sure there is a purpose. But if there is, I won't be privy to it in this life."

"So what do you live for, then?"

"I simply live." His smile became broader. "And what a gift life is!"

Azure's thoughts went to her mom, no longer experiencing the gift of life due to her involvement in an anti-faun protest. She began to well up with tears, suddenly wanting to get something off her chest. Something about Syl's manner made her comfortable, like he could help her somehow, like he would understand. She knew it wasn't his job to help her, and that she probably shouldn't burden him with her shit, but she couldn't help herself.

"I used to hate fauns," she said, looking down.

Syl simply nodded.

"Why?" Brisa asked, taken aback.

"My mom died at an anti-faun protest." She continued to stare down at the deck. "There was a ship coming into Barren, on the Nameless Isles where I live. The ship was bringing a group of faun immigrants. And Pratt, who was just an insanely rich guy at the time, organized this protest against them. My mom was caught up in the idea that fauns were violent and coming to take our jobs and our way of life from us, so she joined the protest.

"As the ship arrived, people congregated on the dock with signs. But the dock was old, and rotten, and it collapsed under their weight. My mom drowned inches from the surface, unable to reach air because of debris and a panicking mass of people." Azure had been trying to hold back the tears, but now they ran down her cheeks. "It was such a stupid way to die. If she would have died being heroic, or even in just a random accident, it would have been easier to take."

Azure composed herself, wiping the tears away with her sleeve.

"So, like most people in my town, I directed my anger, my hatred, at the fauns. I allowed anti-faun propaganda into my heart, having never actually met one.

Azure sobbed, again. "A group of us humans found a teenaged faun alone at the beach, when I was seventeen, only a few years ago. We beat him. I kicked him when he was down and cowering in the sand.

"Afterward, when the group dispersed, I was overcome with guilt. I snuck back to the beach with fresh water and food. I learned the faun's name was Via. I sat on that beach with him well into the night, talking about our lives. I came to realize that I'd been horribly wrong, and that my mom had been wrong, too. I wanted to curl up on that beach and die, ashamed of my inexcusable ignorance.

"I helped Via find his family. He told them that I had helped him, leaving out the part where I had also been the one who hurt him.

"The next day I went back to see him, but he and his family had moved away. I promised myself right then that I would make up for what I had done. I would fight against oppression and bigotry whenever I could. I know it's not enough, but I—"

"You made a mistake," Syl said. "You got caught up in a group you didn't actually belong to. Many are unable to break away from such groups. But you did. And now you found a group the gods intended you to find, or so it seems. I forgive you, and welcome you, for whatever that's worth."

Azure broke down, feeling unworthy of his forgiveness.

Syl stepped forward and embraced her, letting her head rest on his shoulder. Azure cried into it, letting all the unspoken tension of years of guilt flood out. She wasn't sure how long the crying carried on, but when it was done, she felt like she had come up for air after being underwater for far too long.

"Thank you, Syl," she said, backing away and wiping her eyes with her lacy sleeve.

"Do you feel better?"

"Much better."

"Good. Because we'll be arriving on Mirth Island soon, and you should be feeling happy in the happiest place in the islands. I'm glad you decided to share your story with me today. And I'm glad to hear that you're fighting for justice and equality. I've got some duties to perform, but I'll see you once we land."

As Syl walked away, Brisa said, "I'm glad you shared that story."

"I just felt—"

Robin came diving down onto Azure's shoulder. "You alright?" she said.

"Yeah. I'm good."

The Marauder King's bird companion, Nova, drifted down to the rail of the ship and began some kind of mating ritual that vaguely resembled dancing. He slid back and forth across the rail without seeming to move his feet. The sight was strange and giggle-inducing.

"He's insatiable!" Robin said, giddy. "Look at him. He's just gliding across that rail so effortlessly...side to side...and even backwards? Shit! It's too gods-damned sexy. I can't take it!"

She flew over to him, then the two birds sped off up into the top of the sails.

Brisa and Azure looked at each other with confused expressions, then burst out laughing together.

LATER, WHEN MIRTH ISLAND was within sight, the crew gathered around the mast.

"Marauders," the Marauder King said, "let me open our meeting in the traditional way." He ran a hand over his fancy mustache, apparently thinking. "Okay, a marauder walks into a tavern with a ship's steering wheel sticking out the front of his pants. The bartender asks, 'Do you know you have a ship's steering wheel sticking out the front of your pants?' And the marauder says, 'Aye! It's driving me nuts!'"

Some of the crew chuckled, while others groaned and rolled their eyes. The Marauder King looked to Azure and Brisa, and his face reddened.

"I'm sorry, that joke was probably too crude in the presence of ladies."

"It's fine," Azure said, smiling.

"What about me?" called Nargol from the back. "I'm a lady."

"What, was that joke too clean for ya?"

"Exactly!"

At this, a healthier laugh spread through the crew.

"Alright, alright, on to business. And some exciting business I have for ya. We've got a quest!"

A raucous cheer went up.

"We have a lady who needs our help. And in order to give her this help, we must find Old Jonas on Mirth Island."

Another big cheer.

"But we won't have time for our usual shenanigans, because once we have talked to Old Jonas, we're heading straight for—wait for it—Dragon Island!"

The crew lost their collective mind.

"Our new friends believe there is something on Dragon Island that can help young Azure save her dad. So after we go there, we'll head to the Capitol Isles on a life-saving mission. We'll be arriving at Mirth soon, so be ready to scour the place for Old Jonas. Let's fan out and meet back at the sign after an hour."

Chapter 14 Mirth Island

As they approached Mirth Island, Azure noticed a towering structure looming up from its center.

"What is that?" she asked Syl.

"The Fortress," he replied. "It's the biggest casino on the island. By far."

The structure looked like a castle from children's storybooks about the Continent. It seemed to be built from a million light-colored stones, topped with at least ten conical spires of differing shapes, each of them dark blue and almost sparkling in the sun. Thick green ivy clung to the castle from the ground to about half of its height, broken up only by the countless windows cut into the walls. A large flag—depicting a golden crown and two crossed chalices on a dark blue background—fluttered majestically in the breeze. Several ropes extended out from one of the tallest parapets to the ground hundreds of yards away.

"Those are zip-lines." Syl must have noticed her trying to work out what the ropes were for.

"Zip-lines?"

"Yeah. You can slide down those ropes holding on to these wheel things. It's an absolute blast, if you're not too afraid of heights."

"Wow." Azure wished she had more time to try it.

There were some sort of wooden tracks that rose and fell and zigged and zagged just beyond the port area. A cart of sorts ran along the tracks as if pushed by magic.

"What's that?"

"A rollercoaster." Syl's eyes were wide. "I'd tell you more, but I gotta go help take some sails down."

The port at Mirth Island was unlike anything Azure had ever seen. Buildings filled every inch around the busy bay. Ships of all sizes, including several ciguapa ships, sped in and out from innumerable docks. More people than she had ever seen in one place moved busily along boardwalks built over the beach.

After the *Adventure Ship* had completed its lengthy docking procedure, the crew members extended a gangway for debarkation.

"Welcome to Mirth Island!" the Marauder King said to Azure and Brisa, extending his arms out for them to go first. Elijah had decided to stay and watch the ship, and Robin had flown off somewhere with Nova. Mr. Cordingly, Blunderbuss, and Syl came along with them to the island.

The sounds of commerce, of singing, of instruments, of people laughing and shouting, created a cacophony of excitement that was felt as well as heard. Along the waterfront were a countless number of bars, mixed in with places like cardrooms, theaters, dance clubs, and mini golf courses. A statue of the gods Avera and Hime dominated the central boardwalk. Avera held an intricately decorated chalice up with one hand and a string of pearls in the other, while Hime, who had an arm around her waist, stared down unabashedly at her ample cleavage with his one eye not covered with a patch. A large wooden sign just off of the dock read: *Adult Fun* and pointed to the west. Another sign next to it read: *Fun For Everyone* and pointed east.

"It's pretty much just brothels to the west," the Marauder King said. "Reginald Pratt has a second residence over there, too."

"Seriously?" She had suspected Pratt's comments about Mirth Island had been bullshit, but had underestimated his level of hypocrisy.

"Yes. Ya want to go see it?"

"No, thanks."

"Alright. Well, Old Jonas can usually be found at the bars, of which you can see, are many. I think he'll likely be at Wenches, so we'll try there first. Follow me." He led them to the east.

Blunderbuss took a rolled-up paper from his pocket, unrolled it, and posted it to a bulletin board along the boardwalk. On the paper was a surprisingly lifelike painting of himself and Orok with their arms around each other. It read: *Orcs Are Not to be Feared. Ask a Marauder About Our Time With Them,* in beautiful calligraphy.

"Did you paint that?" Azure asked.

"Yeah. I try to post as many as I can wherever we go."

"That's so good of you."

"Eh." He shrugged. "It's the least I can do."

As they walked, Azure took in the sights and sounds with a sense of astonished wonder. Every bar they passed seemed to be playing loud music. There were places called The Scumm Bar, The Admiral Benbow Inn, Sparrow's, The Penzance Dance Club, The Echo Chamber: Hawk, The Echo Chamber: Harmony, and Two-Peckered Billy Goat.

Azure had never felt so out-of-place, although she was enamored with everything she was seeing and hearing.

The next bar, easily the biggest they had seen so far, was called Wenches. Its painted sign depicted a serving girl in a low-cut blouse tilting forward and holding out a mug of beer.

Inside, the high ceilings were held up with impressive heavy timbers. A band playing traditional calypso music entertained from a small stage in the corner.

The place was packed. Serving girls in skimpy outfits rushed back and forth carrying trays of food and drinks. One of them approached and said, "Welcome back, Marauders. Table for seven?"

"No, not this time, Journey. We're looking for Old Jonas. Is he here?"

"You just missed him. I think he headed west if you know what I mean. He said he'd be back in about three hours."

"Thank you." The Marauder King tipped his fancy hat to her as the group moved back outside. "He's in the Adult Fun section, so he's as good as lost to us until he gets back."

"So what should we do?" Azure asked.

The Marauder King shuffled his feet, gazing down at the floor and rubbing the back of his neck. "Well, if ya don't mind, we could have a little fun while we wait. I don't think there's any getting around the waiting part, so we might as well have a good time while we do it?" He looked up to her, eyes wide with childlike hope.

"I'm in," said Azure, excited by the idea. "What do you have in mind?"

"We've been itching to do the Pirate Experience, again. We could do that, then get dinner and drinks here at Wenches while we wait for Old Jonas to return?"

"Perfect." Azure had no idea what the Pirate Experience was, but it sounded fun. "Brisa, are you in?"

"Sure, why not?"

Chapter 15 The Pirate Experience

The Marauder King led the small group through a gauntlet of carnival games and strange, apparently magic-powered rides back to what appeared to be an old shipwreck. A sign across the broken bow read: *The Pirate Experience* in fancy red script. A smaller sign near the built-in door at the bottom of the bow read:

WARNING:

This experience uses magical illusions to create a make-believe reality.

If you are prone to motion sickness, you may want to reconsider participating.

Those with heart problems, or those who are pregnant should not participate in this experience.

Her interest piqued, Azure followed the group into the strange ship.

"Hey, MK," said a ciguapa woman from behind a counter. "Welcome back."

"Hello, Cala." The Marauder King embraced the woman. "I brought some newbies along."

Cala was much older than Brisa, but no less beautiful. She had many more rune tattoos, and her dark blue hair had silver streaks throughout.

Brisa and Cala approached each other, and without a word, simultaneously traced a line from their foreheads, down to the center of their chests, then around in a circle. After the greeting, Cala said, "Welcome."

"Thank you, Cala. My name is Brisa. We are well met."

"May the fire in your chest burn bright." Cala nodded, then turned to the group. "So what will it be today, MK?"

"Well, I was thinking a chivalric experience, maybe a life-saving quest, but let me confer with my crew." The Marauder King pointed to a menu of sorts on the wall. "This is what they offer. Are there any that jump out at ya, or does a good old-fashioned life-saving quest work for ya? I figure maybe we should practice for our real quest ahead?"

The menu read:

The Pirate Experience

1. *A Map to Buried Treasure*
2. *A Casual Day at Sea*
3. *A Rousing Broadside Battle*
4. *Sea Monster Encounter*
5. *Stormy Seas*
6. *Saving a Maiden*
7. *The Pirate Experience for Children Under 13*

NEW 8. The Continent Experience

"Whatever you would like to do," Azure said. "They all sound fun to me, except maybe Stormy Seas." She was particularly interested in the Continent Experience, but didn't want to step on any toes, and the Marauder King made a good point; this could be good practice for the white-knuckle terror that likely awaited them.

"I'm in for anything," Brisa added with a shrug.

"Number six it is, then!" exclaimed the Marauder King.

Azure fished out her coin purse, hoping the cost of this experience wouldn't be too much.

"Your money is no good, here, young Azure," the Marauder King said.

"You sure?"

"Absolutely! And don't think about paying a bent copper for dinner or any drinks tonight, either. You are our guests, and we've got you covered. Alright?"

Azure hesitated, then said, "Alright. Thank you very much!"

"Don't mention it." The Marauder King tried, and failed, to hide his bubbling Chivalric pride.

Cala took the group into a large open room with nothing but a wooden box on wheels inside. "Please remove all weapons, sharp objects, magic wands, or anything that could cause accidental strangulation and put them in the box."

When everyone had complied, Cala wheeled the box into a closet and shut the door.

"In a few minutes, you will be placed under a spell. This spell will affect all of your senses, making you believe that you are somewhere else. For those of you who have not done this before, I must warn you, it is very convincing. You will be able to see, touch, hear, smell, and taste everything around you. At times, you may feel that your life is in danger, but this is only an illusion. In twenty-five years of operating, we have never had more than a few minor bumps and bruises. To that end, please refrain from striking each other while under the spell, because you will also be striking each other in the real world. Any questions?"

Everyone shook their heads.

"Alright. Try to relax as the spell takes hold. I assure you, it's safe, but it will likely be overwhelming at first." She made her way to the door, saying, "Have fun!" before closing it behind her.

The room went dark, except for the subdued glow of silvery blue lines along the ceiling, floor, and all four walls.

Azure heard the rustle of wind in her ear, smelled the sea, and felt the sand under her toes before she saw anything. Then, as if she were opening her eyes, a magnificent scene appeared before her.

The whole crew stood on a black-sand beach in the shadow of a colossal white castle on a ridge.

Azure swayed on her feet, nearly toppling over. She felt like she had when she shot that bolt at the mannequin. Luckily, the feeling passed within seconds, although it was still hard to get her bearings.

"Thank the gods you're here!" said an old man wearing flowing red robes. "The evil Captain Rach has just captured my daughter and taken her on his pirate ship." The man pointed out to sea, to black sails in the sunset, where a menacing black sloop sailed away. A black flag with a white spider flapped violently as the ship sped to sea.

"Your ship is ready!" He pointed to another sloop anchored off the beach. "I'll use my ancient magic to transport you to your ship, but the rest will be up to you. Please don't let us down. The fate of our princess, of our kingdom, rests with you!"

The man snapped his fingers, and the crew found themselves on the ship.

"Weigh the anchor! Set the sails!" The Marauder King barked orders as he took his place behind the ship's wheel. Azure had never seen him so serious, or impressive. It was like he stood a foot taller than usual.

Azure tried her best to help. Mr. Cordingly gave her more specific, easier-to-follow instructions which she carried out as well as she could. Brisa seemed to know what to do, more or less, and jumped from task to task with her usual grace.

In no time, they were in pursuit. They sailed into the breathtaking sunset, the black ship on the horizon. Azure noticed that the sunset wasn't fading, in fact, it seemed to be intensifying in vividness and visual splendor. It was the only thing she sensed that reminded her she was in a make-believe world.

They gained on Captain Rach's ship quickly.

The Marauder King studied the black ship through a spyglass. "Man the cannon! We'll come along broadside to its port side. When I give the signal, fire. And aim high. We don't want to hurt the princess. We'll take out their mast and cripple them."

The crew scattered belowdecks. Azure followed Mr. Cordingly.

"Just do as I do," he told her, picking up a canvas bundle and shoving it into a cannon. "This is powder." He then took a metal rod and rammed the bundle down as far as it could go.

Azure added a canvas bundle to her cannon and shoved it down with a rod.

"Now, the ball."

Azure followed his lead, lifting a cannon ball into the cannon. It was heavy, but Azure managed just fine.

"Now push the cannon to the gun port and aim."

Azure pushed the cannon forward until its tip poked out of the hull. The cannon looked much heavier than it felt. Maybe that was another difference between this world and the real one.

"Wait for the signal." He gripped a cord that came from the back of his cannon. "When we hear it, we'll pull this, as hard as we can."

Azure nodded before poking her head out above her cannon. She could see they were very close, now, so she ducked back in and picked up her cord.

The looming black hull of the pirate ship came into view through the gun port. Azure titled her cannon back, trying to aim for mast-level. She held her breath, muscles tense and ready to spring.

"Fire!"

As Azure yanked the cord, an ear-splitting boom staggered her. Thick black smoke filled the room. She wasn't sure if they had fired or been fired upon. But as the smoke cleared, she saw that at least one of the shots had been successful. The other ship's mast hung broken down to its deck, the sails sagging overboard, dragging in the sea.

Mr. Cordingly held out a hand, smiling. Azure shook it, a warm sense of accomplishment coursing through her.

"Let's get topside," Mr. Cordingly said, hurrying away.

On the deck, Syl handed her a pistol and a cutlass. "We may have to board her. Stay alert."

Captain Rach's ship slowed, and the Marauder King came across its bow, which turned out to be a huge mistake. A cannon on the bowsprit launched a white net over the rescuers' ship. The net clung to everything it touched, as if it was made of glue.

Azure's stomach turned as she watched the pirate crew begin to haul the ships together with a white rope attached to the net, but not just because they had been caught. The crew aboard the pirate ship were spiders; human-sized spiders whose faces were just human enough to ensure the haunting of her nightmares for the foreseeable future.

Before she could process this, the ships had been lashed together with what Azure now understood to be spider webs.

A giant spider holding a woman wrapped in webs approached the rail. It wore a tricorn hat and had patches over four of its eight eyes. Grotesque, coarse hair protruded from its underbelly and covered the bases of its legs.

"I am Captain Rach," the giant spider said, its voice more nightmare fodder. "If you want my prize," he held the princess up with his two front legs, "come and take her."

Spiders holding swords stood on either side of the captain. Above, another spider swung across to their ship's mast on a web, then withdrew four flintlock pistols from its belt and aimed them down at the Marauder King's crew.

Azure looked to the Marauder King, awaiting instruction. The height he had seemed to gain was now gone. He slouched forward, his face a mask of agonized indecision.

"What are your orders?" Blunderbuss asked.

The Marauder King said nothing, his eyes darting from spider to spider.

"We don't have all night," Captain Rach said. "I'm getting hungry." He licked one of his oversized fangs.

The Marauder King seemed frozen in place.

To Azure, the decision was obvious. Why not order an attack? That's what they were here for, wasn't it? This was, after all, just a strange, and extremely convincing illusion. But the Marauder King was caught up. It was clear to Azure that he had forgotten he was in the Pirate Experience.

A spider advanced across the lashed rails, two swords raised high. Blunderbuss charged ahead and swung his sword in a great diagonal arc, slicing off two of the spider's legs. One of the spider's swords clung to the floor as it wailed in agony. With another deft slice, the spider was completely disarmed. Blunderbuss plunged his sword into the spider's belly. A flood of dark brown liquid spilled out onto the deck.

Everything after that happened fast.

Gunshots rained down from above, striking the timbers all around them, sending splinters into the air. Azure ran to her right and dove behind a barrel. From there, she peeked up at the spider pirate on the mast, who was reloading his guns.

Azure stood and aimed her pistol. She cocked the hammer back and fired. Her shot struck the spider in the head. It slumped forward and fell from the mast, landing with a sickening thud.

She was pleasantly surprised to find everything she needed for a reload attached to a leather baldric across her chest. Thinking back to the lessons her dad used to give her, she unfastened the powder horn and poured the prescribed amount down into the muzzle. "Not too much," he always used to say. She pushed a lead ball wrapped in a cloth patch down after it, then tamped it down with the ramrod. After sprinkling more powder into the firing pan, she pulled the hammer back with her thumb as she lifted the pistol to shoulder height. Her dad would have been proud of her efficiency on that reload.

But by the time she looked up, the battle was over. Brisa seemed to have used magic to wrap one of the spiders in its own web. Syl and Mr. Cordingly both stood over the dead Captain Rach, wiping his stinking dark guts from their swords. The Marauder King stood fixed in the same spot.

Azure took the Marauder King by the arm and said, "Let's untie the princess."

"Aye," he said, as if he had just awoken, "good idea."

Together they approached the princess, and, using knives, cut the web that enveloped her.

"Thank you, brave crew, for saving my life." The princess was probably the most beautiful human Azure had ever seen. "And thank you for vanquishing the evil Captain Rach. No longer will he terrorize our fair land." The princess stood and looked pretty for a little too long, seemingly allowing everyone to drink in the moment. Then she raised a hand and snapped her fingers.

The illusion fell away. They were back in the Pirate Experience room.

"Again..." The Marauder King rubbed the burn scar on his cheek. "I freeze up every time I'm faced with a tough decision. I'll never be a true king."

"Oh don't be so tough on yourself," said Blunderbuss. "We got the job done, didn't we?"

"All thanks to you guys."

"Maybe this time, but *us guys* chose you as our leader, and we stick by that, right everyone?"

"Absolutely." Syl put a hand on the Marauder King's shoulder.

Mr. Cordingly agreed, too. The Marauder King forced a smile.

"Now, how about beers at Wenches? I think I saw Chastity working." Blunderbuss winked.

With this, the Marauder King's eyes lit back up.

Chapter 16 Wenches

"Hi, I'm Chastity, and I'll be your buxom serving-wench. Can I start you off with some drinks?" The server put a hand on the Marauder King's shoulder, eliciting a huge grin.

"A beer for me," the Marauder King said, smiling up at her from the table. "The darker the better."

"You know," said Chastity, "I can always tell who the real men in this place are by what they order. Most of our customers are kind of... well, I shouldn't say. But you're different. I like that."

The rest of the men immediately ordered dark beers, as well. Azure shrugged and followed along. Brisa ordered a water.

"Are you seeing this?" the Marauder King asked as Chastity sashayed away. "That lass still fancies me!"

"I noticed that myself." Blunderbuss slapped him on the back.

"Aye, me too," Syl added.

"She laid her soft hand atop my shoulder as she spoke, and she made eye contact with me, and smiled that beautiful smile right into my very soul. It was like the warmness of the morning sun on a still day at sea."

Azure looked to Brisa and shook her head, subtly.

"Shh," said Mr. Cordingly, looking serious. "She's coming back with our drinks already."

"That was quick," Blunderbuss said to her as she handed him a beer.

"On the rare occasion I get a really interesting group like you guys, I try to speed it up the best I can." Her giggle was obviously forced. "Have you decided what you'd like to eat?"

Azure ordered a steak and ale pie, which sounded delicious. Chastity flirted with her as she ordered, but not as much as she flirted with the Marauder King.

A small group of men came in and sat down at the next table. Chastity glided over to them to get their drink orders. She seemed particularly flirtatious with one of the men, a tall, bearded guy with long hair.

The Marauder King watched Chastity's interaction with the man intently, a souring look on his face. When the man put his hand on Chastity's hip, the Marauder King let out an unintentional yelp.

"It seems I have a rival," he said to the group in a low voice.

"You're not going to stir something up, again, are you, sir?"

The Marauder King twirled a finger in the air, bobbing his head, his eyes aimed at the ceiling.

"I think I've got a song brewing." He mouthed some words, still twirling his finger. "Could you guys back me up?"

"Of course," Blunderbuss, Mr. Cordingly, and Syl all replied. "But try not to get into a fight," Mr. Cordingly added.

Azure wondered what the hell was going on.

After mouthing a few more words, the Marauder King stood, as dramatic as a stage actor, and marched around the table to the man, who was sitting and laughing with his friends.

"I beg your pardon," the Marauder King sang.

"HE BEGS YOUR PARDON," the crew repeated in song, as well.

"For I think we are in opposition." The Marauder King stood with chest high.

"Are you singing at me?" the man said, his brow furrowed.

"I'm singing to you."

"HE'S SINGING TO YOU." This time Azure tried to join in.

"For it seems that I have the same goal as you do."

"Of what goal do you speak?" the man said, scowling, but with just a hint of song in his voice.

"I believe we are in competition, though I think it was not our intention. For the lass bringing drinks, it seems methinks, that both of us two are quite smitten."

The man laughed and muttered something to his friends at the table. Then he stood, knocking his wooden chair to the floor, and sang in a mocking voice.

"Well, now I must beg *your* pardon!" He looked to his friends, who roared with laughter. "For I must tell you that you are mistaken. For a waitress at Wenches I'd never be deceived, and my heart could never be taken."

"Deceived?" the Marauder King took a dramatic step back, and threw up his hands as if he were about to engage in fisticuffs. The man formed fists at his sides. "How dare you, good man! To slander the name of the one I adore. She is virtuous, sincere, beautiful, and pure. She showed me affection and now I want more."

"HE WANTS MORE!"

"For my longing, my yearning, in my heart is burning, like the sea in a storm my—"

The man drew back and punched the Marauder King in the face, sending him sprawling across the floor.

Before Azure could register what happened, the marauders had jumped up and attacked. Blunderbuss drove his shoulder into the man's gut, causing both of them to crash to the ground in a heap. Syl came in hot with a flying kick. His hoof caught the ear of the man's closest companion. Mr. Cordingly roared, smiling, and chased another man around the table.

Azure and Brisa looked to each other, then shot up and joined the fray. Azure launched herself into a man who had just gained the upper hand on Blunderbuss and was raining down poorly blocked punches on his grinning face.

In her peripheral vision, Azure saw Brisa approach a man, who turned and sprinted away.

But before the fight could really get going, several large men who worked for Wenches broke it up, separating the two groups and standing between them.

"This place sucks, anyway," said the long-haired, bearded man.

He and his friends left the building with a barrage of insults.

Blood from a small gash over the Marauder King's right eye flooded down over his face, but he never stopped grinning. Brisa took a handkerchief from a nearby table and pressed it to the wound.

"You alright?" Brisa asked as everyone settled back down at the table.

"Aye!" he said, his teeth bloody. "I defended the honor of my dear Chastity, and my crew fought bravely by my side." He took a swig of beer, washing away most of the blood.

Azure shook her head and smiled, thankful she had met these goofballs. "I have to pee," she said, getting back up from the table.

As she searched the expansive bar for a latrine, Chastity said, "Our women's latrine isn't working right now. You'll have to go next door to the Three Lanterns, tough girl." She winked and threw a few fake punches in the air.

"Thank you."

A small, broken-down tavern next door had a faded sign that read: *The Three Lanterns: A Place for Drinks, Understanding, and Insight.*

Inside, the place was dark and musty. As Azure headed back to a marked latrine, the bartender said, "Sorry, Miss, but the latrine is for paying customers only. Tavern policy I'm afraid."

"Alright. What do you got?"

"Our special is grog. Our only drink is grog. But on the bright side, we've got the best grog on the islands."

"I guess I'll take a grog." Azure was crossing her legs, now.

After paying for the drink and leaving the glass on the bar, Azure relieved herself at the stinking latrine.

When she came back out she sat on a stool at the bar and sipped her drink. "Dang. This *is* good!" She held the grog up toward the bartender.

"Told ya."

A drunk older man who was sitting next to Azure chuckled. "It's the best grog on the islands," he said, slurring his words.

"So I've heard." Azure took another drink, savoring the flavors.

"I call it the nectar of the gods," the old man said. "My name is…Favian, and I call it the nectar of the gods."

"Nice to meet you, Fav—"

"And I have some authority in the matter. The gods, that is. I was once among the most powerful people in the church, I was. What's your name?"

"Azure."

"Well, Achur, do you wanna hear something interesting?"

"Sure." Azure took another drink.

"The Epiphany is incom...incomplete."

Azure sat up straight on her stool. "What?"

"I said..." Favian held down the urge to vomit with great concentration. "I said, the Epiphany is incomplete."

"What does that mean?" Azure, a student of the Epiphany, found herself immediately captivated. She had no reason to trust the word of a drunk stranger, but she wanted to hear more.

"The church left out the ending." Favian let that slurred statement hang in the air, possibly for dramatic effect, or possibly because he was suppressing vomit, again. "But...here's the good part. If someone deser... deserving of the revelation climbs Mount Insight, on Para...dise Island, and simply...asks for a new one, the entiiiiire Epiphany will appear to them."

"Really?" Azure was skeptical, but she wanted this to be true.

"Yeah. You know, magic is supposed to be access...essible to everyone. And they...didn't want you to know—" Favian's cheeks puffed up. He threw a hand over his mouth and hurried away to the latrine.

"A religious guy getting shit-faced," a woman sitting on the other side of Azure said. "Big surprise."

Azure turned around. "Do you know him?"

"No. I was just commenting on the hypocrisy of the church." The woman's eyes were filled with disgust.

"Oh." Azure took another drink, preferring to think about Favian's words rather than talking to the woman.

"Are you Harmony or Hawk?" the woman asked, bluntly.

Azure hated this false dichotomy. This idea that everyone fell neatly into one of two political factions.

"Harmony." Azure answered despite herself, even though she found the question, before they even knew each other's names, to be a bit intrusive.

"Good. I think I'd have to go puke too if I had to sit next to another fucking Hawk right now."

"Oh." Azure really wasn't interested at the moment.

"They're all horrible bigots, every one of them," the woman said. "They'd rather see their precious Pratt become a king like back on the Continent than to see our great system of government thrive. I can't stand them. Every last one of them is a fatally flawed human being, incapable of empathy, incapable of one rational thought. I mean, how stupid do you have to be to believe the utter shit that spews out of Pratt's mouth?"

"I tend to agree with that last thing, but my dad voted for him," Azure said. "My friends and I are actually on a mission to go and save him from a horrible death."

"Well I'm sorry, but not sorry. If he voted for Pratt he deserves a horrible death."

Apparently still riled up from the last fight, Azure punched the woman in the cheek, knocking her from her stool.

Before the woman could stand, the bartender rounded the bar and stood between them.

"This place sucks!" the woman said. "I'm going to the Echo Chamber, where there aren't any stupid idiots like you!" She snatched her drink from the bar and left.

Azure wobbled, staring at a dark knot in the polished wood of the bar. She had just punched someone for saying aloud something she had thought, more than once, before. As she rubbed her sore knuckles, she realized it wasn't Pratt's followers that she hated, it was the things they had come to believe. She hated Pratt himself, but not necessarily his supporters. People were flawed and full of emotion. They could be manipulated and lied to. But it wasn't the manipulated Azure despised, it was the manipulators. People like Pratt, who had played on people's fears in order to paint all non-humans as detrimental to humankind. His followers were far from blameless, and she would continue to fight them at every turn, but she would no longer hate them. The hatred she internalized had hurt no one but herself. Like a bootheel stamping out sparks, it had only worked to smother her fire. She had to let the hate die.

With this new understanding blossoming in her half-drunk mind, her urgency to find and help her dad heightened.

Still reeling, she sat back on her stool and took a drink.

"Nice punch." The bartender nodded and smiled.

"Thanks." She looked up at him. "Hey, you don't happen to know a guy named Old Jonas, do you?"

"Old Jonas? Shit yeah I know that old dirty bastard. He was just here a few minutes ago."

"He was?"

"Yeah. He stumbled next door to The Dripping Bucket Inn just before you got here."

"Thank you!" Azure finished her drink before sprinting to the next bar in the line.

The Dripping Bucket looked like something from another era. It was what she imagined an inn on the Continent, in the days when knights quested, had been like. The wooden bar had seen much, much better days, and there were unscrubbed blood stains on a concerningly large percentage of the floor. The inn had only one customer at the moment, an old man in an old green silk shirt.

"Old Jonas?" Azure asked as she approached him.

"Who wants to know?" The old man replied, eyes twinkling.

"A friend of the Marauder King."

"MK? You're a friend of his, eh?" the man looked her up and down.

"Yes. He and I came to Mirth Island to find you."

"And you're Old Jonas?" the old man said. "I thought you'd be older."

"No." Azure deflated. "I'm looking for Old Jonas."

"Why?"

"So he can tell us how to get to the door in the Eternal Fog."

The old man's eyebrows raised. "You're sure you're with MK?"

"Yeah. He's over at Wenches if you want to go see him."

"No, I believe you." The old man scratched his chin. "What were we talking about, again?"

"Old Jonas, and the door."

"Oh, yes. Well, if you haven't figured it out yet, I am he who you seek, I am Old Jonas, although just Jonas works, too. I'm not *that* old."

"It's good to meet you," Azure said, trying not to sound hurried. "Can you tell me how to find the door?"

"Yeah, why not?" He scanned the otherwise empty bar. The bartender, who was loudly washing dishes, was the only other person in the building. "Now, I can't tell you all my secrets, but if you go northeast from the Mirth

Island docks, you'll find that door. And I'm not talking roughly northeast. I mean exactly northeast; no divergences whatsoever, right into the fog."

"That's it?" The information, and the ease of obtaining it, seemed anticlimactic.

"Yeah. That's how I found it."

"Thank you, thank you, thank you," Azure said as she rushed away.

Once back at Wenches, she told them everything in between bites of her phenomenal steak and ale pie.

"I can give us an exact northeast heading," Syl said, "easy as breathing. I'll just use a directional will-o'-the-wisp."

Azure didn't know what this meant, but she didn't care at the moment.

Chastity approached the table with another round of drinks.

"I'm sorry, m'lady," the Marauder King said, "but we must make haste. A mission of extreme importance awaits, and lives hang in the balance." He stood, dramatically. "But I promise, I will not forget you. I shall fight and quest in your name, in your honor, from this moment on. And one day, if the gods allow, I will return to you."

"Sounds great, honey. Here's the tab."

The Marauder King insisted on paying for everyone and gave an exorbitant tip.

After shoveling the rest of her pie into her mouth, Azure followed the crew back to the ship.

Chapter 17 The Eternal Fog

"You got into a bar brawl without me!" Robin was indignant upon Azure's return.

"It wasn't like we planned it," Azure replied. "And to tell you the truth..." she looked down at the deck, "I got into two bar fights, technically."

"I'm gonna peck your eyes out!"

Azure grinned. "Well you wouldn't have missed it if you hadn't been in your little love nest with Nova." She said the last word in a deep, sensual voice.

"You're right." Robin shook her tiny head. "I'm officially taking a break from him." She looked up, then back down, then back up. "After one more romp." She flew up and disappeared among the sails.

Elijah chuckled. When Azure looked at him, smiling, he ducked his head and shuffled away.

As the ship began to move away from the docks, Syl stood on the bow and began to chant in a whisper. Azure listened and watched with great interest. She couldn't understand what he said, but it had a definite magical quality to it.

Out on the calm water, under a darkening sky, a blue flame ignited. The flame flickered just above the surface of the sea. Syl checked a compass, then moved the flame to exactly northeast from their location. Then, with a flourish of hand motions, he was done.

"No matter where we go, that will-o'-the-wisp will stay northeast of us," he told Azure. "So once we enter the fog, we'll simply follow the blue glow."

"Perfect." Azure nodded, impressed and thankful for Syl's magic.

The crew was busy setting sails and doing mariner duties. Azure watched Nargol and Orok set the main sail, trying to soak up as much knowledge as she could. They explained to her what they were doing, and the names of each line and where it went.

"Did you have a good time on Mirth?" Azure asked when the work was done.

"We didn't go," Orok said.

"Why not?" As her words came out, Azure already knew the answer, and felt stupid for asking. Had she not already got an answer from the posting Blunderbuss had put up?

"Mirth Island is probably the most progressive place in the Islands, but our kind still isn't exactly welcome there."

"Oh. I'm sorry."

"Don't be. It's not your fault."

"But I..." Azure didn't know what to say. She felt horrible for being human at the moment.

"Have you ever heard about the Continent from anyone who has been there?" Nargol asked.

"No." Azure's heart raced.

"Would you like to hear about it?"

"Yes!"

"Alright. Once we're under way, we'll tell you a bit about it."

"Thank you!" Azure couldn't contain her excitement. She had been taught a lot about the Continent but had never had the opportunity to discuss it with someone who had first-hand knowledge of the place.

When all duties were complete, the two orcs found Azure and brought her belowdecks. Robin landed on Azure's shoulder as she descended the stairs.

"Where you going?"

"I'm about to hear about the Continent from Nargol and Orok."

"Really? Can I hear?"

"Of course," Orok said as he opened a door at the far end of the hall.

The orcs' quarters—apparently the two of them were cohabiting—were large but cozy. A small shrine sat in the corner along with a painting of an orc sitting with eyes closed under a massive, red-leafed tree, a statue of an orc in the same pose, and two unlit candles with strange writing on them. There was only one bed in the room, which consisted of a straw-filled mattress on the floor.

"Oh," said Robin, "you two are..." She whistled in a provocative manner.

Azure was embarrassed, but the orcs laughed it off. "Yes, we're what humans would call married."

Azure nodded.

"And we've got a little one on the way." Orok gently placed a hand on Nargol's belly.

"Oh, wow!" Azure said. "Congratulations." She hadn't noticed before, but now that she was made aware, she could definitely see Nargol's baby bump.

"Thank you." Nargol motioned for them to take seats.

When everyone was settled in, Nargol began to speak.

"Orok and I come from the western edge of Mor, or the Continent, in a mountainous region we call Arzol Khagh. The mountains there are immense, much, much bigger than anything you'll see on these islands. Most of them are covered in snow all year round."

"You've seen snow?" Azure said.

"Oh, yes. Used to have to clear it away from our door just to go outside in the winter. We have animals there that you wouldn't believe; big-horn sheep, dire wolves, and giant bears. Some of the bears could even beat me in a fight." She flashed a smile.

"So, as you may already know, the race of orcs has been locked into a centuries-long war with the elves, who have recently joined forces with the humans. For most of our childhoods, the war was nothing more than something that grown-ups talked about, and where our older siblings would go off to fight and sometimes never return. But around the time Orok and I turned ten years old, the elves had pushed into Arzol Khagh.

"Orok and I were childhood playmates, and we enlisted in the army together, pretending to be twelve.

"The fighting was awful. We saw atrocities on both sides. We saw orcs tearing the limbs from unarmed prisoners for fun, and our company was slaughtered by elves with glowing swords who laughed and counted their kills as if it were some kind of game. We only escaped by playing dead and laying under orcs who had already passed.

"So after our company was massacred, and the elves had taken Arzol Khagh, we escaped through the mountains to the western coast. Our families were gone, and we had nothing left on the Continent. We found a ship that was heading for the mythical Ring of Islands that was rumored to exist beyond the Great Sea. We knew the voyage would likely be doomed—not many made it long out in the deep ocean due to the sea creatures—but we felt as if it was our only option. Winter was coming, and we were cold, hungry, and alone.

"Four ships of refugee orcs set sail, but only one made it through the gauntlet of relentless monsters. There were creatures out there that will haunt my nightmares for the rest of my days; unspeakable things that drove some to madness by simply looking at them. To this day, I don't know how we made it: a lucky cannon shot striking a tentacle at just the right time, a fight between two monsters, just as one of them was about to take us down. These kinds of things happened countless times on our weeks-long voyage. The other ships sunk, one by one, into the dark waters, but eventually, we made it.

"We landed on the Torsals, where a small colony of orcs had settled. For years we lived among battered, poor, and depressed fellow orcs. And although we too felt the weight of that depression, we were young, and we longed for something else, even though neither of us could have told you what that something else was at the time.

"Then, the marauders arrived in port one day. Compared to other humans, they were unafraid of us. They talked with us, listened to us. They spoke a very strange version of the Common Tongue, but we were able to understand each other well enough. They said they wanted to learn about orcs and do what they could to help us integrate on the islands. But Orok and I could tell their main objective was to sing and have fun, and this objective appealed to our young hearts. Even though they were made up of mostly humans, we asked if we could travel with them, just for a short while.

"They accepted and we've been with them ever since. That was thirteen years ago last week."

"Wow."

"Fog!" came a muffled shout from above. "Fog!"

"Well, that was a quick story," Nargol said. "I can answer any questions you have about the Continent or anything else any time, but maybe we should go see the Eternal Fog."

The others agreed, and they all hurried topside. The first thing Azure noticed was the lack of Ringlight in the night sky. The glow from above was so familiar, it seemed alien not to have it above her.

The fog was so thick that she couldn't see three feet in front of her. Brisa materialized from the fog right in her face and said, "Come with me to the bow. I don't want to go alone."

Arm in arm, Brisa and Azure made their way to the bow, trying not to trip on anything. Once there, Syl's will-o'-the-wisp became just visible in front of them.

"We gotta relay back to MK whenever we start to veer off course," an older marauder told them. He made a circle around his mouth with his hands and called, "Little to port!"

Another voice about midship repeated his message like some sort of ghostly echo. The ship shifted a touch to the left.

There was a small thud from above, and Robin came plummeting down to the deck. Azure dropped to her hands and knees and searched the floor until she found her friend dizzy, but conscious.

"Stupid fog!" Robin said. "Stupid mast!"

"Are you okay?" Syl came running over, his hooves clicking on the deck.

"Yeah. I'm fine." Robin was obviously embarrassed.

"That's good."

In the silence that followed, with the Continent still fresh in her mind, Azure decided to shoot Syl a question, hoping she wouldn't be prying. "Did you ever live on the Continent?" she asked.

"Nope. I was born here on the islands. My parents came over while my mother was pregnant."

Azure started to ask a follow up, but Syl continued.

"I have a pretty legit claim to being the first faun ever born here."

"That's amazing." Azure paused. "Did your parents talk about the Continent much?"

"Oh yeah, all the time. They used to live in the south, in a place that, translated to the Common Tongue, would be called the Wanderwood."

"Why did they leave?"

"It was burnt down. All of it. A casualty of the war."

"I'm sorry." Azure didn't know what else to say.

"The war has ruined a lot of things, from what I gather. It's still going to this day, unfortunately. In the last few decades the fighting has pushed to the south, displacing fauns who just wanted to be left out of it. Things got so bad that my parents were willing to risk the sea monsters in order to start their family in peace. I can't imagine what that must have been like, to set out across the sea with no idea about what they were facing."

"Where are they now?"

"They died. Killed by humans in a dispute over land use when I was ten."

"That's horrible."

"I would have died, too, if not for the marauders finding me and taking me in."

"So you've been with them since you were a kid." Azure winced for stating the obvious.

"Yeah." He looked out at his will-o'-the-wisp. "Sometimes I miss being around other fauns, but the marauders are my family, and I couldn't see leaving them. We've tried to recruit fauns, but they just don't understand what we've got here. We fauns were never a seafaring people. We usually prefer life under a forest canopy." Syl closed his eyes. "I imagine someday I'll feel a stronger pull to be with other fauns, but for now, I'm a marauder."

Azure nodded, feeling so many things but unsure which feeling to express.

"You look exhausted," Syl said, his expression warm and caring.

"I *am* pretty tired." Azure tried and failed to suppress a yawn.

"You should get some rest, then. I think you'll need it."

"Do you need any help up here?"

"Thank you, but no. We've got it covered. You go get yourself some sleep."

Azure yawned again, bigger this time. "Alright. Thank you."

She didn't remember her head hitting her pillow.

Chapter 18 The Door

Azure felt the ship slow to a stop. In her dream, she was still on Pratt's ship, only it wasn't really Pratt's ship, the way dreams go. Pratt and her mom were slow dancing on the deck of the ship. Then there was a band playing.

One moment, the ship was fine, the next, the dance floor crumbled beneath them. Jets of water spurted up from breaches in the deck. A tentacle wrapped around her mom's leg.

Azure tried to run to her, but she could barely move. It was as if the air was viscous, so thick that even the smallest movement took incredible effort.

Sluggishly, Azure crept forward while the breach around her mom grew bigger. Powerless, Azure watched her mom fall into the churning water and rubble while Pratt walked to safety along the tentacle, laughing.

She awoke with a start, hearing a knock on her door.

"A bit early, isn't it?" Robin said, rubbing her eyes with her wings.

"Sorry to disturb you," came Mr. Cordingly's voice, "but we've made it to the door, ma'am."

"We'll be right out," Azure said, jumping up and shaking off the disturbing dream.

It was daytime, although it was the strangest day she had ever seen. Visibility was still near-zero, but now they were enveloped in a soft gray glow.

"Would ya like me to go in and face any trials that await?" the Marauder King asked, a note of hope in his voice.

"No," Azure said, looking down at the vague outline of the door in the water. "I think it has to be me." She looked up at him, eyebrows pinched. "Do you know anything about the trials I might face?"

"Nothing, Miss Azure. I'm sorry. None of us know a thing about it, I'm afraid."

"Shit." Azure mentally kicked herself for not asking Old Jonas about the trials. That was an extremely stupid oversight.

Much of the crew had congregated around Azure, and were looking at her with excited anticipation.

"Well, lower me down, I guess."

"Do you want me to go with you?" Elijah asked.

"No. Thank you, but I think I need to do this alone." That didn't make any sense to her, but it felt right.

Reluctantly, Elijah gave in. "You're right. I'd just mess everything up, anyway. You're better off without me."

"I wish you'd stop talking like that." Azure shook her head.

The crew equipped Azure with a pistol and a sword, then helped her down into a rowboat that hung near the bow. Once inside, they lowered her into the water. Azure gripped her wand in her pocket, making double sure it was there.

The door was a strange sight up close. In one way, it was a normal door that happened to be floating face-up in the ocean, but it really wasn't like that at all. It was more like a door built at the top of an impossibly tall structure anchored to the bottom of the sea. Small waves ran toward it, and just when it seemed as if they would rush over it, they lost their momentum and stopped at the frame. The top of the door was not wet.

The *Adventure Ship* had pulled up so close to the door that Azure didn't need to row. Instead, she pushed off the hull of the ship, then crossed to the other side of the rowboat and grabbed the doorframe.

Awkwardly, she stepped out of the rocking boat onto the door. Sure she would fall backwards into the water, and suddenly aware of the possibility of monsters or sharks, Azure crouched and shimmied her feet to the frame on the knob side.

Slowly, carefully, she reached down, gripped the knob, and pulled the door open.

A wooden staircase led down into total darkness. A waft of air from below reminded Azure of her childhood, although she couldn't quite put a finger on why.

Azure took out her wand and went over the bolt-firing process in her mind. She descended the stairs, wand stretched out in front of her.

As she descended lower, and her head sunk below the surface of the sea, the familiar smell became stronger. It was a mix of capybara fur and flowers and ink. It was the subtle scent of her childhood bedroom.

A magical light blinked on with a snap, revealing her room as it was when she was seven. Crude drawings of capybaras and ships and landscapes decorated the walls. Her bed was small and piled high with blankets and pillows. A desk with a mirror attached stood in the corner, a kid's chair that her dad had built was pulled up to it.

"Welcome," a child's voice said from the mirror. "Come, sit." The voice was that of a little girl, with a slight Nameless Isles accent. The voice was her own voice, when she was a kid.

Azure tucked her wand away and sat on the tiny chair, feeling like a giant. The reflection in the mirror was her present self. For a moment, she admired her appearance. The modified dress underneath the oversized coat was a good look on her. She looked like a proper marauder, which made her happy.

"Why do you seek the island?" the child asked.

Azure was brought back to the time she had lived in this room. She remembered her parents letting her bring wild capybaras inside. She could almost hear the melodic songs her mom would sing to her while tucked into a mountain of blankets, warm and secure and loved. She remembered her dad reading her stories as she sat on his lap on the floor, imagining being on real ships and using real magic.

"I think I need something on the island. I'm not sure what it is, but I think it will help me save my dad's life."

"But Daddy has changed," her younger voice said, matter-of-factly.

"Yeah, he has. But that doesn't change what I have to do."

"Okay." Her voice was so light, so full of joy and wonder and innocence. It lacked the weight of the world and all the complications it brought. "We will be shown the way."

The strange light in the room faded, and a new light appeared at the bottom of the stairs. Azure shook her head. The illusion of her room had been so real she had forgotten she was under the surface of the sea. After regaining her bearings, she followed the stairs up until she stood in the foggy air, again.

To the east, the fog began to melt away, almost as if it were parting, revealing a clear path ahead. At the end of the cleared lane, barely visible, was an island.

Chapter 19 Dragon Island

The island at the end of the strange corridor of fog seemed to sparkle in the sunlight. The effect only intensified as they sailed closer.

"Avera's nipples!" Mr. Threepbrush said, looking through a spyglass. "The island's made of... treasure?"

Everyone looked at the growing island, taking turns with the spyglass. When Azure got her turn, she confirmed Mr. Threepbrush's description. Where most islands would have had a sandy, or rocky beach, this island was coruscant, glittering with gold coins and occasional jewels. Trees stuck out from the treasure further back from the beach, and there were signs of normal island life—a crab walked sideways along the coins, claws outstretched, clutching a strand of pearls, and seagulls circled in the sky above. Eventually, the treasure gave way to a relatively small volcanic mountain in the center of the island. The mountain was much taller on one side and had an uncanny resemblance to a dragon's head with mouth agape. The sporadic puffs of smoke coming from the would-be dragon's mouth enhanced this simulacrum. The Eternal Fog encircled the entire island about a hundred yards off of its coast. The effect was eerie and aesthetic at the same time.

"Remember," called the Marauder King to the animated crew, a fatherly tone in his voice, "this island has been cursed, and not everything may be as it seems."

The ship was steered into the treasure beach, creating much more of a racket than a normal beach landing. The orcs were the first to jump out. They scooped up giant handfuls of treasure and flung it in the air.

"It's real!" They said as the coins and jewels rained back down on top of them.

Azure scanned the island for a treasure chest, or anything that would indicate where this supposed great power that Pratt feared was located. She noticed nothing.

Following Elijah and Brisa, Azure made her way down the gangplank. She found it difficult to walk in the loose treasure as it slid under her feet. Mr. Cordingly slipped and fell next to her. His face red, he jumped back up and kept a wider base.

Just then, a movement from the treasure about ten yards ahead startled the crew. Coins rattled as something seemed to be approaching from underneath them. A skeletal hand rose from the beach, then another, and another.

Three skulls emerged. Treasure cascaded down around three skeletal bodies as they crawled up from under it. Each skeleton held a curved cutlass in one hand and cried out with unsettling roars.

Azure stepped back and drew her wand, raising it to the skeletons and trying to focus her energy. Robin landed on her shoulder, a low growl issuing from her beak.

For a handful of tense, accelerated heartbeats, the skeletons leered at the crew, brandishing their weapons with apparent murderous intent.

Then, the one in the middle dropped his sword arm to his side. "Elijah?" he said in a gruff voice.

"George?" Elijah stepped forward, sword in hand.

The two skeletal beings dropped their swords, ran to each other, and embraced, bones clacking together.

"William and Charles are with me, too," said George, his accent thick and strange.

Elijah shook the bony hands of the other two skeletons as Azure tucked her wand away and breathed.

"What are you guys doing here?" Elijah asked.

"We got hoodwinked by this arsehole 'oo goes by the name of Pratt," George said.

"Really?"

"Yeah. After ya introduce us to your friends, I'll tell you all about it."

Elijah made introductions to Azure, Brisa, Robin, and the marauders. The three skeletons were amiable enough, but a little rough around the edges, and a bit tough to understand.

"So," George said, "the three of us hear about a man 'oo might know the location of our medallion. So we goes to find this prick on the Nameless Isles. He's this rich arsehole 'oo tells us he can get us the medallion, but he needs our help with something first.

"This guy is so bloody full of himself that the three of us could barely stand him, but we decided that this could be a good lead, and we should see it through. Damned if that wasn't the wrong choice.

"Anyway, he takes us on this wild goose chase, eventually ending up here where we stand. He has us use this map of his to dig up a treasure chest buried in other treasure. Seems odd, but why not?

"Oh, and he's got this dragon with him 'oos a right blowhard, too. Two kernels on a cob, those two."

Gooseflesh rose along Azure's arms.

"So we go and get this treasure chest for him because he says he can't step foot on the island for some reason. When we bring it back to the ship, which was no easy task, he opens it with this key and takes out one little ring. That's it! Apparently, that's all there was in this bloody treasure chest! Our capybara medallion was nowhere to be seen!

"And that's the last thing the three of us remember. Next thing we know, we're waking up on the treasure beach and the ship is long gone. The treasure chest had been locked again and thrown down to the island. We were stranded, marooned by this arsehole. I mean, maybe we could have walked somewhere along the ocean floor, but we didn't even know which way to go in all this fog. We were right pissed, but also feeling pretty gullible.

"We've been stuck here ever since. We wouldn't have a clue how long it's been."

"Where is the chest, now?" Brisa asked, stepping forward.

"It's buried right behind us. But you're not getting in it without the right key. It's protected by Old Magic or some such."

Brisa revealed the key around her neck and took it off.

"Oh. Alright, then. Go for it. It'd be great to see if there was anything else in there."

The skeletons showed the crew the exact location, then Orok and Nargol dug the chest out with their hands.

The chest was built with rich, dark wood. It had runes drawn in black on every square inch of its surface. The wood itself looked ancient but showed no signs of wear or rot. There was just something about it that spoke of being very, very old.

Brisa held up the key, worry written on her face.

"Are you sure about this?" Azure asked

"No," Brisa replied.

"Me neither. But we've come this far, and I don't see a better alternative." Brisa nodded and handed her the key.

Azure crouched and slid it into the lock. For a moment, the lock seemed to pull the key into itself. A low thrum permeated the air around Azure, vibrating her skin down through her feet. She felt herself turn the key, although it felt more like it turned itself.

The lock clicked, sending a final jolt through Azure's body, making her jump.

The lid of the chest burst open and a blur of red exploded up from inside.

Azure fell back on her butt and watched as the red blur began to take shape.

Reptilian claws sunk into the treasure beach mere feet in front of where Azure sat. Powerful legs took form. A scaly red body, rippled with muscle like a thoroughbred horse. Two great leathery wings. A thick neck, lined with menacing spikes along the back. And finally, a terrifying face with sharp, bone-white teeth exposed in what could only be described as a wry grin.

A great red dragon stood before them, its head probably thirty feet from the ground.

"Oh, shit it feels good to stretch my wings again!" the dragon said, its voice part thunderclap and part human male.

The dragon looked down at the frozen crew.

"Who are you?" he said, his expression turning contemplative. "I don't know if I should thank you or roast you."

Chapter 20 Zoth-Avarex

"**P**lease don't roast us!" Azure cried, heart thumping. In the space between beats, she decided to attempt an emergency gambit with the horrifying beast. "We can help you get revenge on Pratt!"

The dragon's throat, which had started to glow orange, darkened.

Several of the Marauders reached for their pistols, but the Marauder King thrust out both arms—palms down, fingers splayed—and lowered them toward the ground.

"You know Pratt?" the dragon asked Azure.

"Yes. We know where he is and where he's going."

"Where?"

Brisa helped Azure to her feet. "First, we need to hear what happened here," she said to the dragon.

"Whoa! You're sure easy on the eyes," the dragon said.

After a short, tense silence, the Marauder King stepped forward with a dramatic flourish. "What is your name, mighty dragon?"

"My name is Zoth-Avarex, and I'm the greatest dragon in the multiverse." He looked at the crew as a whole as if it was his first time seeing them. "Oh, you're pirates, huh? Well aaaaarrrgh, Matey! Yo ho ho and a bottle of rum!"

The marauders looked to each other, confused.

"Huh?" Azure asked.

"You know, pirate stuff. Swab the deck you scurvy cur! Stuff like that?"

"We know not of what you speak," said the Marauder King is his kingliest voice. "For we are not pirates, but marauders, and we have brought this fair lady to this island to help her with her quest to track down Governor Pratt and vanquish him."

"*Governor* Pratt? That asshole rose up the ranks quick." The dragon interlaced his claws and stretched his arms over his head, then rubbed the back of his neck.

"Where do you come from, Zoth-Avarex?" the Marauder King asked.

"Some other Realm, another world. But I don't want to get too far into it. If you knew the true extent of the multiverse, it would fry your little human minds like eggs. So, where is Pratt?"

"First, we want to hear what happened here," Azure said. "How you came to be in a treasure chest, and why Pratt fears what is on this island."

"You know what?" The dragon's throat started to glow again, his brow furrowed in anger.

For a tense moment, Azure considered leaping away from the impending firestorm. The marauders fumbled for their pistols again.

"Shit," the dragon said. His face relaxed and the glow darkened yet again. "I guess I wouldn't mind telling you the story. I have been awful lonely in that stupid box." He shuddered, a confused look on his face. "Lonely? Damn, I'm getting pathetic in my old age."

Zoth-Avarex jumped into the air, beating his massive wings with a sudden violence that threatened to knock Azure back on her butt. Preternaturally fast, the dragon flew around the volcano before alighting back down on the treasure in front of the crew.

"That's better." He stretched again and lay down on his belly. "Alright, gather around, you group of misfits."

The dragon snapped his claws and a stack of cut wood appeared. He sent forth a small burst of flame from his nose, igniting the wood and making a cozy little campfire on the treasure beach.

"So, here's my story.

"I was minding my own business in my own Realm when this Pratt asshole conjures me to your world. But the idiot has barely got enough magic to conjure me, and definitely doesn't have enough to bind me. So I'm about to roast him when he says, 'I know about a massive treasure, and I'll give you ninety-nine percent of it if you help me find it.' I was intrigued, to say the least.

"He tells me he needs me to find this door out on the ocean, hidden by this dense fog. He says that if we find that door, we'll be led to a place called

Dragon Island. So, you know... Dragon Island... I'm a dragon. I start seeing the hand of fate in all of this, like a gullible, dewy-eyed moron.

"I read his mind to see if there is anything nefarious going on, but all I see is the lust for treasure and power, which I completely understand.

"Looking back, it's so obvious. Why did he only want one percent of the treasure? That should have been a red flag to me, but I missed it."

"Why didn't you just force the information out of him?" Syl asked.

"I hate to admit it, but I was eager for some interaction, even if it was with a pathetic human who had as big of an ego as I do." The dragon shook his head, obviously disgusted with himself. "Anyway, we find the door and he sends one of those purple girls, like her," he pointed at Brisa, "in. He had kidnapped the girl's family and forced her to go in the door and face some trial. He was as cold-blooded as a dragon. That's kinda why I took to the guy, to tell the truth. But you'd think there would have been a better system for finding the island. Didn't whoever made that door expect someone could force another person to open the way for them?" The dragon shrugged his mammoth shoulders. "I guess it's just another example of the willful naivety of beings who try to live with peace and love.

"Anyway, we get to the island and it looks like what you see here, absolute paradise, right?

"Now, this is where I really messed up. While I'm rolling around in my new treasure, as I am wont to do, and trying to calculate its worth, Pratt sends this skeleton crew onto the island to retrieve his share." He stopped and waved at the reanimated skeletons. "Oh, hey you guys... Anyway, after following this map and digging down through the treasure, they pull up this chest. I ask them what's inside and they tell me it's this gold medallion with a capybara on it. They tell me about this curse that had turned them into skeletons, too, not that I gave a shit.

"So, the funny thing was, I already had a golden medallion with a capybara on it. I mean, that's a story for another time, but I knew they weren't going to find it in that chest."

Elijah and the three other skeletons straightened up.

"While you skeletons were taking the chest back to Pratt, who never set foot on the island, I went and hid my medallion in a pile of treasure so you'd never find it, not even thinking about what was actually in that magical chest.

That was probably the worst mistake of my life. I don't make many, but that one was huge.

"When the crew got back to Pratt, he opened the chest with this key he had and took out this one little ring. As he went to slip it on his finger, I knew. This was a ring of great power.

"I barely got the word *shit* out before I felt the loss of control over my own body. I leaped from my beautiful treasure and flew to the ship, where Pratt was staring me down with the ring glowing bright on his hand.

"I felt him invade my thoughts, and for the first time in my life, I couldn't resist. The loss of control was horrible. I almost felt sorry for all the beings whose minds I had invaded in the past.

"Anyway, as he peeled back the layers of my massive, impressive mind like a gods-damned onion, I decided to try one final ploy. I bluffed him, putting everything I had into one solid thought, making him believe I had the ability to eventually overcome his mind control, even though I did not. I guess in the moment I thought I might make him give up on the idea of controlling me and just leave me alone.

"And it worked, to an extent. Although in hindsight it was probably that ploy that got me stuck in the damn chest. He said, 'I was going to use you for my undertaking, but I don't need you. There is a greater power than you, anyway. A power that actually belongs in the Undering.'

"I felt the mind control become absolute. I found myself flying over to retrieve the chest, and—this is the most embarrassing part—shrinking myself down, shoving myself into the chest, and closing the lid over my own head.

"I knew I was done. The chest was made with an Old Magic I couldn't penetrate. I knew I was stuck there until death, or until someone opened it from the outside. So I slipped into a kind of hibernation mode and waited it out."

"So, that medallion with the capybara on it is here on this island?" Elijah said, looking around in the firelight.

"Yeah, but that's mine. That thing played a crucial part in my imprisonment, and it was the first gold I had laid my hands on in a very long time. I'm going to wear it around my neck until I forget what the dark and lonely inside of that chest was like."

"But if you throw it into the sea, my curse, and the curse of those like me will be broken."

"Sorry. Not my problem."

"How about you go get that gods-damned medallion and toss it in the sea or I'll peck your fucking eyes out," Robin said, jumping down to the ground in front of the dragon.

Zoth-Avarex laughed and let out a burp of flame. Robin zipped away, but not before her tail feather was singed.

"Hey! Hey!" Azure jumped up and threw her hands in the air. "Hold on a second! Before you go blowing fire at anyone, let's have a little chat. I think it's clear that we're going to need each other."

"Why would I need you? I have more magic in a scale on my ass than—"

"Because Pratt has a ring that is more powerful than you. If you show up anywhere near his ship, he'll take control of you again. Is that what you want?"

"Well—"

"And why would we need this asshole?" Robin said, tending to her singed tail.

Azure didn't have an immediate answer. Thoughts of her father and the unknown danger he faced made her heart sink. "We don't know what Pratt has planned, but we can guess it's going to be big. I don't know if we'll be able to stop Pratt without the dragon's help."

"You're assuming a lot by thinking I'm going to help you guys. I mean, I'm grateful you let me out of that treasure chest but helping humans in their trifling affairs isn't really my thing."

"A deal, then?" Azure said. "If we can get the ring away from Pratt, you'll help us save my dad and everyone else aboard the galleon Pratt is sailing on."

The dragon narrowed his eyes, deep in thought. "How about we put it this way: I won't roast the lot of you right here and now if you promise to get the ring from Pratt? And when you do get the ring away from him, I will absolutely take my revenge on his ass."

"But you'll spare the hundreds of people on the galleon?"

This seemed to really annoy him. "Yeah, sure. I guess." He gave Azure a particularly long, creepy look. His expression of annoyance morphed into a smile. "I don't know what it is, but I like you. What's your name?"

"Azure."

"There's something about you that reminds me of a princess I once knew in an emerald city."

"So, we've got a deal?" Azure stared up defiantly.

"Yeah, we've got a deal."

"Then what about that medallion?" Azure tried her best to show a strength she didn't feel. "If you want our help, you'll have to throw that medallion into the sea first."

"No. I don't think so."

"But it would mean so much to my friend. It isn't fair for you to keep it."

"The multiverse is full of injustices. It's not my job to go around fixing all of them. What I want right now is simple: revenge and treasure. And I'm not giving up either for anyone."

"You—"

Elijah put a hand on Azure's shoulder. "It's okay," he said. "The matter with your dad is much more pressing. We've been waiting a hundred years to break our curse, what's a few more days? Let's not push the issue right now."

The other skeletons, through body language alone, looked exasperated.

"The bony guy makes a good point," the dragon said. "I'd—"

"You greedy fuck!" Robin screamed. "I really oughta peck those big juicy eyes out of your big ugly skull!"

The dragon's laughter shook the treasure under everyone's feet.

"You've got spunk! You must have a little dragon in you."

"I'll show you spunk, you fucking prick. I—"

Azure cupped a hand around Robin and smiled at her.

Chuckling, Zoth-Avarex flew to a palm tree, dug into the treasure, and retrieved the capybara-etched medallion, which was connected to a giant gold chain. Elijah let out a lungless gasp when he saw it.

The dragon clasped the chain around his neck.

"Where did you find it, may I ask?" Elijah said when the dragon returned.

"I was flying near these tall white cliffs when I saw a skeleton guy like you throwing something that glinted in the sun. I zipped down to intercept it and caught this beautiful, ornate piece of gold just before it splashed into the sea." Zoth-Avarex chuckled, again. "That was a close one!"

Elijah shook his skull, staring down at the treasure beach.

Chapter 21 Smith Island

Governor Pratt watched his followers from Smith Island pile onto the ship with impatience. He knew this was a needed step, but being so close to his goal, it was an annoying delay.

The people, mostly men, who boarded the ship looked at him with awe and reverence, their stupid mouths hanging open, catching flies. Pratt loved the attention, but he was disgusted by the people themselves. He could smell them from where he stood, waving and smiling next to one of the many League flags.

Instead of continuing to watch them board far too slowly, he focused on the statue of Enzo that greeted visitors to the island. The statue's face was mad with battle lust, with a sword in one hand, and a shield in the other. Pratt wondered what a statue built for him would look like as he absent-mindedly rubbed the ring on his finger. He wondered if Enzo, or any of the gods were really anything more than what he was: a man who combined great ambition with the rare ability to manifest it. He liked that idea.

When everyone was onboard, and the ship was once again under way, Pratt took to the stage for his official welcome.

"People of the newly-dubbed Smith Island, welcome aboard *The Savior*, the finest ship in our great League of Islands."

The newcomers roared and applauded.

"When I say your island is newly dubbed, you know how true that is. I mean, it still has that old name—whatever the hell it was—on our maps. But," he held up a map of the Isles, "many of you clever people have been making adjustments to your maps. The rumor is they're calling them Pratt maps? I mean, I don't know, but that's what I heard they were being called.

So on these Pratt maps, you've got, blah blah scratched out, and *Smith Island* printed boldly and beautifully instead."

The crowd cheered.

"Now, some would say, 'Well, that's just a map. How much can that matter?' My response would be, 'Have you been to Smith Island?'"

More cheering.

"Am I right? Because Smith Island is one of the most civilized islands in the League. Humans outnumber ciguapa five to one, there. Humans are using magic at unprecedented rates, there. Humans are simply thriving, there.

"And what, may I ask, is wrong with the idea of humans thriving?"

"Nothing!" many people shouted, but not in time with each other.

"Exactly." Pratt paused and gazed up at the Ring. "I'd like to take a moment to reflect on Smith Island's namesake, the great General Ebenezer Smith."

The crowd roared their approval.

"General Smith was a gods-fearing family man tasked with a near-impossible mission. You see, humans were meeting unprecedented resistance on...Streya...or, Whatever Island." This elicited a chuckle from many in the audience. "Anyone who has studied their history will know this, but life on this island used to be the other way around. Ciguapa used to outnumber humans about five to one. And believe me, it wasn't much of a place for a human to try and raise a family. And gods forbid you were a human who wanted to assert your right to use a little bit of magic." He ran his index finger across his throat. "So, in comes General Smith, and just in time, too. He wasn't on the island more than a day when an all-out battle erupted." Pratt pointed up to the Ring. "You know, they say that there are no coincidences under the Ring. The gods had placed General Smith there at the right time, just when the ciguapa were planning to attack.

"Now this is the part when the Harm-Phonies like to cry about what happened. They complain that the general's tactics constituted war crimes or some such bullshit. But if the utter annihilation of one's enemies is considered a war crime, then lock me up right now." He held his fists out, together and palms up. "General Smith's sneak attack was a thing of military brilliance. His snuffing out of nearly all ciguapa life on the island helped humans get a much-needed foothold in our gods-endorsed expansion. Enzo himself would have been proud."

Pratt pulled out his wand, barely skipping a beat. "Now, I know many of you brought your own wands, and that's great, but the rest of you aren't going to need wands. We ran a little short due to an attack on our supplies by a militant group of fauns, but that's okay. You see, I'm going to tell you about a secret of magic they don't want you to know." He paused for dramatic effect. "The secret we've discovered is if people are in direct physical contact with a wand user, they too can focus their energy through that wand-user's wand and double the amount of magical power."

A hubbub enveloped the crowd.

"Yeah. It's true. And I think it's a powerful metaphor for what we're doing, here. Only by working together, by relying on each other, can we get what we all deserve." Pratt forced himself to keep a serious face. These people were eating this stuff up. It was almost too easy. What he said was true; if you had a whole group of people who were, say, holding hands, they could all direct their magical energy through one wand. This little-known fact had saved him a fortune on gold wands. The plan had been to give everyone from the first stop a wand, then make up an excuse why no one else was getting one. It hadn't been a hard sell. People were all too ready to act against their own self-interest for the things he pumped them up about. The corner of his mouth turned up a bit, no matter how hard he tried to suppress it.

"We'll be practicing this technique, but not before the wonderful welcome party we've prepared for you Smith Islanders!"

At this signal, confetti was launched out over the crowd, the band began playing, and crewmembers circulated with glasses of various types of alcohol.

As Pratt mingled amongst the newcomers, wearing his biggest, fakest smile, he noticed John Brine sulking out by the starboard rail with his conjured tiger moping behind him. Pratt was amazed at the amount of weight the man had lost in a few days. As far as Pratt knew, John hadn't eaten a thing since his daughter had been sent away.

Pratt grabbed a slice of buttered bread from a tray a crewmember carried and waltzed over to where John stood. "You need to eat something, John, or you're liable to blow away in the wind." His voice was caring, gentle.

John looked up slowly, his face apathetic.

Pratt handed him the bread. "Have you been practicing with your wand?"

John took a small bite, then shook his head.

"Well, I hate to say this, because I know you've gone through a lot, but if you're not able to practice, I'll probably have no choice but to give your daughter's wand to someone else, like one of these Smith Islanders who didn't get one."

At this, John woke up. "No," he said, "I'll practice." He took a bigger bite of the bread.

"Okay. Good. I like hearing that." He patted John on the back. "You're going to have to get back in amongst your fellow passengers. We're going to be working on a new technique in which many people will focus their energy through one wand, so every wand is important."

"Alright." John finished the bread.

Pratt's eyes widened, a genius idea occurring to him out of the deep. "Besides, you're about to be a bit of a celebrity yourself, John."

John looked confused.

"In my next speech, I'll talk you up to the newcomers. The man who sacrificed his own daughter for our noble cause."

"No," John said as his face drained of color. "You don't have to do that."

"Oh, don't mention it. You deserve the recognition."

John tried to speak again, but Pratt shot him a look that stopped him short.

"Yes." Pratt patted John on the back, again. "That will work out quite nicely." He squeezed John's shoulder, then turned to go.

"Are there any scraps of meat I could get?" Thunder Paws asked Pratt.

Pratt's eyes widened as he spun back around. "Do not speak to me, you mangy stray. You're lucky I don't throw you overboard for addressing me like an equal."

The tiger's eyes flashed, then immediately darkened. He looked to the deck, his ears tucked close to his massive head.

"Keep your *pet* in line," Pratt told John, all of the gentleness gone from his voice, "and come join the others."

Head bowed, John complied.

Chapter 22 Ringfall

After a quick conference, the marauders decided not to take any of the treasure from the island, even though their stores were pretty much depleted. They had heard Dragon Island was cursed and weren't sure if the curse involved removing treasure or not. Zoth-Avarex, notably, kept the capybara pendant around his neck.

As they pushed off from the island, a flurry of orange sparks glinted in the clear sky far above where any clouds would have been. At night the sight would have been spectacular, but the sun had just begun to rise out of the east, washing out the contrast.

"Ringfall," Azure said, pointing it out to Robin.

"Oh, nice."

Azure was brought back to her first memory of Ringfall when she was around five years old. She remembered craning her neck back, mouth agape, nestled in between both of her parents.

"Is it dangerous?" she had asked them, looking to their faces for any indication of worry.

"No, Az, it isn't." Her mom had smiled down at her, squeezing her closer. "Let's just enjoy the show!"

Azure had watched those dancing sparks in a state of pure wonder. Nothing else mattered in that moment, safe between her two protectors, enjoying nature's splendor.

"The gods are putting on a show for you!" her dad had said.

Since then, Azure had learned much more about the phenomenon of Ringfall. She knew that it happened when small parts of the Ring would slough off and fall to the Undering. Something about the fall made the pieces burn up, creating the display of fire in the heavens. This was a fairly common occurrence. Azure had seen Ringfall about twenty times in her twenty years, and every instance brought back the warm memories of that first encounter.

There were, however, times when Ringfall was actually dangerous. Every now and then, a larger piece of the Ring would crash down on the world. This usually happened out at sea and didn't cause much damage. But once, way before Azure was born, a small town on Paradise Island had been completely obliterated by Ringfall.

The devout saw the showy, pretty Ringfall as evidence of the gods' happiness, and the fireballs as a sign of their displeasure.

"The gods are pissed at us!" Robin cried, stirring Azure from her reverie.

A fiery, fist-sized rock ripped through the mainsail on its way into the sea to starboard. Another struck the deck, ripping through it like a cannonball through butter. Ahead, Zoth-Avarex was being pelted with dozens of zipping fireballs.

The sea detonated on the port side. The resulting explosion of water deluged Azure and violently rocked the ship.

A harsh, rushing, whizzing sound permeated the air, and a boom like a cannon thundered from above. A massive object, burning with intense red fire, hurtled down directly toward the ship, trailing thick gray smoke as it dove closer. Azure had an instinct to run and jump overboard, but at the same time knew escape was unimaginable.

She ducked and covered her head in what must have been the world's most useless pose.

With otherworldly speed, Zoth-Avarex appeared above the ship. And with the wave of his claws, a glowing sheen, almost like a bubble, formed around himself and the ship.

The fireball struck the bubble and glanced off, crashing into the sea with a staggering splash. The ship rocked harder, threatening to tip over one way, then the other, then the first way again, but somehow managed to stay afloat.

Above the ship, the dragon remained, still encapsulated by the iridescent shield. Smaller projectiles continued to strike the bubble and disintegrate for a long, tense minute or so before petering out. After a few final seconds of sparks above, the Ringfall was over.

"What the hell!" Zoth-Avarex said after removing his protective shield. "Is this something that happens often in your shit-hole world?"

"No," Azure answered. "I've never seen anything like that before." The dragon looked to the sky, shaking his head.

Azure shifted her focus to the people nearby. After quick checks on each other, everyone found that there had been no major injuries. Orok had been struck in the neck by a small fireball, but aside from a human-thumbnail-sized burn, he was no worse for wear.

"Alright ya slackers, the little fireworks show is over, now," the Marauder King barked. "Let's get repaired and underway. We've got to get Azure to the Capitol Isles posthaste."

As the marauders jumped into sailor mode, the Marauder King tried to catch Zoth-Avarex's attention.

"Yes, my liege?" the dragon said, half-mocking.

"I wanted to thank you for protecting our ship, and more importantly, my crew."

Azure had never seen him more earnest.

"Well I couldn't let—" Zoth-Avarex cut himself off. Then, with great apparent effort, he said, "You're welcome."

THE REPAIRS NEEDED to the ship were much easier than they could have been, and the *Adventure Ship* was cutting through the calm sea in no time. With a southeast heading, assisted by another will-o'-the-wisp from Syl, they were out of the Eternal Fog in a matter of hours.

Once back in the open air, Zoth-Avarex flew within sight of the ship most of the day. Sometimes he would zip up into the clouds, and other times he would disappear on the horizon ahead, only to return within minutes.

The crew, which now included Azure, Brisa, Robin, and Elijah, seemed torn on their impressions of the dragon. Robin and a smaller contingent chose to focus on Zoth-Avarex's refusal to give up the golden capybara medallion, but most of the crew found themselves endeared to the dragon after he saved their ship from certain destruction. Azure wavered on the issue. She hadn't forgiven him for his greediness, but she was grateful to him, too. And looking ahead, she was thankful they would have such a powerful ally when they finally caught up to Pratt.

"You're a magic user, huh?" the dragon's gravelly voice said from behind Azure.

She turned to find he had shrunken himself down to the size of the orcs and had landed on the deck.

"Yeah." Her hand went to her wand without conscious thought. "Not for very long, though."

"What can you do so far?"

Azure showed him her limited abilities. He didn't bother to hide how underwhelming they were.

"Would you like a few pointers?" Zoth-Avarex said.

"Sure." Azure didn't bother to hide her excitement.

For several hours, the dragon worked with Azure on her magic. He was not a patient teacher, but he was effective. By the time the sky began to darken, she felt much better with her wand in her hand. She couldn't help but connect with the dragon through the training, even though the sight of the capybara medallion around his neck continued to irritate the shit out of her.

As the sun set behind them, Zoth-Avarex called everyone within earshot to him on the deck. The crew gathered around.

The dragon lifted a claw into the air, paused, then snapped.

Several barrels blinked into existence around him.

"We've got white wine, red wine, light ale, and dark ale," he said, pointing to each barrel in succession. "I figured you all would want to throw me a welcome party, so here's your chance."

The crew cheered, but Azure was slack jawed. Was there no end to the magic this dragon could do?

Zoth-Avarex snapped again and everyone had a cup in their hand. Even Robin had a bird-sized cup in her talon.

Azure shrugged and poured herself a dark ale.

"Well, shit," said the bird. "Give me one of those, too."

Azure splashed ale into Robin's cup and placed it on the bar.

"So." Zoth-Avarex looked in the Marauder King's direction. "What's your deal?"

"We're Marauders, and our *deal* is the simplest thing in the world. We simply sail the islands in search of wrongs to right and adventures to undertake."

"How do you afford to do this? How do you make money?"

"Well..." The Marauder King rubbed the back of his neck and looked to the floor. "Early on in our adventures, a few of us found treasure. We've been living off of that for more than a decade, now, but it's about to run out. We're working on some ideas to earn more money, but nothing is set in stone yet."

"What are your ideas?" Azure asked.

"We've considered becoming a merchant ship," the Marauder King said.

"We still hope to find another treasure, too," Mr. Threepbrush added.

"You just left an entire island of treasure." Zoth-Avarex pointed. "Un-cursed treasure, preferably."

"What other types of magic do you know, here?" the dragon asked. "I forgot, can you travel to other realms?"

"No," Brisa said. "But we know they exist."

"Can you conjure beings? Or is that something this Pratt prick figured out himself?"

"We can conjure." Azure looked at Robin, perched on her shoulder. "I conjured Robin from another realm."

"Oh, yeah. I almost forgot about the dragon in the little bird's body."

"Eat shit," Robin said.

The dragon laughed and took a swig of ale.

The alcohol content in the dragon's barrels must have been high; before long the marauders were feeling no pain. Laughter echoed around the deck as the sky darkened above.

Without any apparent warning, the crew erupted into their song. Azure tried her best to sing along.

When the song was finished, the Marauder King climbed up to the higher deck to address the group.

"Marauders! Guests!" He was well on his way to tipsy. "I am addressing you from the poop deck—" He couldn't contain himself, blurting out a guffaw. A murmur of giggles swept through the crowd. Azure joined in on this, too. "I'm addressing you from...up here to welcome our new guest, Zoth-Avarex."

Most of the marauders applauded, only a few refrained.

"We are grateful to you for saving our ship this morning, and for this wonderful ale tonight." He held up his cup, sloshing out at least half of its contents. "We don't have much with which to repay you."

"You're leading me to my revenge." Zoth-Avarex held up his cup.

"Well, yes, revenge. But allow us, as well, to regale you with songs. For we marauders are no slouches when it comes to singing and merriment."

"Eh..." Zoth-Avarex shrugged and finished his drink. "Sure. Why not?"

"Who wants to go first?"

"Syl!" someone shouted from the crowd.

"Yeah!" someone else agreed. "Marauder's Green!"

After some pushing and prodding and gentle encouragement, Syl made his way up the ladder to sit next to the Marauder King, cloven hooves dangling over the edge. Mr. Cordingly tossed him up a ukulele, which he tuned by ear.

When he was ready, he strummed a chord, and the crew fell silent.

Syl began to sing, softly at first:

As I walked by the dockside, one evening so fair,
To view the calm water and take the sea air,
I heard an old faun, he was singing a song,
'Won't you take me away boys, my time is not long.'
Wrap me up in the canvas of topsails,
No more on the docks I'll be seen.
Just tell me old shipmates, I'm taking a trip mates,
And I'll see you someday on Marauder's Green.
When you get to the Green, and your long trip is through,
There's pubs and there's clubs and there's lassies there too.
The girls are all pretty and the beer is all free,
And there's bottles of rum growing from every tree.
There's fauns and there's orcs and there's humans,
There's ciguapa and elves but no fights.
Just fun, mirth, and laughter, forever hereafter
On calm, warm, and well Ring-lit nights.
Wrap me up in the canvas of topsails,
No more on the docks I'll be seen.
Just tell me old shipmates, I'm taking a trip mates,

And I'll see you someday on Marauder's Green.
Some say, 'Is this really the truth, Syl?'
And I answer them with this same line.
This song will suffice, truth's a roll of the dice,
But Gods! Wouldn't it be damn fine?
So, WRAP ME UP IN THE CANVAS OF TOPSAILS!
NO MORE ON THE DOCKS I'LL BE SEEN!
JUST TELL ME OLD SHIPMATES, I'M TAKING A TRIP MATES!
AND I'LL SEE YOU SOME DAY ON MARAUDER'S GREEN!"

The song built in volume and intensity until the final rousing chorus from the entire crew. It was moving, and fun, and put the crew in an even livelier mood.

"Who thinks they can follow that?" The Marauder King called once the din had died down.

"Nargol and Orok could," Syl said with a grin before jumping down to the main deck.

At this, a deafening cheer went up.

Eventually, after much rowdier encouragement, the two orcs made their way up to the poop deck stage without using the ladder or ramp.

"It's probably a bit early in the night for this one," Nargol said, seemingly blushing. "But the dragon's drinks are quite stiff, so..."

Orok looked into Nargol's eyes and started singing, his voice gritty, but wonderful.

When I met you I knew you were special,
"Your eyes were like two sparkling gems.
Your voice was as sweet as honey,
I knew that I loved you right then.
"When I met you I knew you were special," Nargol sang.
Your words made me feel my own worth.
Your voice was so deep and melodic.
Your pants seemed to bulge with great girth.

Azure let out a guffaw from the pure unexpectedness of the line. Orok put on an embarrassed act, looking to the floor like a teenaged boy at his first dance.

"When I met you I knew you were special," Orok continued.

Your tusks were so pretty and white.
Your hair smelled of lilacs and roses.
You made my dark days much more bright.
"*When I met you I knew you were special,*" Nargol sang.
Right away we just seemed to click.
Your ass was so round and amazing.
Plus you had a really big—
Orok cut in with perfect timing.
"*Darling, I knew you were special,*
And I still know that to this day.
You're pretty and smart and so caring.
No longer is my life so gray.
"*Well Darling, I know you are special.*" Nargol wore an extremely mischievous grin.
You have the key to my lock.
I want you to slip that key to me.
And by key, of course, I mean your big—
Cock-a-doodle-doo? It's the...morning of our love?
And I feel that I've got such good luck."
When Nargol took over with perfect timing of her own, Orok slapped a palm to his face.
"*So let's ignore that interrupting rooster.*
Let's stay in bed all day and—
Fa la la la, la la lala,
Fa la la la lala la,
FA LA LA LA LA, LA LA LA LALA,
FA LA LA LA LA LALA LA!
Everyone on the ship roared with laughter, not the least of which was Zoth-Avarex. He sent a tongue of unintentional flame into the air, just missing the mainsail. Then he doubled over, falling to his side on the deck, cackling like a madman.

His laugh was infectious. The crew, who had already been laughing, grew even sillier. Even Robin found herself infected. She laughed about as hard as Azure had ever heard her laugh before.

Nargol and Orok bowed. Nargol shot back up, though, and slapped Orok on the butt.

"Hey, I didn't get this way with magic," Nargol said, rubbing her belly with one hand and shrugging with the other.

The two orcs embraced and kissed each other on the lips before joining the crew.

Giggling, Azure stumbled starboard and took a seat on a wooden chair near the rail. She sipped her drink and scanned the sky for any more signs of Ringfall. Finding none, she allowed her eyes to drift closed, a vague smile still on her lips.

"Whatcha doing?" the dragon's voice said, startling Azure awake.

She opened her eyes to see the re-sized Zoth-Avarex jump up and sit on the rail, tail hanging overboard.

"Just checking for any more Ringfall."

"On the insides of your eyelids?"

Azure chuckled.

"Can you believe that song?" He laughed and shook his head. "I've been around a long time, and I don't remember ever laughing that much at a performance."

"They were great, weren't they?"

"They really were."

"Kinda makes you glad you found this crew, doesn't it?"

"I don't know about that." His face turned serious, as if he were willing his smile away.

"Well, I am." Azure looked the dragon in the eyes.

"So, what's your story?" Zoth-Avarex said after a pause. "How did you end up with this group?"

Azure told him the story, from the fight with her dad, to the trial at sea, to ending up on Dragon Island.

"So you stood up and faced probable death for some people you didn't know back on Pratt's ship? And they weren't even human?"

"Well, yeah, I guess I did. But it worked out okay so far."

"And then you stood right up to me, the moment we met. I mean, me, a terrifying, overwhelming, extraordinary presence. A gods-damned dragon! Had you ever seen anything even close to me before?"

"No."

The dragon rubbed his shoulder, scaly brow furrowed. "Okay, so back to the thing on Pratt's ship. Why would you put yourself in harm's way for a tiny chance to save people you had just met?"

"Because it was the right thing to do." Azure shrugged.

"And has that usually worked out for you? Doing the *right thing?*" The dragon curled two clawed fingers from each hand.

"I haven't done it enough to know. The gods know I've chosen the wrong thing, the easy thing, most of my life."

"So why start doing the supposed right thing now?"

"Better late than never." Azure mimicked a line her mom used to say.

"But," Zoth-Avarex now rubbed the spikes on top of his head, "it's the concept I've never quite grasped. What compels some people to act against their own self-interest like that?"

"I guess it's kind of like the fire in the ciguapas' chests. They have this fire—I'm not sure if it's literal or not—that waxes or wanes depending on how they act. It guides them to act honorably, I think." Azure was tired, drunk, and unsure if she was getting that right. "I believe we all have something like that inside us, and whether or not we choose to listen to it is up to us."

"That still doesn't answer the question about why anyone would choose to listen to something like that. I mean, yeah it's there, but that shit is so easily ignored."

"That's tough to put into wo—" Azure hiccupped. "—into words. But I did hear this little nug—" Another hiccup. "—nugget of wisdom from a drunken sailor up at the inn one time." She held her breath until the effort was interrupted by a hiccup. "Shit!" She looked at the dragon, hesitant to ask him something. "Could you... cup my ears with your... hands?"

Zoth-Avarex was taken aback for a moment. "Uh... sure?" He jumped down from the rail, shuddering the deck below Azure's feet.

"Just make little scoo—" Hiccup. "—scoops and hold pressure over both of my ears."

Somewhat reluctantly, the dragon did as she asked. His scales were cool and smooth against her face.

With the pressure applied, Azure finished her drink in three big gulps.

"Okay, thanks."

Zoth-Avarex released her and took a step back, looking down at the tim-bers.

Azure waited for about ten hiccup-free seconds, then declared, "Gone." She laughed at the dragon's surprise. "That's an old family trick my mom taught me. Works every time."

"Nice." He jumped back up on the rail. "So what did he say?"

"Who?"

"The drunken sailor at the Inn."

"Oh yeah, he said, 'You shouldn't try to act in a way that makes you hap-py. Instead, you should try to act in a way that makes you *worthy* of happi-ness.' You see the difference?"

The dragon stared across the deck, seemingly in deep contemplation. "Fuck that." He flicked his claws as if shooing the concept away. "I've made it five thousand years without that kind of sentimental shit, no need to start with it now." He looked to the marauders gathered around the stage for the span of a few heartbeats. "These guys sure know how to have a good time, though. I mean, tonight was even more fun than burning a village to the ground."

Azure shook her head with a knowing, slightly disapproving smile— like her mom used to give her when she was younger and in trouble.

"Anyway, what can I do to help with this Pratt shit? You know...my re-venge."

Chapter 23 The Bird and the Dragon

Red-tinted sunlight filtered into Azure's room, waking her to a pounding headache. She wasn't sure how she had gotten back to bed last night. Her mouth felt as if she'd been eating sand, so she pushed herself up and trudged out in search of water.

To the east, the sky was a deep, vivid red, although the sun had not quite made its appearance, yet.

"Red sky at night, prepare for a fight?" the Marauder King murmured to himself, a confused look on his face. "Or is it red sky at night, sailor's delight?"

"I don't know." Azure rubbed her temples.

"Zoura's ass!" He kicked the rail and stared at the striking red sky as if trying to read it for some kind of sign.

"Red sky in the morning, sailor's warning," Mr. Cordingly said as he approached, also rubbing his temples.

"So a storm is coming?"

"Yes, sir. It looks that way."

Brisa tapped Azure on the shoulder. "How are you feeling? You look like shit."

"I probably feel worse than I look."

Brisa put a hand on Azure's forehead. Azure closed her eyes and listened to Brisa whisper a word. The edge of Azure's headache began to wear off, and the throbbing slowly came to a stop. The headache remained, but it was no longer one of the worst of Azure's life.

"Thank you so much, Brisa." She looked to the beautiful ciguapa woman. "Did that cost you anything?"

"No. Not really. Just a tiny drain on my energy. I could probably ease half the hangovers on this ship and still be alright."

"That's good to know."

Just as the first sliver of sun poked up from the horizon, a thunder crack pierced the sky. Dark clouds rolled in unnaturally fast and began to pour wind-whipped rain down on them.

The sea didn't take long to begin swelling and churning under them. The ship rose and fell with vomit-inducing intensity.

Zoth-Avarex, who was still orc-sized, appeared to Azure's left.

"Do you remember what we talked about last night?" he said.

"Uh, no." Except for hiccups and the vague recollection of talking about happiness, she didn't.

"You asked me if I could fly ahead and scope out Pratt's progress. You told me all of the stops he would be making and showed them to me on a map."

Azure mentally kicked herself. She had meant to play that information closer to the vest.

"Well, anyway. I'm going to head out and get away from this shit. So, I don't know why I'm telling you this, but I'll be back later."

"Not without me, you won't," Robin said, appearing out from sheets of rain.

"What?" Azure was perplexed.

"I told you last night. I'm going with him so I can keep an eye on him."

"I thought I remembered you disappearing with Nova?"

"That was after I told you." Robin twitched, obviously embarrassed.

"You sure about going, Robin? Even in this?" Azure pointed up to the building storm.

"Yeah, Az, I'm good. I'll see you tonight."

The dragon and the bird took wing just before a blinding bolt of light-ning struck the tallest mast. For a moment, the ship was surrounded by a blaze of white fire. The boards shook beneath Azure's feet, nearly knocking her down.

As soon as she regained a steady base, she looked in the direction Robin had gone, praying to see her still airborne. To her great relief, Robin flew up and away from the ship in the dragon's wake.

Then, just as quickly as the storm had appeared, it relented.

Well, that wasn't exactly true. It was more like the storm simply shifted away from the *Adventure Ship*, in the direction of Robin and Zoth-Avarex.

The dragon created a protective bubble over himself, with Robin just inside.

A bolt of lightning crashed into the bubble and, in a dazzling display, seemed to spread out equally around the entire construct like a thousand tiny veins, then reform as a single bolt that plunged into the frothy sea.

"WHAT THE HELL?" SAID Zoth-Avarex. "It seems like your stupid world is out to get me."

"I wonder why that could be." Robin's voice dripped with sarcasm.

"Try and keep up." The dragon accelerated at an alarming rate, leaving Robin behind. Then he turned and said, "What is the airspeed velocity of an unladen robin, anyway?"

"Fast enough, asshole."

Robin tucked her legs in closer to her body and flapped furiously.

Several more lightning strikes were absorbed and redirected by the dragon's bubble. Thankfully, Robin was now clear of the storm, which was relatively small and following Zoth-Avarex no matter what his speed.

The image, although hilarious, reminded Robin of a drawing Azure had made when she was a little girl, just after her mother had died. The picture was of a young Azure—dark hair, mismatched clothes, beautiful—with a dark cloud pouring heavy rain down over her head. Her eyes were two black dots, her mouth the black smudge of a frown. The drawing had broken Robin's heart. It was that moment when Robin discovered she loved little Azure.

After a final, ear-splitting strike, the storm dissipated, and the sun regained its full splendor low in the eastern sky.

Down below, the calm sea reflected like a mirror. The real Ring's image meeting its reflection on the horizon was quite a spectacular sight. Robin had never appreciated nature's splendor as much as Azure always did, but she had to admit that this was pleasing to behold. She wished Azure could see it from this angle.

Up ahead, Zoth-Avarex slowed down to let Robin catch up.

"Before you open your annoying little beak, I know I must be cursed. It's not the first time in my life."

Robin shook her head. She liked the idea of the dragon being cursed, but she didn't like the implications for Azure and the crew. She wanted to chide him for it but knew it would be the equivalent of bashing her head into a brick wall.

The two of them flew without speaking for hours. Robin regretted coming along in the first five minutes, but she kept at it, unwilling to show any weakness, although her wings burned and she felt like puking.

"So you like being a conjured imp?" Zoth-Avarex asked out of the deep.

Robin had never heard that word before but figured it must have been derogatory. "I love it. Best thing that ever happened to me. And I know I'm in the minority here, but I was one of the lucky ones."

"So you like having a master, then?"

"She's not my master," Robin snapped back. "She's my best friend, and my sister, and my mom all rolled up in one. She's everything to me, so fuck off."

The dragon chuckled. "So sensitive."

"You can throw whatever you want at me, but if you mess with my friends, we're going to have a problem."

"Noted."

They continued to fly at a pace close to Robin's top speed. She was really starting to feel her wings burn, but she refused to show it, even a little.

"What do you know about the history of this Undering, as you call it?" Zoth-Avarex asked.

"Not a whole lot. There's a place they call the Continent on the other side of the world. I guess there's this massive, everlasting war going on over there between humans, elves, and orcs. So a group of humans packed up and tried to venture out across the sea to find something new."

"Tried? Seems like they did find something new."

"Yeah. A small percentage of them did. I heard a hundred ships full of humans departed from the western shore of the Continent, and only four ships made it here to the islands."

"Why is that?"

"Sea monsters. The open ocean is overrun with horrible, giant sea monsters."

Zoth-Avarex scanned the calm sea below them. "I don't see any monsters down there."

"I said the open ocean. This here, inside the ring of islands, is pretty much monster free."

"Why is that?"

"Hells if I know. Brisa mentioned something about a sleeping leviathan or something, but I don't know much about that."

"Brisa, the ciguapa, right?"

"Yeah. They have lived on these islands as far back as history. Had a good thing going by all accounts until the humans showed up."

"So it goes." Zoth-Avarex shrugged, mid-air. "You know, I could see myself taking a ciguapa princess. I usually go for humans, but that Brisa is ridiculously beautiful."

"You touch her and you lose an eye."

The dragon bellowed laughter, then pointed down below. "I think we're almost there."

They were approaching a group of large islands, bigger than Robin had ever seen. The waters between islands were full of ships traveling in every direction.

"Gods," Robin said. "The galleon we're looking for is giant, but how are we going to find it in all of this?"

Zoth-Avarex snapped and a map of the islands appeared in his claws. "Well, according to what your precious Azure told me, they should be somewhere between Smith Island and First Frontier." He disappeared the map and studied the islands below. "Come on." He zoomed forward and to the right. Robin struggled to keep up.

Before long, the dragon pointed down. "Is that it?"

Robin squinted, straining her eyes. "Yes!" she said. "I think."

"Well why don't you go check it out to make sure?"

"Aren't you coming?"

"No." Zoth-Avarex looked away, fidgeting in flight. "If Pratt sees me, this whole operation will be compromised." His voice gave away the shame he felt in saying this aloud.

"Alright. I'll be right back." Robin tucked her wings and dove toward the galleon below.

As she approached, she confirmed that this was, in fact, Pratt's ship. The flag of the League flew from the stern, and that idiotic carving of Pratt stuck out from the bow. She considered turning around, but an idea moved into the light. She could go down and contact Azure's dad, John. Or, at the very least, she could try to dig up some information about what Pratt intended to do. Her stomach dropped when she thought about whether or not Pratt or that asshole Paul Sancti would recognize her, though. She decided to land up amongst the sails and be as sneaky as possible, her tiny heart racing like a hummingbird's.

A swarm of people milled around on the deck. Many of them were concentrated in the middle of the main deck, around the stage, practicing magic. She tried to pick out Azure's dad but wasn't having any luck. Then, up in the front corner of the ship, she saw Thunder Paws, sunning himself on the rail.

As nonchalantly as possible she bounced her way down the rigging until she landed next to the sleeping tiger. Even though she realized the gravity of her current situation, she had a hard time fighting the urge to startle him and send him flailing overboard.

"Hey, Thunder Paws," she whispered.

The tiger continued to bask in the sun, a deep gentle purr rumbling the rail under Robin's feet.

"Wake up, dumb shit," she said, louder.

The tiger stirred, lifting his majestic head, his eyes still closed. Robin's less majestic head darted back and forth. Fortunately, no one had noticed her yet.

"It's me, Robin. Wake the fuck up."

"Huh?" Thunder Paws said as he opened his eyes, in the loudest gods-damned voice possible. "Robin?"

"Quiet, you idiot!" she hissed.

"I thought—"

"I don't have much time. I need to ask you a few questions."

"Alright, then," he said in his drawling accent, mindful this time of volume.

"How is John doing?"

"Shitty. He's lower than a snake's belly in a wagon rut."

Robin was glad to hear that. He deserved whatever sadness he felt.

"Have you heard anything useful about Pratt, or what he intends to do?"

"Only that he's a pompous ass."

Robin was impressed with the usually vocabulary-challenged tiger's use of *pompous* but brushed it aside. "You haven't heard anything useful?"

"Well..." The tiger licked his paw and ran it over an ear. "I don't think Governor Pratt cares much about John, or anyone else on this boat. I think he's using 'em."

"Ya think?" Robin reined herself in. "But what is he using them for?"

Thunder Paws stared blankly at the rail. Robin could tell his gears were turning, hard. She could practically hear them grinding.

"I don't know if this is useful, but Governor Pratt says if people touch each other, they can direct magic through one wand, or something like that."

Robin wanted to berate him but figured it would be counterproductive. She was about to ask him a more specific question when his head darted to the right. She followed his gaze to see John approaching in a small group. In a moment of panic, wondering if John would possibly turn her in to Pratt, Robin hopped behind Thunder Paws's big paw.

"Shit," Thunder Paws whispered. "Pratt."

Robin didn't even try to get a peek. She dropped from the rail, let herself fall halfway down to the water, then darted along the hull toward the back of the ship. Around the corner, she found a length of rope hanging over the stern to latch onto. After a few deep breaths, she took off and raced up toward the gathering clouds.

As she flew, she expected her mind to be taken over by Pratt with every beat of her wings. She knew the governor would see her and use whatever strange mind control magic he had. He would make her come back and make her tell him everything about Azure. He would discover their plans and be ready for them. Azure would be as good as dead, and it was all Robin's fault for trying, and failing, to get one useful scrap of information.

But Robin plunged into a puffy white cloud, and she still had control of her own mind. Relief washed over her. She didn't care that every muscle in her body screamed at her.

"Couldn't help yourself, eh?" Zoth-Avarex's gravelly voice startled Robin. "Had to go above and beyond?"

"I know, that was stupid," she said to the vague outline of the dragon in the clouds.

"Was it worth it?"

"Not at all. I didn't get shit."

"Oh well. You didn't get caught, either. And now we know where they are and where they're heading."

"Yeah, I guess."

"Did you see Pratt? Was he wearing the ring?"

"No. I didn't see him."

The dragon nodded and took off toward the west. Robin sighed and followed him.

Chapter 24 The Cenote

As Zoth-Avarex and Robin sped away from the *Adventure Ship*, the sudden storm followed them.

The ship still rocked in the waves, but the rain and wind and lightning had all stopped as soon as it had started.

"Is the storm following the dragon?" Brisa asked Azure.

"It sure looks that way."

"He's cursed," Brisa stated.

"Is he?" Azure kicked herself for the stupid question. It seemed obvious that the dragon was, in fact, cursed.

"Yes. But I don't know the specifics. I know that my people put a curse on Dragon Island, but I don't know anything about it."

"Shit." Azure kicked at the mast and almost slipped onto the wet timbers. "Another complication. Just what we didn't need."

Brisa started for the bow of the ship. "I will pray for understanding and enlightenment. Maybe it will help."

Azure watched as Brisa climbed onto the bowsprit and stood, straight legged, with her hands together at her chest. Her balance was impeccable; she never so much as swayed to either side as the ship rocked and cut its way through still-choppy waters.

"Ha!" cried the Marauder King as he inspected the base of the main mast. "Worked like a charm!"

"Aye," said Mr. Cordingly. "That was a great decision on your part."

"What are you guys talking about?" Azure asked.

"We had the ship outfitted with a line of copper down the mast." The Marauder King shaded his eyes as he looked up at the undamaged top of the mast.

"It sends the lightning right down through the ship and into the sea," Mr. Cordingly explained.

"Is it magic?"

"I don't think so. It's more science than magic, I'm led to believe."

"Wow," Azure said, impressed.

"Uncharted island ahead!" called Syl from the crow's nest.

Everyone turned their attention to the bow, where Brisa still stood, unmoving. Just beyond her perfect long indigo legs was the vague blur of land on the horizon. Brisa ran a finger from her forehead to her heart, made a circle around her entire chest, then jumped down from the bowsprit.

"Did you make that island appear?" Azure asked her quietly after rushing over to her.

"I don't know." Brisa was even more beautiful and serene post-prayer. "I'm too young to understand how these things work."

Azure turned to the Marauder King, who was peering at the island through his spyglass.

"I think we should make one more stop," she said.

"May I ask why, m'lady? Is time not of the essence?"

"I think we might find answers there."

The Marauder King shrugged. "Good enough for me." He barked out orders, which were conveyed more thoroughly by his quartermaster.

Azure stood with Brisa and watched the island grow until the ship glided through the gradual transition of deeper blue waters melting into the vibrant aquamarines of the relatively shallow cove. Most of the coves and bays Azure had seen in her life were enchanting, but this one was more so somehow, as if its vividness had been enhanced by magic.

The *Adventure Ship* stopped at a pristine dock nestled into a pristine beach. A pristine boardwalk led up an incline and into a thick, but decidedly pristine jungle.

"I think it would be best if only Azure and I go," Brisa told the Marauder King, her tone straddling the line between telling and asking.

When he nodded, Azure and Brisa debarked and followed the boardwalk into the jungle. The trees—a type Azure had never seen before, with pale green leaves and branches that hung down to the ground as if weeping—formed a tunnel that encircled the boardwalk. Fireflies, glowing green, danced throughout the darkened, enclosed passage. The effect was spellbinding. Azure could have wandered within the charming sylvan tunnel all day but kept pace with Brisa.

After about a hundred yards, the boardwalk became an arching bridge that spanned a murmuring creek. Here, Azure had to pause.

She gazed down at the rushing waters, reminded of her favorite creek back home, and closed her eyes, letting the sounds of the water's babbling soothe her.

Azure's thoughts went back to a time when she and her father sat alongside the creek when she was younger. She had looked to him, his face anything but serene, and wondered why the creek didn't do the same for him as it did for her. She remembered him fidgeting, impatient, unsure why anyone would want to sit and simply watch the water flow by. He was always anxious to move on to the next thing, never willing to slow down and truly linger in a moment.

Azure, on the other hand, loved to take the countless opportunities nature provided to stop and ruminate, or, if she was lucky, to have her mind become devoid of any tangible thought at all.

"Azure."

Stirred from her daydream, Azure turned to see Brisa, smiling and waiting for her well past the bridge.

"Sorry."

Azure followed Brisa until the boardwalk turned into a staircase that led down into a dark rocky cave.

Brisa didn't break stride, descending the stairs with her usual grace. Azure hesitated, gulped, then followed her.

After a minute's descent through a claustrophobia-inducing hollow, they came out into a massive underground cavern. The middle of the cavern's ceiling opened to the sky, streaming sunlight. Thick green vines adorned with white flowers hung down from the opening, some of them reaching all the way down to the crystal-clear water that covered the cave's floor. A kaleidoscope of colorful butterflies flitted across the spaces between the flowers. At the bottom of the staircase, the path continued, although now made of perfectly carved stone. The stone path extended out into the water where it formed a circle just under the opening in the top of the cave.

Sitting in the middle of the circle, still as a stone, was a ciguapa woman with skin covered in rune tattoos. The woman opened her eyes and smiled as if she had been expecting them. Her smile was like a burst of sunlight on a cloudy day. It was warm and welcoming and revealed deep age lines that did nothing to take away from her beauty.

The woman said something in the ciguapa language, and Brisa replied.

"Do you speak the human tongue?" the woman asked.

"Yes, Mother." Brisa approached the edge of the water.

"Is that your mom?" Azure whispered, dumbfounded.

"No," Brisa said. "She's a member of the matriarchy."

"Oh." Azure felt two-fold stupid; for assuming, and for blurting out.

"Welcome to our Cenote. My name is Cono. You have found me because you have asked for understanding with a pure heart. How can I help you?"

"Raci, Mother," Brisa said, her voice unsteady. "I am called Brisa, and this is my friend, Azure. We come to seek knowledge about the curse placed upon Dragon Island, I mean Ersa Trago, if it pleases you, Mother."

"You can relax, Brisa." Cono stood and extended her hand.

Tentatively, Brisa walked across the stone path to the circle and took the woman's hand in her own.

"Come, Azure. Join us under the sun." Sunlight poured straight through the opening, bathing the circle in brilliant warmth.

Although she felt like an intruder, Azure stumbled across the path to the circle and took Cono's other hand.

As soon as she touched the woman's hand, a cozy serenity flowed through Azure's body.

Up close, Azure could see the extent of the woman's tattoos. Her chest, stomach, arms, and thighs were completely covered in two-inch circular runes. Silver ink decorated her body like permanent jewelry.

"I sense you're in a hurry, so I will not take much of your time," Cono said, still holding both Brisa and Azure's hands. "The curse put upon Ersa Trago is this: Those who step foot on Ersa Trago will, from that moment on, live honorably, or face the consequences of a curse. This curse will forever follow you if you choose to stray from virtue. Every day you will have the option to live the right way, to live honorably. If you start the day deciding to be dishonorable, you'll start the day with the curse, which can take many, sometimes hard to understand, forms. Every day for the rest of your life. You'll also face the curse if you try to spend or sell any of the treasure that was put on the island by the wise matriarchs long ago."

Understanding shone on Brisa's face. "Raci, Mother." She bowed to the older woman.

"You have been to Ersa Trago." It was more of a statement than a question.

"Yes, Mother."

"Then I think you have earned yourself a new rune."

Brisa's mouth dropped open.

"If you would indulge an old woman a moment longer?"

"Of course."

The woman took a metal instrument, like a tiny silver wand, from her hair and began to draw on Brisa's left wrist. Brisa made no sign of discomfort, but Azure noticed that her jaw was clenched tight.

When the rune was done it looked like a billowing cloud inside a circle.

"Those who have been through the Sia Nebla have earned the ability to make a fog of their own. The word is *nebla*." The woman let Brisa repeat the word, then continued. "As with all of our runes, you must not use them for personal gain or dishonorable purposes."

"Yes, Mother." Brisa closed her eyes and nodded.

"Alright, give it a try." Her smile became even broader and warmer.

Brisa traced the rune with her finger while whispering, "Nebla."

The cenote vanished. Azure waved her hand in front of her face and could just make out its outline through the fog that had appeared. But before Azure could say anything, the fog was gone.

"You will be able to hold it longer with practice," Cono said.

"Thank you so much, Mother. It is more than I deserve."

"I don't sense that to be true. I sense a great empathy in you. The fire in your chest burns bright. I sense you are bound for great things, young Brisa."

Brisa bowed low.

"It was good to meet you, Azure," Cono said. "But I know you must get going."

"I would have loved to stay here with you all day, Mother." Azure hoped she wasn't being too familiar using that honorific. "But you're right. We have a quest of great importance to carry out."

"May empathy guide you." She bowed to both of them, even lower than Brisa had. "And may the fires in your chests burn bright."

"To you, as well, Mother."

"Bye." Azure waved, then bowed, awkwardly.

Once back outside the cenote, Azure and Brisa hurried down the boardwalk toward the dock.

"So it's the dragon's unwillingness to give up the capybara medallion," Azure stated.

"Yeah. Apparently we'll face tough mornings until he leaves or throws that medallion in the sea." Brisa tried to feign anger but was still too aglow after her meeting with Cono for it to be believable.

"Maybe I'll just take it from him."

"Yeah. That should work." Brisa obviously hadn't even heard what Azure had said.

"And that's why that asshole Pratt never stepped foot on Dragon Island," Azure added. "He must have known about the curse beforehand. He knew damn well he wasn't going to act honorably, so he paid others to step on the island for him."

"Yeah." Brisa nodded, grinning.

Azure found it difficult to build up a proper rage with Brisa being so content, so she abandoned the effort and focused instead on getting to Paradise Island as soon as possible.

Chapter 25 Drawing Close

Governor Pratt was in bed with a young and attractive follower when a knock at his door interrupted him.

"What?" he yelled.

"Sir," said Paul Sancti through the door. "Some of the passengers claim to have seen a red dragon amongst the clouds."

"Shit." Pratt tossed the girl aside and dressed in a maddened rush.

Once outside his quarters, his eyes shot to the sky, but he didn't see anything unusual. He tried to gain control of Zoth-Avarex's mind but could latch onto nothing. If the dragon had been nearby, which seemed incredibly unlikely, it was now too far away for Pratt to control.

"Here are the passengers who claim to have seen it." Paul Sancti presented two passengers to Pratt.

"Did you see it with your own eyes?" Pratt asked the portly male passenger.

"Yes, sir." The man beamed as if he were the luckiest person under the Ring for having Pratt ask him a direct question. "It came out from one cloud, then darted into another. It wasn't more than a flash, but I could tell it was a dragon. It had the wings and the tail and everything."

"You saw it, too?" he asked the woman, who was decked out in an expensive dress.

"Yes, and it was horribly frightening. I tried to point it out to my husband, but by the time the idiot gawked up at the clouds, the dragon was gone."

"When was this?"

"About a half hour ago," the man said.

Governor Pratt spun around and slammed the door behind him. "Get out," he said to the girl in his bed.

She smiled at him as if he were joking.

"Now!"

She scrambled out of the bed, threw on her clothes, and hurried out of the room.

Pratt rushed to his desk and opened the top drawer. He lifted a false bottom, revealing... nothing. He closed his eyes, an anxious tightness in his chest. The key he had hidden there was gone.

He stormed out of the room and called for Paul Sancti, again.

"Get me John Brine."

Several minutes later, Paul Sancti returned with John Brine in tow.

"Did your bitch daughter ever talk to you about Dragon Island?"

John winced. "She's not a bitch."

Pratt slammed his fist on the desk. "Did she talk to you about Dragon Island?"

"Well, we talked about the red dragon that was seen over the Nameless Isles when we discussed changing the name of our inn. It used to be called Two Cappies and a Pup after—"

"I couldn't possibly care less," Pratt said. "Did she ever mention anything about a curse or a key?"

"No. Never." John looked nervously from Pratt to Paul and back.

Pratt took control of John's mind using his ring. It was exceedingly simple to control the mind of a human, and became simpler every time he tried it.

He forced John to talk, knowing that only the truth would now come from his mouth.

"Azure hated you," John said. "She would have done anything to see you fail. But she didn't know anything about a curse or a key or Dragon Island. We lived in the Nameless Isles our entire lives. We never left, even though she wanted to see every island in the League. She—"

"That's enough." He forced John to stand and leave the room. "There may be trouble brewing," he said to Paul.

"Sir?"

"We need to cancel our next stop. We'll head straight to Ridgeback Island."

"But what about your inauguration?"

"Fuck the inauguration. What I'm trying to do is much more important than that."

"But you said we needed five hundred people for our mission at Ridgeback Island to be assured success."

"How many do we have, now?"

"Just shy of three hundred, sir."

"Shit." Pratt had only come to the figure of five hundred people through hearsay, but it was solid enough information, and he didn't want to stray from it. He had heard about it from an old soldier, who had heard it from a ciguapa prisoner during the war on Smith Island.

"Five hundred souls, united in common cause. This is the only way to—"

Pratt shook his head. There was no use in going over those words for the thousandth time. Instead, he calculated probabilities in his head. This dragon business was likely nothing, and even if that brat had actually made it through the Eternal Fog and freed the dragon, Pratt could control it as soon as it showed itself. He would have to remain vigilant. Maybe set up a dragon watch and an alarm bell or something.

"Alright. We'll make one final stop at Whetstone, but only to pick up the last group. We'll postpone my inauguration until after our mission, as you put it."

"Yes, sir."

Chapter 26 The Tsunami

Robin and Zoth-Avarex returned to the ship in the late afternoon.
"Did you see my dad?" Azure asked Robin after a tiny embrace.

"I saw him but didn't get a chance to talk to him. I did talk to that big dumb idiot Thunder Paws, though."

"What did he say?"

"Nothing, really. He mentioned something about people being able to direct magic through one wand if they touch each other, but that was about it."

"Did my dad seem okay?"

Robin paused for just a fraction of a second. "Yeah. As far as I could tell."

Azure left the subject alone, unsure if she really wanted to hear how he was doing, partly because she wasn't sure if she preferred him miserable or happy.

"So Thunder Paws said numerous people could direct magic through one wand?"

"Yeah, if they touch each other or something."

"Huh." Azure took out her wand and pointed it at a nearby barrel. She focused and tried to lift the barrel from the floor. Beads of sweat appeared on her forehead as she poured all of her energy into the task, but the barrel didn't budge.

She called to Syl and Mr. Cordingly, who were having a conversation nearby.

"Could you guys help me with something real quick?" she asked in her sweetest voice.

"Of course," Mr. Cordingly said.

"Could you both touch my arms and focus your minds on lifting that barrel over there?"

Syl and Mr. Cordingly shot her confused looks but shrugged and complied. Syl touched her left shoulder, Mr. Cordingly her right.

She aimed her wand at the barrel and concentrated as hard as before. At first, nothing happened. But then she started to feel something on both of her shoulders, a sort of buzz flowing across her chest and down into her wand hand. The barrel moved, then lifted from the deck. For several seconds it hung in the air.

Azure smiled and looked to her friends, causing the barrel to crash back down with a dull thud.

"I didn't know that was possible," Mr. Cordingly practically shouted.

"This is huge." Azure's mind raced with the implications of this new knowledge. The possibilities of magic used in this way seemed endless.

Azure's eyes wandered to where Zoth-Avarex stood, shrunk back down and talking to the Marauder King. Her temper flared, thinking about the curse. She had half a mind to march over and confront him, but the other half was tired and still a bit hung over. She decided she'd confront him later.

Eleanor and Alistair Covington waddled by, making contented chattering sounds to each other. Azure half-bowed, half-curtseyed to them as they passed. Alistair stopped, squatted, and pooped near a coil of old rope. Azure pretended not to see it happening, fidgeting with her wand as she purposefully looked away. When he was done, and the happy couple had moved on, Azure found a small broom and dustpan, swept up the mess, and sent it over into the briny deep.

As night fell, the Marauders convened around the makeshift stage, like usual. But the mood was much more laid back. No one seemed to be drinking. Azure assumed they were still feeling the effects of the night before.

"What did the ocean say to the marauder?" the Marauder King said from the stage.

He paused.

"Nothing. It just waved."

The crowd collectively groaned. Only a few chuckled at this one.

"Alright, alright. My head is still throbbing. But it would be nice to hear a few songs tonight. Does anyone have anything mellow for us?"

Azure was surprised to see Brisa's hand go up.

"I have a song in my language, if that's okay?"

"Of course," said the Marauder King. "We'd be honored."

Brisa made her way up to the stage.

"So this is what it's like on the poop deck," she said, trying to suppress a grin.

The marauders, seemingly every last one of them, giggled.

Azure nodded in appreciation. She hadn't known Brisa to tell many jokes since she'd met her.

"This is a song my mother used to sing to me when I was young." Brisa took a moment to compose herself, then began to sing.

Azure's mouth dropped open. The marauders no longer milled about. Every one of them stared up at Brisa, unmoving. Her voice was unlike anything Azure had ever heard.

The song needed no accompaniment. It was perfect with just the one voice. Brisa weaved in and out between soft and passionate singing, alternating with flawless transitions. Azure couldn't understand the words, but as she stood transfixed, she could feel every note of the song. Her eyes welled up, and she tried to fight off the tears, unsure why she didn't just let them flow.

When the song was over, the crowd roared with enthusiastic applause. Brisa gave a graceful bow, then melted back into the group.

"That was brilliant," Azure told her. "What was it about? If you don't mind me asking."

"It's about a child asking his or her mother about all the what-ifs of life, and the mother's responses."

"Oh."

Brisa must have been able to see in Azure's eyes that she wanted to know more, but was too polite to ask, because she offered a longer explanation.

"The child asks things like; what if I do something really bad? What if I get lost in the dark? What if the fire in my chest goes out? Will you always love me, no matter what?"

Azure's vision became blurry.

"And the mother responds by saying, 'I will hold you through the darkest night, even if your fire's not alight.' And, 'Call my name any place or time, and I'll come rushing to your side.' I know that doesn't exactly rhyme in your language, but that's the closest translation I can do."

"It's beautiful."

"Yeah. I love it. Always have."

"Anyone else?" the Marauder King said from the stage.

"I don't know if I should try to follow that, but I do have something I've been working on," Mr. Cordingly said.

"Let's hear it!" The Marauder King waved him up to the stage.

Mr. Cordingly sat on the edge, his legs dangling, and pulled a worn concertina from a battered case.

"As you know, this is going to be my last run with you all for a long while."

The marauders playfully booed him.

"So, this is a song about that."

He cleared his throat and began to play and sing. His skill with the concertina was impressive; not fancy or too intricate, but a perfectly played accompaniment. His voice was impressive, as well. It wasn't pitch perfect or beautiful, but it had a rich timbre that resonated warmly around the ship.

Anchor aweigh, oh anchor aweigh,
This ship is soon to be bound for the bay.
Every time I go away,
I have sunshine at home, my radiant May.
And while I am gone, wherever I stray,
The mere thought of her can scatter the gray.
Anchor aweigh, oh anchor aweigh,
This ship is soon to be bound for the bay.
But now another is joining the fray,
For it seems we've got a babe on the way
The crew shouted, "WAY HEY!"
My fatherly duties will soon have me stay,
Back with my young one, back with my May.
So I will drop anchor, back home on the bay,
This marauder is done...marauding today.
Anchor aweigh, oh anchor aweigh,
This ship is soon to be bound for the bay.

He slowed down his playing to half speed.

As you know, I have always loved to roam,
But now it's love that is steering me home.

As the final note rang out, the crowd was silent. Mr. Cordingly set his concertina back in its case and stood. The Marauder King stepped up and embraced him, lifting him off the deck.

The crowd cheered even louder than they had for Brisa. Mr. Cordingly descended the ladder and was rushed with hugs, handshakes, and well-wishes.

Azure shook his hand as he came by and he pulled her into a quick embrace.

"That was really good," Azure said.

"Oh, thanks. Not as good as Brisa's, but not the worst song ever written, I suppose."

An older marauder approached Mr. Cordingly and gripped his hand.

"You're going to love fatherhood," he said. "Those were the best years of my life, they were."

"I just hope I'm good at it."

"If that song is any indication, you'll be better than most."

"Well, thank you."

"You know, kids will assail your coconuts with their knees, assail your nose with the back of their heads, and assail your sleep with screams in the night. They'll assail your nerves with worry of their well-being."

"Wow, you're really selling this for me."

"You didn't let me finish." The man flashed a warm smile. "They'll also assail your heart and soul with every laugh, every dance, and every cuddle. They'll assail the notion that you are the most important person in the world, but to be fair, as a marauder you've already been disabused of that silly notion. Anyway, they'll make you feel a love you'd have never thought possible. At least that was my experience."

"You make it sound fantastic. Thank you, Jim."

The man patted Mr. Cordingly on the back, smiled again, and moved on.

After hearing that, Azure couldn't help considering the idea of having kids of her own. There was definitely a part of her that warmed to the idea, but it was something that would have to be far, far into her future. First, she would want to get married, she supposed, and that wasn't even on her map, yet. Maybe someday, but for now, all that kind of stuff was well beyond the horizon.

Azure yawned, covering her mouth with both hands. She turned and slunk off to her room, completely forgetting about her plans to berate Zoth-Avarex.

AZURE AWOKE TO A COMMOTION in the hallway. She shot up and poked her head out of her door.

"A rogue wave!" Someone called as they ran up the stairs.

"Batten down the hatches!" the Marauder King barked from the deck.

"Zidon's beard!" Mr. Threepbrush said from the top of the stairs.

Azure sprinted up the stairs barefoot. She followed most of the crew members' eyes to the starboard side of the ship, expecting to see a big wave on the horizon.

But there was no horizon.

A wall of water higher than Azure could have ever imagined hurtled toward them, impossibly fast. The sight was disorienting, making Azure wobble on her feet. What she saw was surreal. She hoped she was only dreaming but didn't think herself capable of imagining something this insane.

Her heart dropped. Her mind told her there was no way they could possibly survive this. They had seconds to live before being broken apart and sunk to the bottom of the sea. She looked for Robin, hoping that at least she could fly up and away from the impact, but couldn't find her.

Although it was a futile gesture, Azure wrapped her arms around the mizzenmast.

Orok and Nargol held each other, facing the wave, unflinching. Both of them placed a hand on Nargol's belly.

Elijah hung his head, his bony shoulders sagging.

Brisa closed her eyes and placed her hands over her chest.

Just before the tsunami hit, Azure caught a flash of red from the corner of her eye. Zoth-Avarex, grown back to full size, waved his claws and one of his protective bubbles encapsulated the ship.

The wave enveloped them, rocking the ship, but not smashing it to pieces. Daylight darkened as the water surrounded the dragon's bubble. Azure could see fish swimming frantically all around. A pod of dolphins zipped over the main mast. There was a blur of what could have been a mermaid, but she seemed to have the tentacles of an octopus instead of a fish tail.

The dragon floated among the sails, claws outstretched, concentrating hard on maintaining the bubble's integrity. The ship was bounced around, but not very much. Azure may have been able to keep her feet, even if she hadn't been clinging to the mast.

The ship burst out the other side of the wave. It rocked even harder as it was set back down on the rough water. The protective bubble disappeared, letting a deluge of sea water down on the ship like a heavy rain.

Zoth-Avarex shrunk himself and landed on the deck.

Chapter 27 Abandoned

The Marauders rushed to thank Zoth-Avarex for saving them, again. Azure rolled her eyes and turned away to see Elijah sulking along the rail.

"Well, that was something you don't see every day," she said as she approached, trying to cheer him up.

Elijah shook his head. "This is all my fault. If me and my crew hadn't stolen that medallion in the first place, none of this horrible stuff would be happening."

"That's not true. This is that greedy ass dragon's fault, not yours."

"He's a dragon. He can't change the way he is. You can't blame him for being thrown into this." He sighed. "No. All the blame falls squarely on me, like usual."

"That's bullshit." Azure's fists clenched. She turned to look at Zoth-Avarex, still getting recognition for saving them from something he created. "It's not your fault, Elijah."

Azure stomped over to the dragon and pushed her way through the small crowd.

"You can literally break two curses by doing nothing more than parting with a shiny piece of fucking metal!" she shouted.

"Seriously?" Zoth-Avarex said. "You're going to come at me with that right now? I just saved all your lives."

"Our lives wouldn't have needed saving if you'd just acted honorably and thrown that stupid medallion in the ocean. We found out that Dragon Island was cursed, and something like that wave is going to happen every day as long as you're acting dishonorably by keeping that thing around your neck."

"Dragons are not known for giving up something they want for the sake of others, and I'm the most dragon-like dragon you'll ever meet." He pumped up his chest. "We're also notoriously stubborn. Once my heels dig in, nothing can pull me out. You could prove beyond a shadow of a doubt that I should toss this medallion into the sea and I'll refuse because I already said I wouldn't."

"But the curse is going to keep coming for us, for you, unless you do the honorable thing."

Zoth-Avarex shrugged. "The curse hasn't been all that bad, and if it gets too annoying, I'll just create a portal to another world. I'm guessing the curse can't travel across realms."

"But you said you would help us. And what about your revenge?"

"Good point." He rubbed the spikes on the back of his neck. "I do have to stay until I get my revenge."

"But you're not going to give up the medallion?"

"Nope."

Azure pulled out her wand, rage clouding her judgement.

The dragon burst out laughing.

"Give me that medallion," she said through gritted teeth.

"Or you'll do what? Hit me with a bolt?" He chuckled. "Go ahead. Give me everything you've got."

His mocking infuriated Azure beyond reason. She channeled her anger through her arm and into her wand. She imagined a burst of powerful energy striking the greedy dragon in his stupid face.

A bolt that seemed bigger than the bolt of lightning that struck the mast discharged from her wand. With an ear-splitting crack it struck the dragon on his smirking mouth.

When a puff of black smoke dissipated, the dragon was still smirking, completely unscathed.

"Don't feel too bad," he said. "Even if this whole crew linked arms and channeled their energy through your wand, you couldn't scratch a single scale on this handsome face."

Azure dropped her wand and lunged forward, roaring and reaching out for the medallion around his neck.

Zoth-Avarex leaped into the air and hovered ten feet above the deck.

"You know what?" His expression mirrored that of an angry, hurt, reprimanded child. "I don't need this shit. I can get my revenge on that Pratt asshole without you."

"We don't need you either!" Even as she said it, Azure knew she was making a mistake, but she didn't care.

Wordlessly, the dragon grew to full size, turned, and beat his massive wings, sending a gale across the deck.

"What a coward," Robin said as the dragon disappeared into the clouds.

Chapter 28 The Stranded Ship

E ven with Zoth-Avarex gone, the Marauders plowed ahead. "We'll just have to stop Pratt before he enacts his plan," Azure had said, trying to sound confident. "That's all."

"Exactly, young lady," the Marauder King had replied.

With the waters calm and the wind directly at their back, they had made good time since that little conversation.

The crew was at constant work—in a constant state of song—making minor adjustments to maintain full speed.

"Ship!" Called Syl from the crow's nest. "Dead ahead!"

The Marauder King jumped down from the ship's wheel and sprinted to the bow. He extended his spyglass and peered at the horizon directly in front of them.

"It's flying a distress flag," he said loud enough so most could hear him. "Looks like a merchant sloop from here. It's in amongst a couple of huge rocks jutting up from out of nowhere. It could be sinking."

Mr. Threepbrush approached him. "What do you want to do, sir?"

The Marauder King flashed a quick look to Azure with an expression of regret, then addressed his quartermaster. "Do we have *any* time to spare?"

"Not much, sir."

"But some?"

"Well, Yrus has been good to us today. We've made it farther than I expected. And the winds won't be as good for Pratt as he tries to sail north. So yes, we have a little time." Mr. Threepbrush cleared his throat. "But we have to consider this could be a trap."

The Marauder King gazed back into his spyglass, studying the ship. Then he handed it to Mr. Threepbrush.

"I don't see any indication of it being a trap. Do you?"

Mr. Threepbrush looked through the spyglass, then said, "No, sir."

"If they're in true distress, the entire ship could be sunk to the bottom of the sea before anyone else comes along. That means the crew..." The Marauder King shook his head. "No. We'll swing by and see what the problem is. If it's anything short of sinking, we'll tell them we have to press on, and we'll report their location the first chance we get. But if they're sinking, it's our duty as marauders to get them aboard. As fast as possible, of course."

Azure nodded, worried, but not willing to show it, or fight him on this point.

"Aye, sir." Mr. Threepbrush barked orders to the crew

As they got closer, Azure could see the massive brown rocks off the stern and starboard sides of the ship, which was facing a forty-five-degree angle away to port. The flag flying from the stern was bright red with a black star in the middle. The rocks towered over the ship, maybe three times as high. A lone pine tree clung to the side of the biggest rock, growing out then up in an amazing display of resiliency. Seagulls circled above the rocks like vultures.

Men appeared along the port side waving to the marauders. A woman wearing a bright yellow dress waved, as well.

Sails were dropped, adjustments were made, and the *Adventure Ship* began to slow as it pulled up near the distressed ship.

The red distress flag started to come down as they approached. Azure waved to the people from across the water, noticing, to her surprise, that the woman in the yellow dress had an unusual amount of facial hair. The name across the bow, which was just now becoming visible, read *Widow's Lamentation*.

Another flag shot up in the red flag's place. This one was black and depicted a white skeleton slicing a red heart in half with a massive white sword.

An explosion echoed off the rocks as the stranded ship shot one of its port side cannons.

The bell of the *Adventure Ship* began to ring furiously.

"Roberts! Roberts! Roberts!" shouted Orok.

"Aye," said the Marauder King, looking defeated. "We got it."

"Surrender or be destroyed," shouted a man who appeared alongside the man in the yellow dress.

The man must have been six and a half feet tall, and broad as an ox. He wore all black, from a black bandana tied around his head, to his knee-high black boots. He was clean shaven and wore the wryest of grins on his scarred but handsome face. At his belt hung a sword damn near as tall as Azure, and was shaped like a cross. At his shoulder floated a menacing gargoyle, its bat-like wings lined with horn-like spikes.

The Marauder King looked to his quartermaster, then his sailing master, then at Azure, his face panicked.

"He'll destroy us," he said, hanging his head.

Mr. Threepbrush removed a white handkerchief from his pocket and waved it over his head.

THE PIRATES FLUNG ROPES with hooks across the gap and pulled the two ships together, jeering and laughing at the marauders as they heaved.

Orok and Nargol looked ready to charge and fight, but the rest of the crew was sullen.

Eleanor and Alistair Covington stood, stoic, watching the invasion unfold.

"Stand down," the Marauder King said, not even half-heartedly.

The ships crashed together, sending a shudder through the timbers.

Captain Roberts put a hand atop the rail and bounded over onto the *Adventure Ship*, his gargoyle and two of his men following close behind. Azure turned her head as the stinging smell of old sweat saturated the air around them. The captain didn't give Azure a second glance, but his men looked her up and down, the carnality in their eyes sending a shiver through her core.

"Who's the sailing master on this pathetic ship?" Captain Roberts said.

Mr. Cordingly must have given some sort of subtle indication, as the captain made a b-line straight for him, grabbing him around the upper arm.

"What are ya doing?" demanded the Marauder King.

"Not that I owe you an explanation," Captain Roberts said, his voice booming and authoritative, "but I am in dire need of a competent sailing master. As you can see, we've had to remove the *ing master* from ours, so now he's just a sail." He pointed across to his mast, where a man was splayed out among the sails, all four limbs tied to ropes. The two men with the captain chuckled.

"Well ya can't take ours!" the Marauder King said, defiant.

"I can't?" He turned to his crew. "Men!"

At least twenty men along the rail aimed pistols—most holding two of them— at the marauders. In addition, they manned three mounted swivel guns at regular intervals along the rail that looked quite menacing.

The Marauder King's shoulders slumped even further.

"That's what I thought." Captain Roberts pulled Mr. Cordingly away.

Mr. Cordingly's face was surprisingly serene. He stared ahead as if he had no idea what was happening.

Every marauder now looked as if they were ready to pounce, to face certain death if necessary, but they all remained still.

The Marauder King stepped forward, then stopped himself. He put a finger in the air, then dropped it back down.

"Stop!" he finally shouted. "Captain Roberts, I challenge you to a duel!"

Chapter 29 The Duel

Captain Roberts spun around and made eye contact with the Marauder King, his face serious.

Then, a grin broke out. The grin grew wider and wider until loud, repulsive belly laughter curled him forward.

At this cue, the rest of his crew began to laugh and shout taunts.

Although the Marauder King's legs were visibly shaking, he held his head high and continued to meet Captain Roberts's eyes.

The laughter continued for an obnoxious length of time. When it finally died out, Captain Roberts asked, "And what, may I ask, would be the terms of this duel?"

"If I win, ya leave us alone, empty handed." The Marauder King gulped. "If you win you can take all the spoils we have left but leave Mr. Cordingly to go back to his family."

"Although I'm sure your spoils might add up to enough to get me a dinner and maybe even a drink on Mirth Island, I think I'll be inclined to decline that offer." He looked to his crew. "*If* he wins, you will respect my dying wish and leave his crew and his ship alone, as he says." The crew nodded assent. Captain Roberts turned back to the Marauder King. "But if I win, we will take our new sailing master and leave the rest of you idiots to your own devices."

"I—"

"This is my one and only offer of a gentleman's duel. If you refuse, we'll take what is ours by right of strength."

The Marauder King nodded.

"Now, what shall we use for weapons; guns," Captain Roberts pulled a pistol from his belt, "magic," he pulled a golden wand from his belt with his other hand, "or swords?" He nodded down to the monstrosity at his hip.

"I was think—"

"Or our bare hands!" The crew whooped and hollered as the captain tucked his wand and pistol and threw his hands up like they were cat's paws, slashing at the air.

"I was think—"

"Or we could have our conjured companions fight in our stead." His gargoyle dove in front of him, teeth bared and claws splayed.

Nova, who stood on the Marauder King's shoulder, looked as if he might faint.

"Guns," said the Marauder King, his voice cracking.

"You would suggest that, wouldn't you? It's the most cowardly option to be sure. And you probably couldn't afford a proper wand, anyway." He paused, smoothing out his eyebrows. "No, I think we'll use swords. And before you object, let me be clear that this is also non-negotiable."

The Marauder King lowered his hand, slowly, to the hilt of his cutlass.

"Don't do it, MK!" Mr. Cordingly called out. "I'll go with them. It'll be fine."

"You've got yer baby coming, yer family to look after." The Marauder King drew his sword.

Captain Roberts took off his coat, folded it, and handed it to one of his men. He turned and pulled his giant, heavy sword from its sheath and held it with both hands.

"It's like a sword in old stories from the Continent, like the one Griffin the Unrivaled wielded," whispered Mr. Threepbrush. "Gods..."

The two men approached each other, swords raised in front of them. Captain Roberts's sword was at least twice as long.

For a tense, silent time, the two of them turned crabwise around each other. The Marauder King's legs were still shaking.

Azure's inner voice screamed at her to do something, to stop this from happening.

Without knowing what she intended, she discreetly drew her wand.

"For Chastity's honor!" roared the Marauder King as he lunged forward, striking out with his sword.

Captain Roberts took a deft step back, although it was probably unnecessary. "Who?" he asked with a smirk.

"There is no maiden fairer than the peerless Chastity of Mirth Island. I fight in her name, in deference to her virtue, always."

"You fight in the name of a whore. Perfect."

"How dare you besmirch the name and the honor of my fair and decent lady!"

Again, the Marauder King lunged forward, swinging his sword in a wide arc from his right.

With little effort, Captain Roberts moved his sword inches to his left to block the blow. The clanging of metal rang out around the ship. The sword almost slipped from the Marauder King's hands.

Captain Roberts lifted his heavy sword with surprising speed and agility. He brought the sword up over his head, and in one fluid motion, meant to bring it down on the Marauder King's skull, likely severing him in half. The Marauder King was wrong-footed and seemed stuck in place.

Azure gripped her wand and concentrated all of her energy into pushing Captain Roberts's sword away from the Marauder King.

As the sword plunged down, it moved to the right, just missing the Marauder King's shoulder. It continued down, a blur of steel, until it lodged into the deck with a thunk.

Captain Roberts pried it from the wood and stepped back. "Who did that?" he shouted to the Marauders.

Azure concealed the wand in the sleeve of her coat.

"If I detect another sliver of magic, I will order my crew to kill every last one of you!"

The marauders looked at each other with confused expressions. Azure tried to play along, acting as innocent as possible.

Captain Roberts looked up at the gargoyle, floating above the dueling ground. "Watch them and disembowel any who meddle."

The gargoyle nodded its horrible green head.

"Let's finish this," Captain Roberts said, raising his sword, again.

The Marauder King charged with a flurry of quick slices, all of which Captain Roberts blocked.

Captain Roberts reared back and swung his sword from his side, aiming at his opponent's hip.

The Marauder King dove for the rail and rolled over, onto the *Widow's Lamentation*. The pirate crew backed up, giving him room to stand, while jeering and feigning at him.

Captain Roberts leaped onto the rails, then down to his own deck. His crew backed up further.

Again, the Marauder King unleashed a flourish of strikes, although they were much slower as he was obviously winded. The captain blocked them all, again. Then, as if he was done toying with his prey, he struck the Marauder King's sword with such force that it flew from his hands, clanging against the main mast and dropping to the floor. Captain Roberts lifted his sword over his head again, bringing it down with terrible speed.

The Marauder King lunged to his right, but not fast enough.

The giant sword bit into the Marauder King's leg, just below the knee, completely severing it from his body.

A collective groan went up from both crews.

The Marauder King fell to the deck and gaped at his bleeding stump in disbelief.

Captain Roberts stood over his conquered foe and put the point of his bloody sword to the Marauder King's throat. He turned and looked at Mr. Cordingly. "Get over here, now. Or he dies where he sits."

Chapter 30 Tactical Decisions

"Detach from their pathetic ship," Captain Roberts ordered as Mr. Cordingly climbed awkwardly over the rails.

The pirate crew unhooked from the *Adventure Ship* and coiled their ropes on the deck. The ships began to separate.

"What about our captain?" shouted Mr. Threepbrush.

"He'll make good shark food." Captain Roberts laughed and turned away. "Man the cannons! Let's sink 'em, boys! It's been too long since we've had a bit of practice at the guns. We wouldn't want to get rusty, would we?"

The men cheered, and most hurried belowdecks. The lids of at least six gun ports lifted along the hull.

"That wasn't the deal," Azure yelled.

Captain Roberts poured himself a drink, pretending not to hear her.

The ships were now about two feet apart. The Marauder King still sat on the *Widow's Lamentation*, bleeding.

With an air-rending growl, Orok leaped onto the barnacled warship and snatched up the closest crew member. He threw the man like a child's toy, striking the would-be operator of the nearest swivel gun and sending them both to the deck in a heap of tangled limbs. Nargol was right behind her husband, snatching another man and tossing him overboard into the ever-widening gap between the boats.

Syl jumped across with a short sword in each hand and engaged two men wielding cutlasses.

Two pistol shots sounded off. One of them struck Orok in the shoulder but didn't seem to slow him down. The other grazed Nargol's thigh. In the span of a heartbeat, Orok closed the distance to two other men who were about to shoot and knocked their heads together.

Robin zipped across to the other ship, dipping and diving and trying to find an opening to one of the pirate's faces.

Azure peered over the side of the ship, paying close attention to the gun ports, where the pirate crew was busy loading the cannons. Her mind raced. She didn't know how long they had until the ship sunk and all was lost.

Syl cried out as a pirate's cutlass nicked his arm. He dropped one of his swords and kicked the man in the chest, sending him flying backwards. The other pirate swung his cutlass at Syl's head, but he ducked and slashed the pirate's arm with his remaining short sword. The pirate screamed, fell, and dropped his cutlass.

Syl grabbed the stunned Mr. Cordingly by the arm. "Help me get MK," he said, pulling him aft.

Captain Roberts smashed his glass against the mast, drew his sword, and charged forward to stand in front of the Marauder King. Syl lashed out at him, but Captain Roberts's heavy sword knocked the weapon from Syl's hand. The captain put his sword to the Marauder King's throat as the horrifying gargoyle loomed overhead.

"Shit!" Syl backed up, pulling Mr. Cordingly away from the captain and toward the rail. The gap between ships was now more than ten feet. Syl opened the pouch that he wore around his neck and poured something that looked like sand into his hand. He said an unrecognizable word and tossed the sand into the gap. Instead of falling to the sea, the sand spread out at rail level, as if it had been thrown onto a pane of glass.

Syl stepped out confidently onto the floating sand and it supported his weight. He tugged Mr. Cordingly behind him. A gun shot whizzed just over Mr. Cordingly's head, causing him to duck and stumble ahead. When they were both back on the *Adventure Ship*, Syl spoke another word and the sand—along with a trailing pirate— fell into the water.

Orok and Nargol panicked and dove across the gap, just catching the rail of the *Adventure Ship* under their arms and scrambling up and over it. They looked back to the Marauder King, crestfallen.

"What are you waiting for?" Captain Roberts clamored, stomping on the deck. "Fire those cannons!"

Azure looked up from the gun ports and noticed the *Adventure Ship* had drifted much closer to the giant rock formation that jutted out of the ocean behind them. As she looked back and forth from the rock to Captain Roberts's ship, an idea formed in Azure's mind, almost fully realized.

"Man the cannons!" she shouted to anyone within earshot. Most of the marauders began to scramble belowdecks without so much as a second look. "But I need Brisa, Syl, Orok, Nargol, Blunderbuss, Threepbrush, and Cordingly up here with me."

They followed her command.

"Brisa!" she said. "I need you to conjure a fog, as much as you can."

Brisa nodded, and without hesitation, began to trace her new tattoo.

"Syl, focus one of your will-o'-the-wisps at their ship, at mast level."

Syl looked to the mast of the *Widow's Lamentation* and began chanting.

Azure took out her wand and pointed it at the rock formation.

"Threepbrush, man the ship's wheel."

He climbed up to his ordered position.

"The rest of you, get over here and put a hand on my shoulder."

They did as she asked. Nargol and Blunderbuss took her right shoulder, Orok and Mr. Cordingly her left.

"I need you to focus all of your thoughts and energy on the idea of pushing against that rock formation. Imagine pushing against it with all your might."

Brisa's fog enveloped everything. Azure could no longer see the rock, and could barely see her wand, or the people next to her.

"Keep pushing!"

She couldn't tell if it was working. It didn't feel like they were moving.

"Use—" She was about to tell them to use anger to increase their magical power, to imagine toppling the rock onto Captain Roberts's head or something. But that wasn't right. That wasn't going to work. Instinctively, she took another approach. "Focus on the love you feel for the Marauder King. Think about him over there, injured, alone. Think of what you would do to save him if you could. What would you sacrifice so he was no longer hurting? No longer alone?"

Azure's shoulders and chest began to thrum with a boundless energy. She sent that energy down her arm and into her wand.

The ship lurched forward.

"Keep going!"

The ship moved faster.

Ear-splitting cannon fire resonated through the fog. Bursts of dull orange pulsed along the hull of Captain Roberts's ship, but there was no shuddering under Azure's feet, no sounds of splintering timber.

Azure looked up to the faint blue glow of Syl's will-o'-the-wisp.

"Turn to starboard, Mr. Threepbrush! Aim our broadside at that glow!"

She felt the ship turning, heard Captain Roberts cursing from across the fog.

"Men belowdecks, as soon as you're ready, fire at the blue glow as best you can!"

A marauder at the stairs relayed Azure's message.

In the silence that followed, Azure wondered if the men would be able to perform this duty with fog blurring their vision.

But the deck rumbled as a cannon fired. Then another, and another. There was a crash, and the sound of creaking and snapping wood, then another, bigger crash, and finally, a resounding splash.

Brisa's fog cleared, revealing the *Widow's Lamentation* with a toppled mast, crippled in the water.

The marauder's ship had rounded the bow of the pirate ship and was now directly in front of it.

"What do we do about MK?" Mr. Cordingly asked Azure.

Without pausing to consider how strange it was that he was asking her what to do, Azure began to go through their options, none of which were any good.

They could continue to fire on the ship, possibly beating Captain Roberts into submission, but she didn't like that idea at all. For one thing, they could accidentally kill the Marauder King. And another, they would undoubtedly kill more pirates, and she wasn't resigned to killing anyone, except maybe Pratt himself.

They could set sail and get away, leaving MK behind. This, of course, was a horrible idea, but possibly the most practical. Everyone else would be safe, and he was likely doomed anyway. But she couldn't imagine leaving him like that. If she were in his spot, she was sure he wouldn't leave her behind.

Captain Roberts appeared near the bowsprit with the Marauder King held in front of him, a pistol pointed at the side of his head. "That was a clever bit of tactics," he called across the water, "but I am done playing with you. Stand down or your *king* will be missing more than a leg."

The marauders looked to Azure as if she was supposed to answer him.

"I..." She looked each one of them in the eyes, unsure if standing down meant they would all be killed. She closed her eyes and tried to draw a calming breath. When she opened them, she caught a flash of red in her periphery.

Zoth-Avarex dove down between the ships and floated at rail level.

"What do you need, Azure?" he said.

"We need to get the Marauder King back."

The dragon turned to Captain Roberts. "You heard her, asshole."

Color drained from the captain's face as he gaped at Zoth-Avarex. He nearly stumbled backwards, but kept his grip on his hostage. Extreme confusion mingled with terror in his expression.

"You take orders from her?" Captain Roberts spat, pressing the pistol into the Marauder King's temple and ducking further behind him.

"I don't take orders from anyone, but I will roast your ship to cinders if she asks me to."

"What power does she have over you?" Azure could see his eyebrows pinch from across the water. "Does she know binding runes strong enough for a dragon?"

"No, she earned my respect through her actions. I have seen very few who could match that human. I mean, she's still a pathetic human, but she's one I will...de...fend?" Zoth-Avarex shook his massive head. "Gods-damnit, I'm getting soft."

Azure felt the moment was right for a bold bluff.

"Hand over the Marauder King to the dragon or I will have him burn your ship into the sea."

As if they'd rehearsed it, Zoth-Avarex unleashed a torrent of flame into the sky. The heat from the fire made Azure narrow her eyes and turn her face away.

Captain Roberts's eyes flitted from Azure to the dragon, to the Marauder King, and back. He bared his teeth and closed his eyes, then, with a roar of frustration, he dropped the Marauder King and took a step back.

Zoth-Avarex flew in and scooped up the Marauder King in one claw. He zipped across to the *Adventure Ship* and lay him down on the deck. The marauders converged on their captain, each of them apparently torn between wanting to embrace him and wanting to help with his severed leg.

Azure gave them a moment, then called, "Set sail!"

The crew jumped up and got to work. The Marauder King, although weary and bloody, winked at her and flashed a warm, genuine smile.

"So, I should burn their ship into the sea, now, right?" Zoth-Avarex said, a tinge of hope in his voice.

"No," Azure said, "I don't intend to become one of them. Let's just go."

The dragon sighed, his massive shoulders drooping.

As they sailed away, Azure stared across at Captain Roberts. As they locked eyes, she tried to keep her face completely emotionless, even though she felt like laughing, or crying, or both. She subtly hid her shaking hands behind her back. Captain Roberts remained impassive as well. But then, just before he turned away, he gave her a slow nod heavily laden with respect and conciliation.

When he turned his back, Azure couldn't keep the corner of her mouth from lifting.

Chapter 31 Race to the Whetstone

B risa rushed to the Marauder King and took a knee. Her face was panicked at first but softened when she noticed that he was just barely bleeding.

"You placed a ligature around your leg," she said. "Good."

"I don't know what that is, but I did tie my favorite scarf around my leg. Probably ruined it with blood, too." He shook his head.

Brisa studied the wound. "The cut is as clean as I've ever seen, perfectly straight. You're—"

"My leg!" the Marauder King cried. "I left it on the other ship."

Brisa didn't respond.

"Oh well." The Marauder King shook his head. "I guess Captain Roberts has himself a souvenir to remember me by. Gods know I won't be forgetting him."

Zoth-Avarex—shrunk down to orc size, again—poked his head in to see what was going on. "We should probably cauterize that," he said. The dragon snapped his fingers and a bottle of rum appeared in his claw. He handed it to the Marauder King. "You're going to want to start in on this."

The Marauder King took the bottle and downed several gulps.

"I need a sword," Brisa said to anyone within earshot. "Preferably a clean one."

Mr. Cordingly appeared at Brisa's side, holding out his unused cutlass. Brisa took it and held it out in front of Zoth-Avarex's face. The dragon spit a curl of fire that momentarily encompassed the blade.

"Here." Mr. Cordingly held out a chunk of wood to his captain. "Bite down on this, sir." He took a place behind the injured man and wrapped his arms around his chest.

The Marauder King took another swig of rum, then placed the wood between his teeth.

"I'm going to count to three." Brisa moved the glowing sword close to the wound. "One..."

Brisa pressed the sword against the end of the Marauder King's leg. He fought and squirmed, his face going beet red as he chomped down on the wood, but Mr. Cordingly held him fast. The wound sizzled sickeningly, and a smoke that smelled far too close to cooking meat filled the immediate area, causing Azure to take a step back and gag.

When it was done, the Marauder King spit out the wood and took a long pull off the bottle.

"I know I'm alive, now!" he said, his face still flushed.

"Would you like me to help you with the pain?" Brisa asked.

"Aye!"

Brisa nodded, then began to trace one of her runes while whispering a word. She placed both hands on the Marauder King's head. His eyes began to flutter, then closed. A contented smile spread across his face as his body went limp.

Brisa bandaged the wound, then Nargol carried the Marauder King to his quarters like a sleeping child, his head resting on her muscular shoulder.

When Brisa went to get cleaned up, and the rest of the marauders dispersed, Azure and Zoth-Avarex were left alone together on the blood-stained deck. Both of them looked to each other, then looked away. The wind whistled around the sails as the ship sped east.

"I'm..." the dragon started. He seemed to make a great effort of swallowing. "I've never in five thousand years said these words, and to tell you the truth, I don't know what form of weakness has me saying them now, but I'm... sorry."

Azure met his eyes, seeing sincerity in them. She wanted to berate him, again, to tell him that if he hadn't flown away to pout, the Marauder King would still have both of his legs, and if he was truly sorry, he would toss that gods-damned medallion in the sea, but she simply nodded. Time was too short, now. They were likely reaching Pratt tomorrow, and they'd need all the help they could get.

"I flew out ahead to get a look at Pratt, again. He seems to be heading straight for Whetstone. He'll be there by this time tomorrow."

"How far away from Whetstone are we?" Azure asked.

"Much closer. We'll be there by just after sunrise tomorrow if the winds hold."

Azure rounded up a few people who weren't working on sailing and brought them back to the dragon. She ended up with Elijah, Brisa, Mr. Threepbrush, Blunderbuss, and Robin.

"We need a plan," she told the group. "Zoth says that we'll beat Pratt to Whetstone by several hours. Any ideas?"

Each of the impromptu meeting members appeared deep in thought.

"What if we could sneak a few people onto his ship?" Elijah said. "I would volunteer, but I'm not exactly welcomed there, or easy to hide."

"Great idea," Azure said, causing Elijah to look down and kick at an imaginary pebble.

He looked back up and took off his green vest. "Here. Someone could wear this and pretend to be a fresh crew member or something."

Azure grabbed the vest. "I'll do it."

"But he knows what you look like, too," Robin said.

"Not if I disguise myself."

"It's too dangerous." Elijah tried, unsuccessfully, to pull the vest back before Azure snatched it from his outstretched arm.

"I'm the only one here who has seen that ship, and knows all the people involved." Azure's face reddened. "The only human, I should say. I don't think we'd be able to get Brisa on board either."

"If you're doing that, I'm going with you." Blunderbuss stepped forward.

"I am, too," Mr. Threepbrush agreed.

Zoth-Avarex snapped and both men were holding green vests in their hands.

"No," Azure said. "I don't want anyone to get hurt, or worse. I can do it alone."

"Ms. Azure." Blunderbuss sounded rather grandfatherly, "I understand the sentiment, but—and I'm sorry to put it this way—this isn't just about you and your father. This is also about stopping Pratt from whatever it is he's about to try. We understand the risks and accept them whole-heartedly." He looked to Mr. Threepbrush, seeking confirmation.

"Well put." Mr. Threepbrush nodded.

"But how will you get on?" Brisa asked. "How do we know that they'll be taking on new crew members? I would guess that they'll be very particular about who they're letting on that ship."

"What if I fly ahead and talk to Captain Hornigold?" Robin said. "I know he's not exactly in charge of the ship anymore, but he might be able to help."

"Yes, Robin," Azure said. "That would be a huge help. Tell him who we are and what we plan to do. I believe he'll be sympathetic to our cause. Tell him there will be three of us dressed as crew members coming aboard at Whetstone. When would you be ready to do that?"

"Shit, I'll go now. Love ya, Az."

"I love you, too. But hold on. Let's think this whole thing through."

Robin, who had already taken wing, landed back on Azure's shoulder. "Good point."

"So, if and when we get on board, our goal will be to get the ring away from Pratt. It won't be easy, but we've got to find a way to get it from him."

Everyone nodded.

"Once we get the ring, we can send Robin, who will be hiding nearby, to go get Zoth-Avarex, who will be hiding up in the clouds."

"What if it's a clear day?" the dragon asked.

"Then we'll improvise."

Zoth-Avarex nodded.

"Hopefully we can get all of this done before the asshole awakens an ancient powerful *Old Magic* or whatever it is that he's doing."

More nods.

"Should I go now?" Robin asked.

"Yeah. I think we're good here."

Robin jumped from Azure's shoulder and took wing. She made it about a hundred feet before she banked and came back to the ship.

"Uh... which way should I head?"

Zoth-Avarex chuckled. "I can show you. Come on." He waved a claw and launched into the sky. Robin followed.

"I think I should go in separately from you two," Mr. Threepbrush said. "Just in case. I can carry my wand and pretend to be a Pratt follower. That way we're not all in one group if something goes wrong."

"Great idea."

"And if they don't let me on, I'll just hurry back and get on this ship."

A spell of silence ensued. Everyone seemed to be happy with the plan.

"I have a friend in Whetstone who owns a tailor shop," Brisa said. "We can get you a disguise there."

"Perfect," Azure replied.

The rest of the day rolled by fast as Azure imagined and reimagined different scenarios that could play out back aboard the galleon. The one she enjoyed most was the idea of walking up to Pratt, punching him in the nose, and taking the ring from his fat finger while he blubbered on the deck, bleeding, in the fetal position. She knew this probably wasn't going to be the best course of action, but it was fun to consider.

The more she thought about it, the idea of getting back on that galleon with Pratt and Paul Sancti was anxiety-inducing, but she didn't see a better alternative. They'd have to make it work or go down with the rest of Pratt's followers.

Azure stood alone, gazing without focus out at a beautiful day at sea. Clouds of different shapes and sizes, interspersed with patches of deep blue sky, stretched out beyond the skyline, giving the impression of a rich, vast infinity.

As she took in the seascape, her mind was clear of racing thoughts for several blissful breaths, an ephemeral calm before the coming storm.

An hour after the sunset, Nargol came out of the captain's quarters holding the Marauder King in her massive arms. Word spread fast, and in no time at all, most of the crew had surrounded him. He looked them in the eyes, lingering for a handful of heartbeats on every single crewmember.

"I'm seeing a lot of sullen faces," he said with a warm smile. Slowly, his smile became more mischievous. "But I know what you need to hear from me: one of my hilarious jokes." He ran his forefinger and thumb along his mustache. "You know, I've been trying to come up with a good one, but I'm stumped..."

Nargol shook her head, trying to suppress a smile of her own. Azure blurted an awkward guffaw. Only a few of the marauders chuckled, but all of them had lost their sullen expressions.

"Anyway, I was thinking about regaling you with a story," the Marauder King said. "One I've never told before."

A quiet hubbub swept through the group.

"What do I always say when one of ya asks me about my life before I bought this ship?"

"I was a merchant, rich but miserable," the group recited in monotone unison.

"Would ya like to hear a more detailed version?"

The noise the group made wasn't a cheer, but the strange sound of muzzled, unanimous enthusiasm. They took seats, legs crisscrossed, in front of the makeshift stage. Azure joined them, sitting in the back row next to Brisa.

As Nargol carried the Marauder King up the incline, Azure felt something soft on her elbow. She turned to see Eleanor Covington sidling up next to her. The capybara plopped down on the deck, her head resting on Azure's knee.

"Hello, m'lady." Azure felt herself both smiling and, unexpectedly, getting somewhat emotional. She tentatively reached down and stroked Eleanor's head. "Where's your husband?"

As if on cue, Alistair waddled up from behind her and slumped down, his head laying across the hem of Eleanor's gown.

On stage, the Marauder King cleared his throat, and the crowd became silent.

Chapter 32 The Marauder King's Story

Even though I'm now known as the Marauder King, my real name, as many of you probably still remember, is Jacob Blimey. I was brought up in a wealthy merchant family on First Frontier.

A strong sense of wanderlust filled me as a child, but I was always taught to suppress it. I was taught that the most important things in life were money and prestige. My father had zero imagination but a lot of creativity when it came to finding new ways to make more money.

Once, as a boy of about six, I stalked through a nearby creek and caught a big green frog. I brought it to my father, who was in his office, working like usual.

"Father!" I said, bubbling over with pride. "Look what I found!"

He didn't look up.

"I found a frog in the creek." My excitement was quickly bleeding away as he kept working.

Then, my heart leapt as he stopped what he was doing and looked up at me.

"Get it out of here," he muttered before refocusing on his work.

That is the earliest memory I can conjure.

Well, that's not exactly true. I can remember vague images of my mother, smiling and laughing and playing with me before then, before she too became as lifeless as her husband.

Anyway, I don't mean to whine, I'm just trying to set the scene.

The real meat of the story starts when I turned seventeen. By then, I had this lovely burn scar from a black powder accident aboard one of our merchant ships, and I was consigned to the idea of one day taking over the family business, of being rich and prestigious like my father before me.

That's when I met Calliope.

She was a poor girl who I saw on the beach as I rounded up our workers to load an incoming ship. She was out near the water, frantically waving her arms and calling for someone to help her. There was something lying on the beach behind her, but I couldn't tell what it was.

"You!" she called, pointing at me. "Get over here!"

For a moment, I hesitated. I actually considered turning around and going back to work. But she stared me down until I complied and reluctantly jogged over to her.

As I approached, I realized that the thing lying on the beach was a dolphin that had become stranded.

"Help me push her," the girl said, dropping to her knees in the sand.

I paused again, this time because I was staring at the girl. She was the most beautiful person I had ever seen. I'm sure that my mouth hung wide open as I gawked at her.

"Come on!" she said.

I snapped out of my daydream and began helping her push the dolphin back toward the waves. It was not easy. That creature weighed a lot more than I would have guessed, and by the time we got it into the water, I was soaked with sweat and covered in sand.

The girl squealed with delight as the dolphin swam out to sea.

"Thank you!" she cried, wrapping me in a rough embrace.

I couldn't have been more awkward if I'd tried, patting her on the back and hoping to the gods that I wouldn't become aroused.

"I'm Calliope." Her voice was a sweet melody, brimming with a joy for life. She barely even registered the existence of my burn, instead locking eyes—those milk chocolate eyes—with me.

"I'm Jacob," I said.

We shook hands.

Calliope lived in what we referred to as the village, a poor area down the coast from the main town. Even though she was the same age as me, and had lived there for several years, I had never seen her before. And although we were opposites in many ways, we seemed to hit it off right from the jump. She always had a song in her heart and on her lips. I was absolutely mortified at the idea of singing in front of anyone, but she was able to coax a line or two out of me from time to time. She lived for fun and adventure. She thought it the most natural thing in the world to do so. I envied her for that but knew it wasn't the smart way to live, and that it wasn't the life for me.

I say we hit it off, and we did, but that didn't mean we spent much time together. I was busy with work, which was still my first priority. A momentous day was fast approaching. My father was to step down and I was to take over as head of the company on my eighteenth birthday.

I kept my work mostly secret from Calliope, not wanting to brag about how wealthy my family was, even though she probably knew because of my last name, which was relatively famous at the time. I didn't tell her what was going to happen on my birthday.

Two days before my birthday, Calliope greeted me with a gleam in her eye.

"I think I know where Captain Cadd's shipwreck is!"

I laughed. Captain Cadd's shipwreck was a legend from as far back as I could remember. He was supposedly a pirate back in the days when the League of Islands was new. His ship was rumored to have wrecked somewhere amongst the small cluster of islands off the east coast of Final Frontier. It was said to contain a tremendous amount of gold and jewels.

"I'm serious!" she persisted. She showed me a detailed notebook and a map she had drawn. She told me how she had been taking every bit of information she could find and pooling it together. She made a damn compelling case, really.

"There's this boat at the docks we can...borrow," she continued. "I've got it all figured out. It should just take a couple of days. I thought—what better birthday present than to lead ya to Captain Cadd's treasure?"

The inherent adventure of the idea stirred something in my soul. It reawakened my wanderlust. It reawakened something inside that, unfortunately, fell right back asleep.

I declined her offer, deciding instead to stay and accept my new position as head of the company.

I never talked to Calliope again.

She ended up being gone for more than a week. At that time, I had to travel to a nearby town to secure a deal. When I returned, I went looking for her in the village, but I heard she and her family had moved away.

I don't know why they moved. Maybe she had got in trouble for stealing that boat, or maybe they found work somewhere else.

The worst part was that I had never told her how I felt about her. I had grown to love her, but I had always suppressed that feeling, for many reasons. I felt unworthy of her, and at the same time, knew my family would find her an unworthy match for me.

Anyway, years passed, and I built our merchant company and became even richer. But every day was torture as I thought about what I had passed up, watching ship after ship sail off into the great unknown.

One day, the captain of one of the ships was in my office.

"A girl on Paradise Island asked about ya the other day," he said, giving me a lascivious wink.

My heart did a backflip.

"Who?" I tried to act nonchalant.

"Someone by the name of Calliope. Beautiful, too. She saw yer flag at my stern and asked if I knew ya. Wanted to know how you were fairing."

"What did ya tell her?"

"I told her you were about the richest bastard on First Frontier, if you'll excuse my harsh language."

"She lives on Paradise Island?"

"I guess so," he said.

I finished up my business with the man, then rushed to charter a boat to Paradise Island.

When I arrived, I began searching for Calliope, asking locals if they knew her. It didn't take long. I was told she lived on the beach just to the north of the docks, so I set out on foot.

And just like that, there she was, more beautiful than ever, hanging clothes on a line in front of a modest, dirt-floored house.

I sprinted toward her, my mind racing with all the things I would say to her.

Then, a man stepped out of the house and embraced her from behind. She turned and kissed him. I stopped in my tracks.

I watched the two of them from afar. They seemed so happy together. They couldn't even afford a real floor in their home, but they had each other.

There were two small canoes on the beach in front of the house. She had found someone willing to share adventures with her.

I was crushed.

I decided in that moment that I would never again listen to my head over my heart.

I would never again pass up an adventure.

I would never again pass up love.

I gave the business back to my father, keeping only enough money to purchase the ship we're sailing on, and to pay for a crew to man it. I searched the pubs of the town and rounded up a crew, most of which are still with me.

And the rest, I guess, is history.

"YOU'RE NOT DONE, ARE you?" Brisa protested.

"Aye. That was the story of how I became what I am today."

"Keep going. I mean, you're just getting started, really. You've got the boat, you've got the crew, but what's next? You can't leave us hanging like that."

"I'd like to hear more, too," Azure said. "If you're up to it."

The Marauder King itched his leg above his bandages. "I suppose I could tell about what happened next."

USING ONLY WHAT I REMEMBERED from Calliope's notes and map, I set out with my new crew to find Captain Cadd's treasure. Lucky for me, I found some brilliant people. I was pulled toward people who smiled easily and liked to sing and be merry. People like Calliope. They helped me come out of my shell, and they taught me what it meant to be the captain of a ship.

For over a year, we searched those islands for that shipwreck, but couldn't pin it down. We were just like the countless other treasure-hunters who had tried and failed to locate Captain Cadd's ship.

With the money I had taken drying up, I knew we would have to find another means of earning a living. I refused to go back to my father with my tail tucked between my legs, and to be honest, I didn't want to stop being Captain Blimey. By that time, we had quite a rapport on board. We had the beginnings of what we are today, with the nightly singing and all of that.

We held a meeting and decided that we would have to try our hand at piracy if we were to buy ourselves more time to find the treasure. We would do our best not to hurt anyone, and we would only take enough to get us by for another month or so. We felt we were so close to finding the shipwreck.

So, as we approached a merchant ship, I saw the flag of my father's company flying from its stern. Ya might think this would have dissuaded me, but in fact, it had the opposite effect. I knew my father could weather losing one of his shipments without it causing any real damage financially. And there was something rebellious in the act, as well. This would bring a permanent end to my old life, and would force me to make this new life work.

But as we got closer, I had an idea.

"I need a new name. I can't have them hear ya calling me Captain Blimey."

"How about something fearsome?" Mr. Threepbrush said. "A name a mighty pirate would have. Like Captain Kraken, or Captain Plank, or Captain Bloodclot?"

"How about Captain Dreadful, Captain Nauseating, or even Captain Unpleasant?" chimed in Mr. Cordingly.

"How about Captain Char?" I said, rubbing my burn scar.

"What about the Pirate King?" Blunderbuss cut in, his voice grandiose.

"Yeah, that's perfect," Mr. Threepbrush agreed.

"Alright," I said, having more pressing issues to deal with, "Pirate King it is."

Well, ya know from Blunderbuss's wonderful song how the raid went. All we got out of it was a horrible ass wound and some bruised pride.

That's not exactly true, though. We learned a valuable lesson that day. Like I've told ya before, that's when we drew up the Marauder's Code. We started calling each other marauders instead of pirates or treasure hunters or sailors. We liked the way it sounded. And my name stuck, kind of. They changed it from Pirate King to Marauder King, and we haven't really looked back since.

After our botched attempt at being pirates, we sailed back to the cluster of islands, consigning ourselves to living off the land if necessary until we found the shipwreck.

As we were searching for clues one day, I noticed a dolphin jumping out of the water, doing these fantastic flips over and over, again. I know the crew doesn't fully believe me on this point, because when I called them over, the dolphin was gone.

We cruised over to where the dolphin had been and looked into the crystal clear, aquamarine water, and there it was. The vague outline of what could have been a wrecked ship at the bottom of the relatively shallow waters between two islands. My mind's eye perceived Calliope's map. She had been right all along.

A few pieces at a time, we dove down and pulled up the treasure from the shipwreck. Time and rumor had inflated the amount, but there was still enough to keep us comfortable for many years to come.

Then, when all the treasure had been drudged up, I set a course for Paradise Island.

Once there, I brought enough gold to buy whatever Calliope might want. I left it there in the night with a small wooden carving of a dolphin that Blunderbuss had carved for me on top.

And the rest, I guess, is history.

THE CREW APPLAUDED at the end of the story.

"Do you know what became of Calliope?" Azure asked, stroking Eleanor Covington's neck.

"Well, I heard she and her husband took the money I left and opened an orphanage on Paradise Island. It sounds like something she would do." He gazed out at the sea, his eyes unfocused and wistful. "I've put that chapter of my life behind me." He flashed a grin, part sincere and part wry. "I've got my sights set on another, now. A true beauty who has called me *honey*. My Chastity." He gave an exaggerated sigh, eliciting chuckles.

"That *was* a nice story," Brisa said.

"Thank you." The Marauder King shook his head. "Now I'm just an old, washed-up guy with one leg."

"Lots of pirates in the multiverse have one leg," Zoth-Avarex said. "When you get yourself a peg-leg you'll finally be a proper pirate. I'll just have to teach you some lingo."

"Aye, MK," added Syl, "you'll be up and thumping around the deck with a nice new wooden leg in no time."

The Marauder King's smile was at least half forced. "Let's save Azure's father first. Then, we'll worry about my new leg."

ROBIN AND ZOTH-AVAREX, who had returned during the story but hadn't wanted to interrupt, told everyone about how they had successfully contacted Captain Hornigold. He was more than willing to cooperate with anything they needed. His authority had been greatly diminished, but he still had many loyal crew members on board. His exact quote was, "I will do whatever I can to get that asshole off *my* ship."

Chapter 33 The Three Maidens

When the Marauder King finished his story, the crew, still restless, wanted more entertainment.

"Zoth-Avarex," said the Marauder King in grand fashion, "you have no doubt led an extremely interesting life. Might you regale us with a story?"

As the dragon hemmed and hawed, the marauders encouraged him, evolving into a chant of "Drag-on stor-y, drag-on stor-y."

"Oh, alright." Zoth-Avarex scratched his scaly chin. "I got one for you." The crew cheered.

"So, one time I tricked some morons on this backwards planet called Earth to conjure me there. They thought they were going to use me as a weapon for their military." He let out a snorting laugh with an unintentional burst of flame.

"Anyway, a bunch of shenanigans ensued. For instance, reality split in two, and in one of those realities, I ended up becoming President—which is pretty much like a governor, here—of their most powerful country. I got this stunning human princess to willingly stay with me, and more importantly, collected the biggest hoard the multiverse had ever known!"

The dragon looked to his audience with great expectation and seemed disappointed when there was very little reaction.

"I'm talking the greatest hoard ever, by a long shot. I am the current record holder, and I don't know if it will ever be broken."

Azure gave him a thumbs-up, a toothy smile, and an exaggerated nod, like an overworked mom reacting to her toddler's seventh art project before noon.

"I feel like you guys aren't understanding the scope here. The multiverse basically goes on for infinity, you know?"

"This *story* feels like it's going on for infinity," Robin said, sighing.

"Screw you guys, then." Zoth-Avarex folded his arms and turned his head away. "I can't help if your under-developed minds can't fathom what an accomplishment that is. It's not like you could do any better, Robin!"

The deck was silent, the only sound the steady whoosh of wind through the sails.

"Shit." Robin rubbed her face with her wing. "I could do better than that, just give me a second."

Just as the silence was becoming awkward, she flapped her wings. "I got it." Azure could have sworn she was grinning.

"So, one time Azure and I were up late just talking. It was really late, and we were getting a little loopy. We wandered outside and saw that the sky had begun to lighten in the east." She sighed. "I can still remember what the view looked like that day—like you could see the entire Azure Archipelago from where we were."

"Gods," said Azure, "I haven't heard that term in a long time."

"So—"

"Why'd you call it the Azure Archipelago?" Blunderbuss asked, hand half-raised.

"That's what I used to call this place—these islands—when Azure was little," Robin said. "Now shut up and listen to the story."

Blunderbuss gave her a thumbs-up and a sheepish grin.

"Alright, so we were up all night and feeling loopy..."

Robin giggled.

"This capybara was out there just spinning in circles for no apparent reason, and it got us to really giggling. 'I guess we're not the only ones feeling loopy,' I said.

"So Azure says, 'I dare you to ride it,' and I'm like, 'Ride it?' and she says, 'Yeah, why not? On to adventure!'

"So then we really start giggling. 'On to adventure?' I said, watching the confused capybara turning in slow circles.

"After I got control of myself, I puffed out my chest then flew over and landed on the cappy's back. Well, it does another half turn or so then slumps down in the dirt to sleep.

"I raised my wings and shouted, 'Adventure!' and we just lost it. I have never in my life laughed so hard. Azure was doubled over with true belly laughter. It was so great seeing her so happy and carefree." For just a moment, Robin became serious, wistful.

"And then—I kid you not—the capybara farted."

The giggles had completely retaken both Azure and Robin now.

"Azure literally fell to the ground in tears. It was so great."

The two of them continued to giggle uncontrollably while the crew sat and watched. Many of them wore smiles, some even pretended to chuckle.

"On to adventure!" Robin cried, and the giggling intensified.

Azure wasn't sure how long it went on, but when she finally looked up at the crew, she was thoroughly embarrassed.

"Wow," said Zoth-Avarex, "that was quite a story. You're right, that was much better than mine." He shook his head.

"You had to be there," Robin retorted.

"Mm-hmm."

"Why don't you tell a story or sing a song, Elijah?" Blunderbuss said, obviously trying to steer away from the awkwardness. "It would be interesting to hear about something from back in your day, wouldn't it?"

There was a general agreement and nodding of heads.

"Well, I'm not a good singer, but Robin's story got me thinking about a very old pirate song we used to sing on board. I guess I could sing that for you."

"Let's hear it," said Syl.

"Alright, but just so you know, it was made up by this captain who was obsessed with capybaras."

Elijah cleared his non-existent throat, then began. His voice was way out of tune.

The kindest of all creatures, the capybara is king.
They're the cutest, cuddliest critters, underneath the Ring.
They're caring and courageous, they make me want to sing.
The kindest of all creatures, the capybara is king!"
Cappies are my kindred, they form my coterie,
They're cunning, not conniving, like humans tend to be,
They're sometimes calm and cautious, sometimes cuddly,

Oh the kindest of all creatures, the kingly, kind cappy!"

There was a smattering of polite applause.

"How about a story?" said Mr. Threepbrush.

"I could tell one about Griffin the Unrivaled, I suppose?"

"Yes!" Mr. Threepbrush exclaimed, blushing afterward.

"That'd be great, Elijah," agreed the Marauder King. "I'd like to hear a good faerie tale from back then."

"Oh, they're not faerie tales," Elijah said. "My father served with Griffin in the Iron Company."

"The Iron Company was real?"

"Yeah."

"Tell that one, then!"

"That sounds great," agreed Robin.

Elijah looked as if he was about to start when a bony finger shot into the air. "No! I know which story to tell. The Three Maidens. Have you heard it?"

"No," said the Marauder King, "but I was hoping to hear about Griffin the Unrivaled."

"Oh, you'll like this one even better."

No one in the crew seemed pleased with this last second change, but Elijah rolled ahead, a childlike giddiness in his voice.

"Alright, this is called The Three Maidens. It's a classic tale from my time..."

THERE ONCE WAS A MARRIED couple, a hunter and his wife, who had a baby boy in their cottage in the woods.

When the child was born, the wife was so delighted that she died.

The hunter, distraught, married another, more beautiful woman. But this woman hated his son.

When the boy was old enough to speak, the stepmother would whisper in his ear, "Don't fall asleep tonight, for if you do, I shall cut your throat."

In fear of his life, the child fled to the castle, where the king took him under his protection.

At the castle, he learned to be a fine nobleman, swordsman, musician, and all-around great man.

Years later, the lad decided to pay a visit to his father and stepmother. He wished to stay a few nights there, for old time's sake.

So the young man set out—

"WAIT A MINUTE," ROBIN said, interrupting the story. "I'm sorry, but he's going back to spend a few nights in the home where a lady said she was going to slit his throat while he slept? Is this guy stupid?"

"I don't know," Elijah said. "I'm just recounting the story as I remember it."

"And the wife was *so delighted that she died*? What the fuck is that?"

"Come on, Robin, let him tell it," Azure said with a smile.

"Alright. Sorry. My beak is sealed."

ON THE WAY TO HIS CHILDHOOD home, he happened upon a great blue lake. In that lake, he saw something swimming toward him on the surface of the water. He squinted but couldn't tell what kind of creature approached.

As it got closer, the boy exclaimed, "It's a bat!"

The bat climbed from the water, then climbed up the dock until it stopped to sun its wet wings along the rail.

"I will share with you great knowledge of something you might find precious," the bat said. "But only if you deserve it."

"I deserve it," spoke the youth.

"Alright, sounds good. Beyond the lake there are three maidens hidden in three caves. These maidens are as pure as snow and fair as a summer day. But to get to the maidens, you must first pass the cave of the hideous old hag who has captured them. If you can best her, you shall have your choice of the maidens." The bat shrugged its wet, leathery wings.

"I shall find the cave, best the hideous hag, and marry the fairest of the maidens," stated the lad.

When he approached the hag's cave, he was weary. He began to hear a strange sound in the dark woods surrounding him.

Vip, vip, vip... The strange swooshing sound was preternaturally loud. He drew his sword and crouched behind a tree.

Vip, vip, vip...

The sound was everywhere and nowhere. He cried out, "Show yourself!"

Vip, vip, vip...

His weariness made it difficult to concentrate.

He stumbled.

Vip...

Toward.

Vip...

The hag's.

Vip...

Cave.

The hag emerged from the cave swinging her magic broom through the air.

Vip, vip, vip...

The hag used her dark magic to turn the lad into a half-man, half-squirrel. He fled into the woods and made his home in a tall fir tree.

Eventually, after storing nuts for the winter, he met and married a beautiful young squirrel maiden. After they said their vows to the local hedgehog minister, the hag's curse was broken.

The youth, now human again, went back to the castle to see the king. But he learned the king had died and left a will in a heavy-lidded chest, and according to the will, the boy was the new king!

The king met an old barefoot wizard in his gardens who helped him catch the sun using trickery and ancient magics.

The king married the sun and lived joyfully from then to never.

The end.

"WHAT THE FUCK DID WE just listen to?" Robin said, beak gaping open.

"What do you mean?" Elijah tilted his head.

"I'm sorry, Elijah. I mean, you're great, but that story made absolutely zero sense."

"Really? I used to love that story when I was a kid."

"I have never in my life heard a story with so many loose threads."

"Loose threads?"

"Like what happened to the wicked stepmother, or the squirrel wife, or the gods-damned titular three maidens?"

Elijah tilted his head back, apparently thinking. "Well, I think it's a story for a different era. I know it was full of allegory about different political happenings on the Continent at the time, but I never understood any of that. I just liked the imagery, I guess."

"And that bat was pretty easy to convince, wasn't he? He just takes this dipshit's word that he deserves the information about the maidens. And then he assumes one of them will marry him. Typical."

"Uh..."

"I think it was good," Azure lied.

"Thank you, but I'm sorry I wasted everyone's time. I should have remembered that I'm horrible at telling stories. I mean, I forgot the whole part about the talking tree and the seven ravens. That might have tied it all together better." Elijah slapped his bony palm on his forehead. "Maybe I should have just told the story about Griffin the Unrivaled."

"No," said Robin, "you did fine. I mean, the *vip, vip, vip* part was very well done. It's just the story itself I have problems with. I shouldn't have said anything. It's not like my story went over any better."

"Alright, everyone," said the Marauder King, trying his best to not look disappointed in the evening's entertainment. "Let's get some sleep. We've got a big day tomorrow."

Chapter 34 An Annoying Curse

Z oth-Avarex awoke before dawn, guilt ticking like a magical, internal alarm clock.

He considered ignoring it and slipping back into sleep, but only for a moment.

The sky was already brightening in the east. It wouldn't be long until the next variation of the curse of Dragon Island manifested itself. When this happened, he intended to be far away from the marauder's ship, even though the resounding voice in his head thought this intention to be sentimental and pathetic.

Bones creaking, he stretched his wings and yawned. After wiping the sleep from his eyes with scaly knuckles, he leaped off the rail and took flight.

As he flew through the crisp morning air he gazed down at his reflection in the calm sea, wondering what form the curse would take this time. He looked up at the Ring, wondering if gods truly resided there. He'd seen crazier things than that in his five thousand years of life.

Zoth-Avarex was so busy staring at the majestic Ring he didn't notice the sun peek over the horizon.

A vague shape grazed his peripheral vision. He turned his head in time to see a strange floating door, but not in time for evasive maneuvers. He cringed and squeezed his eyes shut as he cannoned through it.

The light went dark as he crashed into ground that wasn't there a second ago. More embarrassed than hurt, he stood and brushed himself off. As his eyes adjusted to the lack of light, he took in the familiar cave surrounding him. He watched the volcano he had been born in outside the cave's entrance as it spewed lava into the air. This was his cave. The closest thing he had to a bedroom growing up.

Before he could take a nostalgic look around, the entrance of the cave darkened. The form of another dragon landed on the lip and entered.

"Welcome," the dragon said. "We need to talk."

Zoth-Avarex stared at himself, but in a younger form, from sometime before he turned one thousand. He was impressive as hell, all shiny and rippled with muscle.

"You've got some disturbing, pathetic thoughts rolling around in that old head of yours," the younger dragon said. "You're making it tough to be proud of the dragon I'm going to become someday."

Zoth-Avarex's first instinct was to kill this little shit, but he wasn't sure how this curse really worked. Would killing a younger Zoth-Avarex, in effect, be killing himself. Instead, he said, "Piss off."

The other dragon laughed. "I get it. You were alone for a very long time. Then you were cooped up in that treasure chest, not knowing if you'd ever see the light of day again. But you're taking a wrong turn. Instead of letting those experiences make you weak, use them to become stronger. Double down on your—our—desire to be the greatest, strongest, richest dragon in the multiverse!"

"But what about my... friends?" The last word was difficult to get out. It felt extremely strange to say.

"Friends?" The dragon scoffed. "What is a friend?"

Zoth-Avarex started to answer, assuming the question wasn't rhetorical, but was cut off.

"It's someone who can, and likely will, betray you. It's an enemy in temporary false clothing. You know that true greatness can't be obtained by the weak who trifle with things like friends."

"How dare you call me weak! You're just a hatchling. You haven't done shit yet. Meanwhile, I am the current record holder for the biggest hoard in the multiverse!"

"And where is that hoard now?"

Zoth-Avarex looked at the cave floor.

"You could be on top, again. This world you're in is rife with opportunity. You could betray these so-called friends of yours and amass another record-breaking hoard. Get everything you can, whenever you can. Come on, you've always been the strongest, and the smartest. You've always been the best. Why stop now?"

The speech his younger self gave, although rousing, was missing something that Zoth-Avarex couldn't quite put a claw on.

He thought back on his life, all the highlights and lowlights. There had only been one constant throughout it all: the overpowering desire to have it all. This desire had driven him for as long as he could remember, and he was tired of it, tired of always wanting more, of never being the slightest bit content.

The words of his younger self were compelling, but revealed an underlying truth; there was no true joy in domination. Even when he had subjugated an entire planet, and owned the multiverse's biggest hoard, he had only wanted more. There was no endpoint. The only possible solution was a shift in perspective.

The idea was scary as shit, but he knew, somewhere inside, that it was necessary. Maybe that made him weak, but for the first time in five thousand years, he didn't give a shit.

Zoth-Avarex pushed past the younger version of himself and took wing, flying out from the cave and up over the volcano where he had been born.

This iteration of the curse had been strange and unlike the others, but he felt like it was the most challenging yet.

Another door appeared, floating just ahead.

Zoth-Avarex lowered his head and barreled through it.

Chapter 35 Disguises

Azure awoke, later than usual, to the sound of a bell ringing. It wasn't the high tinging of the ship's warning bell but a deep, resonant chime that permeated the air around her.

Disoriented, she made her way up to the deck. After rubbing the persistent sleep from her eyes, she looked out ahead. The sight about knocked her over.

The *Adventure Ship* was entering the harbor of the biggest city Azure had ever seen, by the magnitude of at least a hundred. It made the city along the bay of Mirth Island seem small in comparison. On each side of the ship, high up on rocky ledges, were castles that looked similar to the huge casino on Mirth Island, only much more utilitarian and formidable. Rows of cannons lined the ramparts, and gigantic League of Islands flags whipped in the wind from the parapets.

The harbor was a forest of masts. Most of them bare and belonging to ships at anchor, but countless ships moved under sail as well. Azure counted at least ten ciguapa ships, with their bold, black runes stitched to their sails.

Palm trees swayed along the beach, which was packed with buildings, almost all of them white with red clay roofs. The city rose on a massive slope, filling as big a hill as Azure had ever seen with an impossible amount of structures. On top of the hill loomed an awe-inspiring stone church; each of the thirty-seven steeples must have been bigger than the church she had gone to as a kid. The Ring ascended up from the church in its constant arc as if it were a direct line to the gods.

Off to the east, the hill flattened out, and the area was absolutely packed with tumbledown structures made from all sorts of different materials. The difference between that area and the opulence of the city on the hill was staggering.

The amount of people scuttering about the city was overwhelming, too. Azure had never seen this many people in one place at one time. She had always known that there were thousands of people on the islands, but it was much different to imagine it than to actually see it. Azure felt a strange mixture of anxiety and excitement at the idea of immersing herself into a crowd like that.

As they got closer, it was plain there were more than just humans moving about the city. There were ciguapa and fauns milling around each other without second looks, all living and working in the same spaces. At least one in every five people was ciguapa, and maybe one in every twenty a faun. Azure felt a tug at the corner of her mouth.

"It's really something, isn't it?" Brisa said from Azure's side.

"It's unbelievable."

"I didn't realize how much I missed it until we got here."

"Are you from here?" Azure hung her head, devastated that she'd been so self-centered as to not know where Brisa was from.

"Yes." She pointed to a white building with a steeply pitched, dark blue roof. "That is the church I attended growing up."

"I should have asked you where you were from at some point. I'm so sorry."

"We both could have strived to learn more about each other," Brisa said. "In our defense, we have been a bit busy since we met."

"Does your family live here, too?"

"Yes. My parents live in a different part of town, now. I'd like to go see them, but we don't have enough time."

"Do you have any siblings?"

"I did. My older sister was killed in the battle for Streya; the second one." Brisa's features hardened as she looked to her childhood church.

"Oh, I'm sorry."

"I was very young when it happened. I only have vague memories of her. I remember the day she left to join the freedom fighters on Streya. She gave me candy and let me ride on her shoulders all around the house. I remember her arguing with my parents. And then she was gone."

Azure didn't know what to say, so she repeated, "I'm sorry."

Brisa smiled. "She's with Teus, now. I will see her again."

Azure was jealous of Brisa's confidence in this, a confidence she didn't share when it came to the idea of ever meeting her mother again on the Ring.

After a spell of silence, Azure pointed to the poorer area east of the hill. "What's that over there?"

"It's known as Shantytown. More people live there than any other area of the city."

Azure nodded, not knowing what to say.

The ship eventually came to rest at a dock system bigger than Azure's town. A magnificent statue of Saga rose out from the center of the docks. He was holding a roll of parchment and had a crown of woven grass on his head. Azure closed her eyes and said a silent prayer.

"Best of luck to ya," the Marauder King said from Nargol's arms, interrupting Azure's reverie. "I hope you know that it pains me beyond explanation that I'm in this state," he glanced at his missing leg, "and that I won't be able to help you in this quest."

"I know, MK." Azure wore her most sincere expression. "You would be there by my side if you could, like you were with Mr. Cordingly."

The Marauder King gave her a solemn nod.

"We'll follow Pratt's galleon out when it leaves here," Nargol added, her expression pained. "We'll be close if you need anything."

"Thank you," Azure hoped to the gods this wouldn't be the last time she saw the marauders she was leaving behind.

Elijah seemed as though he wanted to reach out and embrace Azure, but he stopped well short. "I hope you have much better luck without me around."

"I wish we could stay together," Azure said, meaning every word.

Before Elijah could respond, Syl took the pouch from around his neck and handed it to Azure. "The true name of this sand is harenae. Say it."

"Harenae." Azure was intrigued by Syl's naming magic. She wanted to know more, but would have to wait.

"Good. Did you see me use it to get across from ship to ship?"

"Yeah."

"Call it by name and it will do what you ask of it."

"But won't you need it?"

"You'll need it more. I expect you to come back with my fellow marauders, you know."

"Thank you." Azure held back the sudden urge to bawl as she slipped the pouch over her head.

"Say it one more time."

"Harenae."

Syl nodded and moved on to embrace Mr. Threepbrush.

After several more earnest goodbyes and well wishes, Azure, Robin, Brisa, Mr. Threepbrush, and Blunderbuss debarked. Brisa led them down the dock and into the bustling city. Buildings towered overhead, taller than the tallest palm trees. People rushed back and forth, zigging, zagging, and dodging horse-drawn carriages on the cobblestone roads. The smells were overwhelming, too. The pleasant spices of ciguapa food mingled with smoke, horse manure, and several scents Azure couldn't identify.

Many of the people rushing about had conjured beings with them. A small girl holding her father's hand had a glowing faerie zipping playfully around her head. A gargoyle—much like the one with Captain Roberts, but with a much warmer smile—flew alongside a middle-aged woman while carrying a basket of mangoes and chatting about dessert recipes.

Azure could have stood and people watched all day, but Brisa opened the door to one of the buildings and held it for everyone to go inside.

The shop they entered smelled of lavender and cloves. Racks of clothes lined three of the four walls, and tall mirrors on wheels were set up on either side of a large table that was stacked with folded shirts in the center of the room.

A very tall, very handsome ciguapa man stepped out from a back room.

"Brisa?" he said, his voice so rich and melodic it gave Azure goosebumps.

"Moso!"

The two stood close together, then traced a line from their foreheads to their chests, making circles there.

Moso asked her something in their language. Brisa responded while shaking her head, then turned and introduced everyone. Azure caught herself staring at Moso more than once during the introductions. His face was mesmerizing. He was just as beautiful as Brisa, but in a different way.

"Azure needs a disguise," Brisa said. "She needs to be a common girl who is going to work on Governor Pratt's ship." Simultaneously, when Pratt's name was mentioned, both of them made a gesture that looked like a circle with their right hands, their beautiful faces twisted in disgust. "Quickly, if you can manage it."

Moso looked Azure up and down, making her blush a deep red.

"I love your style." His accent only added to the appeal of his voice. "I've never seen anything like it. Very bold."

"Uh... thanks." Azure looked down at her torn dress under the oversized coat. He was right, it was pretty great.

"I've got just the thing." Moso threw a finger in the air then rushed away to the back room.

"Gods!" Azure said when he was gone. "Are you *with* him?"

"No." Brisa shook her head as if the idea was ridiculous.

"Why not? He's gorgeous."

"Eh." Brisa shrugged. "He's alright."

"Alright?"

Moso came back out holding off-white skirts and a bonnet encircled with red and white flowers. "Here. You can try these on in the back room."

Azure took the clothes and motioned for Brisa to follow her back. As she changed, she said, "So there's nothing between you and him?"

"No."

"Why not?"

"Well, I'm not interested in people like him."

"What, extremely attractive, tall guys with kind eyes?"

"I'm all for extremely attractive, and tall, and kind."

Recognition bloomed on Azure's face.

Brisa stared at the floor, seemingly embarrassed.

"Two friends of mine got married to each other, and they were both guys," Azure blurted out.

"Is marriage like this allowed by your church?"

"Well, not exactly. Not yet, anyway. I mean, it's pretty clear in the Epiphany how the gods feel about it, but the church is extremely resistant to change."

"Mine, too."

"Really? I thought the ciguapa had it all figured out. I thought you lived with love and empathy. I didn't think you had...problems." Azure knew this was silly, but she had believed it anyway. She had never known anyone as together as Brisa.

"Are you kidding me?" Brisa said, shaking her head and smiling. "We don't, as a people, have it all figured out. We're just like anyone. Some of us are doing better than others, and it's all subjective. Sure, we have our elders like Cono with all her hundred tattoos, and yeah, they're obviously very wise, but most of us are just trying to figure life out like everyone else. Not all of our fires have the fuel to sustain themselves, unfortunately. Some of us have deeply-ingrained prejudices, too."

"Oh." Azure had finished changing and Brisa began tying her corset in the back.

When the corset was tied, Azure put on the bonnet and went out to look in the mirror. She looked like a proper working girl, but it wasn't much of a disguise. Pratt would notice her, even with the bonnet pulled down low.

"Do you have anything that would disguise my face?" Azure asked Moso, gazing dreamily into his dark purple eyes.

"I do!" He disappeared to a different back room and returned with a yellow-haired wig and an eye patch. "The yellow hair is all the rage in Whetstone right now. I don't think a girl of your character's financial status could afford one, but I seriously doubt that Pratt," again with the gesture, "will know the difference."

Azure tucked her black hair under the wig and fixed it on her head. She pulled the yellow hair down around the sides of her face, covering much of it. Then she slipped the eye patch over the yellow hair, covering her left eye, and replaced the bonnet. Last, she put Elijah's green vest over her shirt.

"Now that is a good disguise," Blunderbuss, who had been hanging quietly in the corner of the room, said.

"You think it'll work?" Azure asked no one in particular.

"I think so," Moso said. "And you can leave your blue dress here if you want. I can clean it and sew it up to make it look like it's supposed to be cut that way. You can come back and pick it up any time."

"Really? Thank you so much!"

"You're welcome."

"How much do I owe you for all this?"

"Nothing. I'm assuming if you're on some kind of secret mission with Brisa, you're probably doing something I'd be proud to support in any way I can."

Chapter 36 Back on the Galleon

Back at dock, in front of the *Adventure Ship*, Azure and Brisa shared a long embrace. Brisa then hurried aboard as the crew began the process of readying the ship to set sail.

A nervous buzz permeated Azure's chest. No turning back, now. The galleon would sail into Whetstone soon, and she would have to get on it.

Azure, Robin, Blunderbuss, and Mr. Threepbrush made their way to the lively place where all of the docks converged. A massive fountain in the center of the square depicted an intricate stone carving of Henry Whetstone holding a sword aloft. It reminded Azure of the ridiculous carving Pratt had ordered to be placed on the *Savior,* only the man depicted in this statue actually looked the part. Around the fountain, and the whole square, were flowers of every color lining every walkway.

Street performers with a small but captive audience played an upbeat and danceable song on steel drums to the west. To the east was a line of food carts intermixed with merchants selling everything from flags to conjuring wands. Azure found herself drawn by her nose to a brightly painted food cart run by a female faun.

"Hello," the woman said, voice as bright as her cart, "what can I get you?"

Azure hesitated. This interaction was so strange in her experience, yet the faun acted as if it couldn't have been more normal. The mere presence of a faun back in Barren would have been the scandalous talk of the town. One of them running a business would have been unheard of. "Uh...what do you recommend?"

"Do you like spicy food?"

"Sure?"

The woman smiled. "I'd recommend the cibum, then. I'll go easy on the spice." She winked and moved vegetables around on her grill.

Azure dug out her coin purse, paid the woman a copper, and took a plate of delicious-smelling food.

"Oh! if I could be trying cibum for the first time, again!" the woman said as she handed over the plate. "I sure hope you enjoy it as much as I do."

"Thank you. It smells great."

Azure turned to see Blunderbuss and Mr. Threepbrush posting their orc flyers wherever they could fit them. She grinned, feeling lucky to know those two, then took a seat on a nearby wrought iron bench.

Her plate was separated into three parts; one was filled with a yellow rice full of chopped vegetables, one had a piece of flat, grilled bread, and the other held a steaming portion of what she assumed was chicken in a vibrant orange sauce.

"Would you like some rice?" Azure asked Robin, who was perched on her shoulder.

Robin opened her beak wide.

Azure spooned a few grains of rice into Robin's mouth.

"Oh that *is* good," Robin said, mouth full.

"You want more?" Azure looked around for something to put a scoop of rice into.

"Oh, just put it on the ground. I used to eat worms from the mud, this won't kill me."

Azure chortled, then did as Robin said before digging in herself. The food, without hyperbole, was the best Azure had ever tasted. The flavors were bold and new, with just the right amount of kick. She finished the entire plate and considered going back for another.

When she was done she leaned back, put both hands on her belly, and burped with her mouth closed. Even the burp tasted good.

She watched as an eclectic mix of people came and went and carried on in the square. Off to her left, she noticed something that looked like a shiny golden statue, but there was no way it could be real. It depicted a man who looked like Pratt—overweight, powdered wig, fancy clothes—stepping on the head of a faun, while pointing a pistol at the head of a ciguapa woman. Pratt's other hand was hidden behind his back, where a furtive priest secretly handed him a bag of money. Azure stood and wound her way through the crowd to get a better look. Upon closer examination, she could see the hint of the rise and fall of breathing under the gold paint on the ciguapa woman's chest.

Azure was so impressed and entertained, she dropped a full Copper into a box they had set up for donations.

As the coin fell, a man in a uniform stepped up next to Azure.

"Alright, that's enough," he said.

The performers remained absolutely motionless.

The man drew a baton from his belt. "You've got about ten seconds to—"

A commotion around the square distracted the man. He and Azure both looked around, wondering what was going on.

Azure followed the eyes of a nearby woman to the bay.

The governor's galleon approached the docks.

Azure didn't know what became of the man in uniform or the performers. She rushed over to the faun woman who had sold her the food and quickly told her how great it was. The woman gave her a knowing nod and thanked her.

Azure bolted for Blunderbuss and Mr. Threepbrush, who were scanning the crowd for her. Robin alighted back on Azure's shoulder.

"I'll approach from the north," Mr. Threepbrush said. "You two approach from the south."

Azure nodded, and she and Blunderbuss took off toward the southern docks.

"Good luck, Az," Robin said. "I'll be watching from up in the sails."

"Be careful, Robin."

"You too."

The two of them shared a long look laden with a lifetime of meaning before Robin took to the sky.

The buzz of the crowd was much different than it had been when the galleon had pulled into Barren. There it had been a celebration, with only a few dissenters. But here in Whetstone, the ratio of celebrators to dissenters was about one to one.

As they neared the docks, Azure heard things like, "Finally, someone is here to clean up this disgusting city," and, "I hope he's not as big of an asshole as I've heard he is," and, hopefully, "The ship is here early, maybe that means he met a tragic death en route?"

Azure and Blunderbuss pushed their way to the front of the growing crowd on the dock.

When the massive galleon finally came to rest, Paul Sancti marched halfway down the gangplank. "People of our great capitol," he said, his voice amplified by magic, "our great new leader has finally arrived where he belongs!"

Some cheered, some clapped, some booed, some hissed.

"But Governor Pratt and the League of Islands needs help, and they need it fast. We are looking for two hundred volunteers to board this ship and depart immediately for Ridgeback Island. Those with gold wands will be given preferential boarding."

The hubbub on the dock was deafening. Within seconds, several humans began to ascend the gangplank. Mr. Threepbrush among them.

Azure watched as Paul Sancti spoke with each person who approached. She held her breath as he talked with Mr. Threepbrush but let it out as he was welcomed aboard with a handshake.

Captain Hornigold stood further up the gangplank, his arms crossed and expression unreadable.

"Well," said Blunderbuss, "here we go, then."

Azure nodded and followed him into the growing mass of people heading up the gangplank. She pulled the yellow hair around her face and made sure her eye patch was in its proper place. She worried they wouldn't be expecting new crew members. The ship had come early. How were they supposed to know to board if they truly were part of the crew?

As they ascended, Captain Hornigold came down to greet them.

"The fresh crew I requested," the captain boomed. "Welcome aboard. We'll get you a cabin and a job assignment, just follow me."

"Hold on." Paul Sancti held up a hand. "I wasn't informed of any new crewmembers."

"With all due respect, Mr. Sancti, there's probably a lot that goes into the daily operations of a ship that you haven't been informed of." Captain Hornigold smiled, but it didn't reach his eyes.

Paul seemed taken aback for a moment, straightening his golden chains and narrowing his eyes. "Well, we're here a few days early. How did they know to be here and ready?"

Azure tried to not let the panic she felt show on her face. She bit down on her tongue and dug her nails into her palm.

"Word travels fast around here, and the League's finest ship doesn't go unnoticed by many." Captain Hornigold's eyes bored into Paul Sancti without a hint of doubt in them. "I'm proud of these sailors and their ability to read the wind. It's the kind of forward thinking I've come to expect of people I hire."

Paul Sancti turned to Azure and Blunderbuss. "Are you willing to help Governor Pratt's cause in any way you can?"

Azure's nails dug in deeper.

"Of course!" Blunderbuss bellowed.

Paul studied their faces, squinting his eyes and pursing his lips.

Azure forced herself to breath normally.

"Fine." Paul waved a hand. "Get to work."

Azure and Blunderbuss followed Captain Hornigold back aboard the galleon. After a huge sigh of relief, Azure searched the deck for her father. It didn't take her long to find him, moping along the opposite rail, with only Thunder Paws nearby.

Before she could step in her father's direction, Roger approached her, and for a terrifying second, she thought he had recognized her.

"Hey," he said, trying his best to appear laid-back, "welcome aboard. My name is Roger. With whom do I have the pleasure of meeting?"

Relieved, Azure tried to think of a fake name.

"I'm—"

"Beat it, Roger." Captain Hornigold shooed him away like a pestering child. "Let the girl get settled in a min—"

"Captain," called Pratt's voice. "Who, might I ask, are these folks?"

The captain turned to the approaching Governor Pratt, face still stoic. "New crew members, sir." He turned back away.

"Well, don't hurry away too fast," Pratt said with feigned joviality. "Let's not neglect proper introductions."

Captain Hornigold's eyes widened, almost imperceptibly. He spun around and boomed, "Of course! I just figured you were too busy at the moment."

"I'm never too busy to meet the people responsible for *my* ship's operations." He said this as if it were a perfectly natural thing for him to say, even though he likely couldn't name one crewmember aboard.

"This is," there was the slightest of hesitations, "William Davis and Grace Fernsby. William is an old hand at sailing and Grace here is an excellent serving girl."

"Pleased to meet both of you." Pratt's smile was as wide and fake as ever.

Azure attempted a curtsy, her heart hammering.

"Alright, you two," said Captain Hornigold, "enough schmoozing with famous people. Time to get to work."

Azure and Blunderbuss turned to leave.

"Just one more minute," Pratt said. "I have some questions for the—what are they calling it?—*blond* girl, Grace, here."

Azure eyed the rail, considering sprinting and leaping off the side of the ship. "Yeah?" she said, trying to keep her mouth closed unless her teeth were somehow recognizable.

"Well, first off, you can lighten up. You don't have to be all tensed up in my presence, little lady."

"Alright." Azure did her best to look less tense.

"I was curious about what happened to your eye."

"My eye?" Azure said, stupidly. "I got into a fight with a faun when I was younger." The words just blurted out.

"Did they get you with a horn or a hoof?"

"A horn."

"Wow. You must really hate fauns, then."

Azure was as still as one of the statue performers. Her heart beat even harder, but it was driven by both rage and fear, now. This, right in front of her, was the core ignorance of Pratt's message. The actions of one faun—fictional in this case, as it was with many of the cases Pratt cited in his speeches—had nothing to do with fauns as a whole. If she had been in a fight with a human, and that human had put her eye out, no one would dream of blaming humans in general for the actions of that one human. No one race was inherently good or bad. They were all made up of individuals who were capable of both.

"What?" Pratt let out a high-pitched, staccato snicker. "Don't worry. You don't have to concern yourself with being so careful on this ship, or really anywhere now that I'm governor. We're doing away with all that nonsense. Feel free to speak your mind, little lady. Just say it. Say, 'I hate fauns.' It's quite liberating to be so openly honest."

Azure wanted to play along, to say anything to get his attention off of her but couldn't force the words out. She glanced at the gaudy ring on his finger, wondering if she could possibly lunge and rip it away, but she remained still.

"Oh alright." Pratt laughed again. "If you won't give me the satisfaction of hearing a pretty little thing like yourself speak out against the faun that took your eye, you can at least show me the empty socket."

Azure's jaw dropped open.

"What?" Another irritating laugh. "I know it's a bit of a strange request, but I must admit, I've got a macabre fascination with such things. Can I just get a little peek?"

"I don't like to let anyone see it." Azure looked down.

"Oh, come now," Pratt said, his smile grotesque. "I just—"

"She said she doesn't like anyone seeing it, sir," Blunderbuss said, face beet red, staring Pratt in the eyes.

"Yeah," added Captain Hornigold, "that's about enough. It's time my crew got this ship ready for our trip to Ridgeback Island."

Pratt maintained his smile while pulling his wand from its holster on his belt. Then, with the flick of his wrist, Azure's bonnet, wig, and eye patch flew off her head.

"I don't know how stupid you think I am," Pratt said, his tone both triumphant and mocking. "Seize these two!" In an instant, Azure and Blunderbuss were held fast by several armed men.

Pratt looked to the captain. "I want someone to stay with Captain Hornigold. If he strays so much as a hair's breadth from my orders, you have my permission to shoot him in the head."

Chapter 37 Ridgeback Island

Azure was thrown against the main mast, the back of her head bouncing off the hard wood, causing an instant headache. Her and Blunderbuss were tied to the mast with thick, rough ropes around their legs, waists, and chests, pinning them in an unescapable position.

"Everyone," Pratt shouted as he tucked Azure's wand into his belt, "keep your eyes on these two. If they so much as try to wiggle out from their bonds, let me know immediately."

Azure felt the hateful glares of the countless people surrounding her.

Pratt turned and marched away to the bow, but many of their captors remained.

Azure's eyes darted, taking in everything she could see from her stationary vantage point. She looked for the faces of her father or Mr. Threepbrush in the crowd. She searched the sails for any sign of Robin. Part of her hoped to see them rush in and initiate a daring rescue, but the bigger part just hoped they would remain undetected.

"What do we do, Azure?" Blunderbuss said in a low, shaky voice from the other side of the mast.

"I don't know," she said through clenched teeth, barely moving her lips.

She moved her hands around, groping blindly for anything that could be used as a means of escape, but found only the smooth wood of the mast and the tips of Blunderbuss's fingers.

"Quit yer moving around, traitor!" came a voice from the crowd.

Azure instinctually turned away as a man rushed toward her.

"I'd quit moving those hands around unless you want 'em taken off," the man said, inches from her face.

Azure narrowed her eyes and turned her head to face the man, refusing to show weakness. She gasped when she saw Mr. Threepbrush.

"Yeah, that's right, little lady." He brandished his knife. "I'm watching you like a hawk." He turned to the crowd with a sadistic, victorious smirk. If anything, he was overacting, but his audience cheered at the display, unaffected by the over-the-top theatrics.

"What can I do?" he whispered up close before backing up and yelling, "What did you call me?" He put a cupped hand to his ear and dramatically put it close to Azure's mouth.

"Too many people around," Azure said, not knowing what else to tell him. "Wait."

"What? Does a capybara got your tongue?" Mr. Threepbrush turned to the crowd. "I guess she's going to clam up now. Figures." He shrugged and slipped his knife back into its scabbard. "I, for one, am not going to waste my time with these two. They couldn't escape a wet paper bag with a cutlass in each hand. They'll never break free from Governor Pratt's strong bindings." He rubbed the rope, almost affectionately. "No, I'd rather spend my time at the bow with our leader. Ridgeback Island is nearly within sight." He stood on his tiptoes and looked toward the bow. "Hell, I can't see shit from here."

As Mr. Threepbrush started for the bow, a shout came from the crowd.

"What the?" a man said, looking up with a scowl, a glob of runny, white bird shit sliding down his forehead.

"Aww!" another man said, wiping bird shit from his bare arm.

A woman who was tilting her head back, gawking, got struck just below her nose.

People began to scatter for cover, their arms up over their heads.

Mr. Threepbrush backed up to the main mast, his knife held so that it was concealed behind his arm. With a quick glance back, he began to cut the top rope. He stood, his back to Azure, and sawed at the thick rope, all the while searching for anyone who noticed what he was doing.

He wasn't halfway through when Paul Sancti's voice—magically amplified—said, "Ridgeback Island is dead ahead!"

The crowd cheered, minus the people who had been shit on.

"Soon," Paul Sancti continued, "we will be debarking. Everyone should have their wands with them at all times, but if you've left yours in your room, now would be the time to go and get it." A few red-faced people snuck quickly away. "We will line up to starboard, ten straight lines alternating a person with a wand and a person without. Twenty of the governor's most loyal followers, who we've already talked to, will be staying aboard, but the rest of you, go ahead and begin this process now. We will be arriving soon and Governor Pratt does not want any delays."

Mr. Threepbrush, who had continued cutting the rope as Paul talked, was now almost through the first line.

A drunk-looking man approached, a drink in his hand. "Are you gonna practice what you preach?" he said, throwing an arm over Mr. Threepbrush's shoulders. "Come on! Let's go get a good spot in line. Never mind these prisoners, right?"

"Well..." Mr. Threepbrush said. "On second thought, Pratt did tell us to watch them. I mean, it's a less exciting job, but someone's got to do it. You go ahead. I'll take one for the team, here."

"Oh, bullshit," the man said, grinning and pulling Mr. Threepbrush away. "A real follower like you deserves to have a little fun, too. Let's go."

Mr. Threepbrush resisted, but the drunk man eventually led him into the crowd.

Azure's dad was lining up, Thunder Paws at his side. His face was emotionless as he stared down at the deck. She called for him, but he couldn't hear it over the gathering din. "Dad!" she cried, as loud as she could, desperate to keep him from disembarking with the rest of them. His face remained aimed at the floor.

Azure struggled against her bindings, and felt Blunderbuss struggling behind her, but couldn't create a finger-width of space. Even though the rope was mostly severed, it held fast.

"My followers!" Pratt's voice now boomed overhead. "This is the moment we have all been waiting for. You will, very soon, be a part of history. But I want you to think smaller at the moment. I want you to focus on what you've been taught on this cruise. Remember your magic and concentrate on making it as big and strong and powerful as you can. Only then can we, as humans, finally get what we deserve."

Azure lost sight of both her dad and Mr. Threepbrush as hundreds of people swarmed the deck, milling about and getting into their positions. Robin fluttered from one sail to another, looking anxiety addled.

"Now," Pratt said, "it is time for the awakening!"

Chapter 38 The Awakening

J ohn Brine trudged along, following the person in front of him mindlessly. He felt like a sheep but didn't care.

Permeating the air, the voice of Pratt gave a self-aggrandizing speech as the passengers aboard the galleon debarked onto the barren Ridgeback Island.

"When you get onto the island, keep hiking up the ridge to make room for everyone," Pratt's voice droned magically overhead. "And keep close together. Form a nice, tight group. Get comfortable with your fellow Pratt followers."

John kept putting one foot in front of the other, barely listening to Governor Pratt. He just wanted to get this over with. He would play his part in whatever Pratt was doing, then get back home as fast as possible. He would, hopefully, find Azure there. He would apologize to her, admit his mistakes, and beg for her forgiveness. That was the only thing that mattered to him, now.

He fought back tears as the pervasive idea that she might have died reemerged in his mind. He pushed it away and kept moving. Ahead, to the west, a brilliant sunset stretched out along the horizon. Azure loved sunsets. He and her used to sit out on the beach together, watching the sun sink into the western sea.

"Can you hear it?" he used to say. Then, as discreet as he could, "Sssssssss."

Azure would laugh every time, probably just humoring him. Her laugh was so full of joy back then.

"Alright, everyone take out your wands!" Pratt's voice was manic. "Everyone who doesn't have a wand needs to put their arms around the shoulders of the two people next to them. All five hundred of you need to be touching each other."

A man with a bushy beard and a tall woman put their arms over John's shoulders.

"Isn't this exciting?" the woman said, rubbing his back.

Thunder Paws sat behind John and pushed his head through the space between his master and the bearded man.

"Now, focus your energy. Those of you with wands, point them down at the ground. Every single one of you, focus on firing the biggest bolt you've ever seen directly into the ground."

John thought this was strange but did as he was told.

"Now is the time that we, as humans, will take back the power that has been taken from us!" Pratt was really loud now. "On my count, release the energy!"

An intense surge coursed through John's entire body. Everything from his feet to his head buzzed with a powerful, vibrant tingling. It was almost too much. His body felt more alive than it ever had, but he felt as though he might literally explode. The tingling became so violent that it seemed as if it would push his insides out of his body in a forceful burst.

"One!"

Someone in the group screamed in either ecstasy or pain.

"Two!"

John's knees buckled, but the people next to him held him upright. There were several more screams and a few shouts.

"Three!"

John sent the overwhelming energy down his arm and through Azure's wand. He closed his eyes as blinding light erupted all around him.

The ground shifted, causing everyone to collapse onto each other in a sprawling heap. In a daze, John pushed himself back up and tucked the wand into his waistband. He stumbled again as the ground continued to move. The people closest to the water began to slide off the island into the churning sea.

The land began to rise up further out of the water. The violent shift sent many more people tumbling off the side. John threw himself to the ground and searched for something to cling to. For the first time, he noticed that the ground was unlike any he'd seen before.

Right next to John, Thunder Paws had spread out all four limbs and dug every claw into the strange soil.

John thought he saw something like a massive head emerge from the water to the north but was unable to look for long.

As the island tilted, a man flew over the top of John, kicking and flailing as he fell into the water below. John felt himself sliding. He tried to push himself as low as possible, to increase friction in any way he could, to hold onto anything. But there was nothing to hold. The mass of humanity picked up momentum until they were all thrown down toward the sea. John watched as Thunder Paws climbed over several people but was unable to stay on the land.

Freefalling, John held his breath in the second before plunging into the turbulent water.

Pain and darkness were the only things he knew as people fell on top of him, pushing him deeper into the churning sea. He opened his eyes to chaos, an effervescent tangle of bodies thrashing wildly all around.

Panicked, and already feeling low on air, John fought his way toward the vague light he hoped was the surface. He struggled against the writhing multitude of bodies, unable to make any progress. Pressure built in his chest as his lungs begged for a breath.

An image entered his mind, something he had awoken to—sweating, heart pounding—on countless nights. The horrible image of his wife dying under the collapsed dock. This was exactly how he had pictured her last moments of life.

Blackness began to creep into his vision from the periphery. He let out the air in his lungs with a rush of bubbles as he tried again to climb up through the bodies. He was nearly through to the surface when the pressure in his chest became too much, and everything went dark.

JOHN AWOKE TO THUNDER Paws's voice.

"John!" the deep, drawling voice said. "Are you alright?"

John coughed and spit seawater from his mouth. He turned and vomited into the water.

When finished, he lifted his head and looked around. He and Thunder Paws were bobbing up and down on a floating scrap of wood right next to the hull of what John assumed was *The Savior.*

"What..." He found it difficult to speak. His chest throbbed. His whole body ached.

"I found you in that mess of people," Thunder Paws said, panting. "I pulled you to this floating log and kicked us back to the galleon." The tiger paused and looked up. "On the way, I think I saw Azure's bird flying up in the sails."

"Azure is here?" John forgot any pain he had been feeling. When Thunder Paws had told him about his conversation with Robin on the rail, he wasn't sure he believed his conjured tiger. It had happened while he was napping, and Thunder Paws hadn't been fed well on this voyage. John had convinced himself the conversation was nothing more than a dream. But now he held onto a sliver of hope. Maybe Azure really was nearby.

"I don't know. I think I just saw Robin."

"Well, let's get back on board, then." John saw a rope ladder dangling in the water. He pushed himself off the wood and swam to it.

"I can't climb that, John, but I think you need to."

"But what will you do?"

"I can make it back to Paradise Island... probably."

"Probably?" John looked into the tiger's tired eyes. There was intelligence there, and a fiercer loyalty than any he had ever known. He should have recognized these things long, long ago.

John checked his pocket as he dangled half out of the water, relieved to find his small conjuring wand still tucked safely within.

"Do you still want to go back home? To your realm?"

Thunder Paws swallowed. "Yes, sir."

As John drew ancient runes in the air, they began to glow, suspended just above Thunder Paw's head. John tucked the wand away and reached for the tiger. As gentle as a house cat, Thunder Paws put a paw around John and drew him close. The two embraced as they were rocked gently by small rhythmic waves.

"I'm sorry I kept you here so long," John said, choking away tears. "I'm sorry about so much." He hadn't fully realized the tiger's importance in his life until this moment. His relationship with Azure had been fraying for longer than he would have liked to admit, and in that time, Thunder Paws had become nothing short of John's closest friend. The thought of losing him forever was devastating, but it was something he had to do.

"Go get yer daughter back," Thunder Paws said, as if it was an order.

"I will." John gave the tiger a final squeeze. "Thunder Paws, I send you back to the realm from whence you came."

The tiger blinked out of existence. The water on his head fell like tiny droplets of rain.

John closed his eyes and breathed a mournful sigh. Then he turned and began to climb the ladder.

About halfway up, an ear-splitting roar rent the air around him, rattling the ladder under his hands and feet. The hull of the ship creaked as the unnatural sound permeated the Undering.

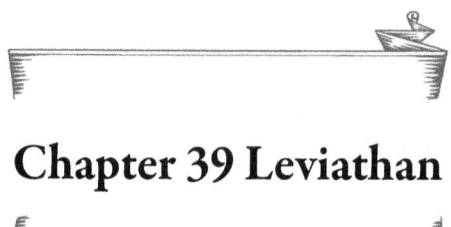

Chapter 39 Leviathan

Azure continued to struggle against the ropes throughout the debarking process. She watched as everyone, including her father, congregated on the strange island.

There was a blinding flash of hundreds of bolts.

The island moved as if alive.

Just as a massive, surreal head shot up from the water, Mr. Threepbrush appeared at her side.

"I'm sorry I took so long. I had to hide and wait for the right moment." He unsheathed his knife and made quick work of the ropes that bound Azure and Blunderbuss. Without a word, Mr. Threepbrush handed his golden wand to Azure.

Pratt, Paul Sancti, and the twenty or so people who had stayed back on the ship were all staring over the starboard rail. A dark shape approached the ship, but Azure couldn't make out what it was. Pratt's ring glowed a bright green.

Azure took a step toward him but was immediately stopped in her tracks. She felt her legs wobble underneath her as an unreal image took shape in front of her.

Rising high above the ship was a vision that didn't seem possible. The head of a colossal creature that made Zoth-Avarex look small in comparison loomed above. It was a lot like a dragon's head, but the face was more elongated, like that of a crocodile. It had rows of four vacant, eldritch eyes on each side of its head. Its scales were a green so dark it was almost black. Tentacle-like appendages stuck out from its neck writhing against the backdrop of the fading sunset.

In a dreamlike stupor Azure watched the head lower itself to Pratt's level.

"Leviathan!" Pratt said, maniacally, his ring glowing brighter than ever. "With you, I will be absolutely unstoppable!"

Chapter 40 Mind Control

A zure considered firing a bolt into Pratt's back. She could do it right now, and all of this would be over. Hand shaking, she raised her wand, aiming it at his spine, at heart level. She tried to conjure the necessary energy for a bolt. Narrowing her eyes and gritting her teeth, she remembered everything Pratt had taken from her, and thought about everything he meant to take away from the League of Islands. She tensed every muscle in her body, willing the energy to appear, but it would not.

For a moment, she wondered if it was due to having Mr. Threepbrush's wand, but she knew that wasn't it. No matter how much he deserved it, Azure couldn't bypass the part of her conscience that disallowed shooting someone in the back.

Disgusted with herself, she abandoned the idea, and instead creeped closer to him. She may not have been able to kill him from behind, but she could smash him in the ear with her wand without reservation. Or, if lucky, she could snatch the ring from his finger as he stared up at the abomination he'd awoken.

Slowly, carefully, she moved closer to Pratt. The leviathan's breathing was loud enough to cover the sounds of footsteps, but she sensed Mr. Threepbrush and Blunderbuss following close behind her.

Azure visualized what she would do when close enough. She would take the ring, slip it onto her own finger, and immediately try to take control of Pratt's mind. If she could, she would make Pratt tell the twenty men on board to stand down. She didn't have a plan beyond that.

She was about ten feet away, heart thrashing, when Pratt turned around, eyes closed, smiling.

"Hello, little lady," he said, opening his eyes.

Azure raised her wand, finding the energy she couldn't create moments ago now thrumming through her.

Most of the twenty men along the rail raised guns or wands.

Blunderbuss shouldered the gun he'd found, aiming it at Pratt. Mr. Threepbrush held his knife out in front of him.

"Stand down," called Pratt, throwing his hands to either side, one of which held a wand. A mocking grin spread across his face. "If you were coming back for your father, I'm afraid you're too late. He's probably on the bottom of the sea by now."

A jolt of sadness and rage coursed through Azure's body. Without conscious thought, she felt the energy travel down her arm, into the wand.

"You killed them all?" she said, voice quavering, not really wanting to hear him answer.

"Well, not technically. You could say they sacrificed themselves, unknowingly, I'll admit, for my, I mean *our* cause."

Azure had come all this way to fall just short of saving her father's life. The man who had sat by her bed on countless nights, reading her stories. The man who had carried her on his shoulders during countless hikes through the jungle. All of his negative traits were forgotten. The pain of his loss, Azure's second parent to die in this way, was world-shattering.

She cried out—a deep, guttural scream.

As if in mercy, Azure's pain was instantly transformed into rage as she looked across the deck at Pratt's smirking face. Her scream of agony morphed into a roar as she unleashed a bolt at Pratt's head. It was the most powerful bolt she had ever created. Magic seemed to electrify the air around her, causing her skin to tingle and hair to rise slightly off her head. This was more power than she had ever felt, much more.

Pratt ducked and slashed his wand to the side. Azure's bolt shot off into the air, ripping through one of the yards of the main mast on its way into the darkening sky. Splintered wood rained down from above.

"Oops," Pratt said with a chuckle. He looked at the shattered wood around Azure's feet, his grin growing bigger and more sinister.

Azure saw Pratt's ring glow green just before she lost all control of her own mind.

Devoid of thought, Azure knelt and picked up a shard of wood with a particularly sharp end, then stood back up. She lifted the wood, then, slowly and deliberately, began to bring it toward her own neck.

As understanding blossomed in her mind, she tried to fight against the unwanted impulse. For a fleeting moment, she was able to stop her hand. But Pratt's ring glowed brighter and her hand began to move again. Her eyes darted back and forth as she tried to push against Pratt's irresistible will. Mr. Threepbrush and Blunderbuss were completely still, eyes wide like startled rabbits, obviously under Pratt's spell, too.

Azure tried to yell as she focused all of her attention on resisting Pratt's mind control, but the shard kept moving closer to her throat. She realized Pratt was only playing with her. He could have made her stab herself to death by now, but he was enjoying this, elongating the moment, like a cat toying with a downed bird.

A small flash of movement came down from above. Robin, hurtling downward, slowed herself just enough to extend her talons in front of her as she barreled toward Pratt's face.

Pratt swatted Robin out of the air. She tumbled awkwardly before striking the deck with a tiny thud.

Azure gasped, and her hand stopped moving, but just for a moment. Pratt refocused, smirking more than ever before. The point of the wooden shard bit into Azure's throat. After an initial pressure, she could feel her skin breaking, could feel a trickle of blood running down to her chest. She put a final desperate effort into stopping her hand, or moving her head away, but had lost all control of herself. The pulse in her neck felt strange against the increasing pressure.

As her eyes went to Robin's lifeless body, she saw another sudden movement, this one from Pratt's left. A glint of metal flashed as it carved through the air. The blade of a sword cut into Pratt's hand, severing at least three of his fingers, one of which wore the ring.

As Pratt bellowed in agony, Azure's eyes followed the sword to its wielder. Her father—soaking wet; rage and desperation in his eyes—turned to face her.

"Azure, run!" he said, before swinging the sword at the closest one of Pratt's men.

Her mind and body her own again, Azure darted back toward the main mast.

Several guns fired. A ball whizzed by her ear and smashed into a small structure behind her. A bolt, as big as the one she had fired, sailed just over her head.

Azure dove behind the small structure and pushed her back into it. For a moment, there was relative silence, then Mr. Threepbrush and Blunderbuss came flailing to join her behind the structure.

"What do we do?" Blunderbuss said.

Azure grabbed the pouch of magic sand Syl had given her, but before she could answer, Zoth-Avarex appeared, seemingly out of nowhere, on the port side of the ship. He lowered his neck to the rail and let Brisa, Elijah, Orok, and Nargol onto the deck.

As the last passenger stepped off, a giant green tentacle wrapped itself around the dragon's body and pulled him down into the water.

Chapter 41 Blood on the Timbers, Blood in the Water

Nargol and Orok rushed into the mob of flat-footed men who stood with Pratt, the orcs' battle cries cowing even the strongest of the humans. Several shots were fired, and again, one of them struck Orok in the shoulder, but it didn't slow him down.

In between shrieks of pain one might have thought were coming from a toddler, Pratt bellowed out orders to his men.

"Kill them!" he screamed as he dropped to his knees, scrambling for his ring finger. "Kill them all!"

Azure popped out from behind the structure, sprinted across the deck, and kicked Pratt's severed fingers toward the bow.

Elijah swung into view, sword drawn, and blocked the blow of someone about to slice into Azure's arm. She watched the sword fight between skeleton and human as Elijah backed the man away from her.

"You!" Pratt roared, standing now. He turned on Azure's father, wand drawn. "You fucking traitor! I should have killed you and your brat long ago!"

Pratt's wand, crackling with energy, was pointed directly at John's chest.

In one motion, Azure poured the sand from Syl's pouch into her hand and launched it between Pratt and her father.

"Harenae!" she shouted, glad she had remembered the name.

As the impressive bolt left Pratt's wand, the sand froze in midair, creating a wall between him and her father. The bolt smashed into the mostly-invisible wall and fizzled.

THRASHING CHAOTICALLY underwater, Zoth-Avarex fought to extricate himself from the tentacle's grip.

He had been around for more than five thousand years. In that time, he had battled more magical creatures than he could count, but he had never encountered anything as strong, or as hard to fight as this gods-damned leviathan.

For five thousand years, his mind had almost never known panic. But now, under fifty feet of water, he had reverted back to his lizard brain. He struggled to think of anything to do other than squirm. Even with damn-near unlimited magical powers, he couldn't decide on a single spell to try.

An idea finally came to him. It wasn't the best idea, but it would have to do. He concentrated on conjuring the biggest sword he could think of, hoping to slice one of the leviathan's tentacles with it.

CAPTAIN ROBERTS GAZED up, inspecting the main mast the crew fished together. They had done well. It would hold together until they got back to Whetstone.

Whether or not he would hold together until then was quite possibly a different story. The crew had been more disgruntled than ever, not even bothering to hide their mutinous musings. They were not very happy with their haul these last few months, they rumbled about the captain being beaten by what looked to be a teenaged girl, and they hadn't had a proper stop at Mirth Island for weeks. And now, all of a sudden, they had a problem with the treatment of their former sailing master. They had laughed their asses off at the time, but now they seemed to have collectively concluded that it was decidedly not funny, and possibly even cruel.

His ungrateful gargoyle, whatever his name was, even got in on the whinging. Apparently, he wanted to go back to his own realm, back to his lover. The thought was not only disgusting but disheartening. It seemed harder and harder to find good help these days, in this or any other realm of existence.

Captain Roberts kicked a splinter of wood, straining his calf in the process.

"Gods' blood," he said.

As he limped to his quarters, he rubbed the hilt of his sword, the only thing that brought him real comfort in this thankless world; an ancient remnant from the Continent handed down for generations. Legend had it that it once belonged to Griffin the Unrivaled himself. Now, it stood as a representation of Captain Roberts's power over these islands. His flag was known and feared in every corner of the League.

As he looked up to that flag, whipping proudly in the wind, he felt his hips shift to the left. He suddenly felt much lighter, not understanding what had happened at first.

It dawned on him before he looked down.

His sword had vanished.

The scabbard remained on his right hip, but the sword was gone.

"Shit," he said.

MR. THREEPBRUSH CHARGED at the mass of Pratt's men, sword raised over his head. One of the men sidestepped his blow, then smashed him in the temple with the hand guard of his cutlass. Mr. Threepbrush dropped to the deck, as heavy and limp as a coil of rope.

Blunderbuss, who was right behind him, brandished the gun he had found, aiming it menacingly at the man who had knocked out his friend.

"You gonna shoot that bloody blunderbuss or wave it at me all day?" the man said, his accent thick.

"I'm—" Blunderbuss took a step back, put off by the man's complete lack of fear.

As he stepped, his heel caught Mr. Threepbrush's foot. He floundered, trying to keep his footing, but lost his balance. As he teetered back, the gun fell from his hand. In midair, he gasped and tried to turn away from the gun. Before he hit the ground, he heard the shot. The blunderbuss he had found struck the ground and fired. The shot caught him in his only remaining butt cheek.

The pain was the same as before, the shame possibly greater; although he was able, in some remote corner of his mind, to see the humor in it. If he lived through this battle—doubtful now—he would live in infamy.

He grabbed at his wound to find most of the cheek gone. His hands were warm and wet.

The man in front of him laughed, then turned and shot Azure's dad in the arm, spinning him to the floor.

Azure used her wand to pull the man's legs out from under him. The unexpected fall sent his head crashing into the deck with little resistance. He was out cold next to Mr. Threepbrush.

Nargol cried out. Blunderbuss turned to see her collapsing, at least six men wrestling her to the ground. Orok tried to pull them off of her, but had several humans on his back, as well.

Blunderbuss ripped off his shirt, pressed it to his ass wound, and tried to rejoin the fight.

ZOTH-AVAREX WAS UNDERWHELMED by the size of the sword he had conjured. He had seen swords wielded by giants in other realms, but, in a panic, had only managed to think of the last sword he had seen. The Claymore-looking sword of Captain Roberts was like a toothpick in his claw, but it had a good, sharp edge. As well as he could under water, the dragon sliced at the tentacle that enveloped him. Dark green blood spilled out and dissipated in the churning sea.

After about twenty hacks, he had made it about halfway through the tentacle. Still it held on. The air in Zoth-Avarex's lungs was depleted. His strength and energy waned dangerously. With a final effort, he shoved the tip of the sword into the end of the bleeding tentacle. A cry part whale song, and part banshee scream permeated the water. Mercifully, the leviathan released its grip.

Zoth-Avarex swam up with wings and claws and burst into the air with a gasping breath.

Another tentacle reached for him, but he ducked under it, then dodged to the right, avoiding yet another. He took in a deep breath and unleashed a rush of dragon fire at one of the writhing tentacles. As the the scorched tentacle retracted into the water, the leviathan's massive head shot up from below.

An explosion of pain erupted near the end of his tail. The leviathan's jaws had clamped down on it, pulling him back into the sea.

"Shit," said Zoth-Avarex.

A MAN KICKED AZURE in the gut with the bottom of his boot, causing her to double over, a strained, wheezing noise issuing from her mouth.

Elijah slashed at the man with his cutlass, slicing into his shoulder.

"Freak!" came Pratt's booming voice from the right.

Both Azure and Elijah turned just in time to see Pratt fire another bolt. The bolt smashed into Elijah's chest, exploding him into pieces.

"No!" Azure cried, turning on Pratt, wand upraised.

Before she could fire a bolt of her own, Pratt's wand was lifted out of his grip. He lunged for it as it floated away, past Azure's head, and into Brisa's hand.

Pratt had never looked so incensed. As his eyes darted around the battle scene in front of him, his face became redder and redder.

Azure spared a quick glance at the battle, too. Pratt's men had the upper hand, by far. Both orcs had been swarmed and bound. Mr. Threepbrush was still out cold, and Blunderbuss was grievously injured. Her father clutched his bleeding arm. Robin was limp on the deck—protected from trampling by a fortunately placed cannon, hopefully still alive—and Elijah's bones were scattered everywhere.

"That fucking ciguapa *took* my wand from me!" Pratt said to his men, spittle flying from his mouth. "You see what *they're* doing? She literally took my wand from me. From me!" He let this hang in the air as if it were the ultimate justification for all he had done. "Now," he said, his face contorted with hatred, "I want you to tear that ciguapa limb from limb! I want you to stomp out the *fire in her chest* or whatever the fuck they call it!"

The remaining men looked to each other, vague looks of disgust on most of their faces.

"Do it!" Pratt shouted. "I want her torn apart!"

Azure took a step forward, sensing an opportunity in their hesitation.

"Is this who you want to follow?" she said, scanning the men, looking each one of them in the eyes like MK always did. "Did you not see what just happened to most of the people who followed him?" She pointed to the former Ridgeback Island. "He used them, and he's using you. He wouldn't piss on any one of you if you were on fire. He's only out for himself, for his own power. Isn't that obvious now?"

One of the men nodded.

"He has played on your fears in order to sow hate and division. He's using our religion as something it is not. You know the words of Saga. You know what Pratt is doing isn't right. Don't you?"

Maybe she was being hopeful, but the scales seemed to be tipping her way. Subtle changes in the men's demeanor led her to believe she was getting through to them.

"He literally just killed hundreds of people who followed him, just so he could—"

Pratt roared and charged forward, hands outstretched at Azure's throat.

Without thinking, she drew back her fist and punched him in the nose.

With a whimper, Pratt clutched at his face and fell onto his butt, blood gushing from between the fingers he had left.

Sitting on the deck, legs outstretched, Pratt spat unintelligible curses as tears streamed down his face. Azure resisted the urge to kick him and looked up at his followers, all of them staring at her in apparent shock.

In a bold gambit, which she gave herself a coin toss chance of winning, Azure said, "Tie him up." She paused. "Please?"

Pratt's men didn't move for a long moment. Then, one of them grabbed Pratt by the arm. Another seized his other arm and they pulled him away.

ZOTH-AVAREX TURNED and yanked his tail from the leviathan's mouth, noticing that he had lost a few feet of it. But before he could mourn the loss of his beautiful tail, the leviathan's jaws opened again, preternaturally fast, and snapped down over the dragon's head.

About half of Zoth-Avarex's body was now inside the leviathan's mouth. The bright line of pain around his midsection was intense, but the worst part of his situation may have been the leviathan's breath. The putrid, rotten air within the ancient maw was revolting, a sickening morning breath a hundred years in the making. Zoth-Avarex somehow held back the urge to vomit and struggled to push himself into fresh air.

The leviathan's jaws clamped down tighter. Several tentacles wrapped around the dragon's hind legs and what was left of his tail. As they pulled, he felt as if he was about to be ripped in half.

Struggling was futile, and the ability to do magic seemed to have left him. As his life flashed before his eyes, he lingered on his record-breaking hoard, and how utterly pointless it had been.

His eyes closed as his body began to tear apart.

AZURE RUSHED TO THE bow and scooped up Pratt's severed finger. Gagging, she slipped the bloody ring from the detached digit and pushed it onto her own finger.

A surge of energy coursed through her. She had an instant understanding of the power she now held and how to use it.

The leviathan's head stuck out of the water to starboard. Zoth-Avarex's legs and tail protruded from its enormous jaws. Several tentacle-like appendages gripped every part of the dragon Azure could still see.

Azure concentrated on controlling the leviathan. She found herself inside its mind. She could perceive its immense weight, feel its intense hunger, and taste Zoth-Avarex against its tongue.

Gagging again, she forced the leviathan to spit the dragon out.

Zoth-Avarex's limp body arced gracelessly across the sky before crashing down into the sea hundreds of yards away.

Azure forced the Leviathan to plunge under the surface and swim inside the eastern edge of the Eternal Fog. Its unreal speed had it arriving there in no time. Then she made it dive down and find a trench at the bottom of the ocean much deeper than the place it had slept before. Unsure how she knew how to do it, Azure coerced the leviathan back into a long, restful sleep. She could sense it fading away, back into utter unconsciousness, into total oblivion.

Knowing the job was done, Azure took off the ring, and without ceremony, tossed it into the ocean. It struck the surface with a tiny kerplunk, then vanished into the depths.

She looked out to where the dragon had landed, but wasn't going to be able to help him. Instead, she sprinted aft, to Elijah, to Robin.

Chapter 42 Robin and Zoth-Avarex

E lijah's bones rattled on the deck, then started to move together. They be-gan connecting to each other, quickly rebuilding his skeletal body.

"Gods!" he said as his jawbone attached, rubbing his ribs.

Azure, happy to see Elijah alive, knelt and scooped up Robin.

She was still breathing, but her breaths were shallower than usual, and hard to see in her breast. Her body was deformed, but Azure couldn't tell what, if anything, was broken.

"Robin." Azure shook her gently. "Robin." Louder.

Robin's eyes fluttered open.

Azure closed her eyes, relief flooding over her.

"Hey, Az," Robin said, her voice weak.

"Hey."

"I hate to tell you this, but I'm not going to make it."

"You don't know that."

"Yeah, I do." She looked Azure in the eyes. "I just do."

"But..." Azure's throat was tight, her eyes burning.

"I want to say something before I go." Robin swallowed. Her wing twitched in Azure's hand. "First off, I'd just like it to be acknowledged that, pound for pound, I was the toughest being the Undering has ever seen. And I don't even weigh a pound."

Azure couldn't help but smile.

"I was probably the sexiest, too," Robin continued.

"Save your breath," Azure pleaded.

"I love you, Az. And if I had to go, I'm glad it was in the process of trying to save your life. There is no higher honor in my eyes. I would choose your life, your happiness, over mine every time I was given the chance." She coughed. "In a way, you've always been that kind, beautiful little girl to me. The one I fell in love with the day you conjured me." Azure's eyes completely blurred. "But I'm so proud of the woman you have become, too. You're such a badass. I just wish I could have pecked someone's eye out for you at some point."

Azure chuckled, a tear falling onto Robin's feathers.

"Alright, one more thing," Robin said. "Put your ear closer."

Azure did as she was told, leaning her head so her ear was directly in front of Robin's beak.

"Elijah wants to bone you."

Azure pulled her head back, trying to suppress the smile that was attempting to force its way through the tears.

"Get it?" Robin said with a head tilt that was her equivalent of a wry smile.

"I love you, Robin. Let's—"

"On to adventure." Robin's eyes closed. The rise and fall in her tiny chest ceased.

"No." Azure shook her head. "Robin." She brushed her friend's cheek with her forefinger.

A hollowness unlike any she had ever felt took residence in her chest.

None of this had been worth it. Absolutely. Fucking. None of it.

ZOTH-AVAREX'S LIMP body sunk into the sea. He had a vague sense of pain and darkness, but was devoid of conscious thought. He was alive, but well on his way across the veil.

In an unexplainable way, he began to subconsciously welcome the darkness, the total oblivion that was so near. The cold water began to feel warm and inviting as he sunk deeper, the building pressure a formless embrace.

Still, something was calling for him to fight back. The sense could have been from inside of him, in the water next to him, or some yet unknown plane of existence, but a nameless voice was urging him to resist the welcoming darkness.

At first he ignored it. Whatever it was trying to pull him back to consciousness seemed insignificant inside death's soothing caress.

But the voice was persistent, and growing more tangible.

AZURE GLANCED UP FROM Robin's lifeless body, only then realizing that a tight circle had formed around her. Sorrowful faces looked down on her and her friend with excruciating pity. She lowered her eyes, unable to acknowledge them, unwilling to share her crippling grief. An overwhelming sense of unworthiness filled the emptiness inside her. A friend like Robin was so much more than she had deserved, but she was not ready to give her up.

Brisa knelt beside Azure and extended a hand. Without thinking, Azure set the bird into Brisa's palm.

With one hand, Brisa traced one of her rune tattoos, while the other brought Robin up to her lips. She whispered a word, then attempted to breathe life back into Robin's lungs.

Nothing happened.

Azure closed her eyes and prayed to Saga. Although she knew it was likely useless, she prayed for Brisa's magic to work. She prayed to have her friend back. She would give anything in return.

When Azure opened her eyes, she saw a forlorn look on Brisa's beautiful face.

"I'm sorry, Azure. I couldn't..." She handed Robin back to Azure with eyes closed tight.

The bird's tiny body no longer looked deformed, but she still didn't show any signs of life.

IN A SERIES OF STRANGE flashes, the dragon transitioned into the hazy realm of conscious thought. He wasn't yet awake, but somewhere inside the liminal space between waking and sleep.

The strange voice still called to him, but it sounded like it was coming through leagues of churning water. It was distant, warbled, and completely unrecognizable.

In his dreamlike state, Zoth-Avarex knew he was underwater. He could feel himself falling deeper. The pressure was unbearable, so was the excruciating pain that enveloped his midsection. He was no longer being eaten alive by that horrible leviathan, so that was good. But death was very close, now.

What the hell was that voice saying? It seemed important.

AZURE BROUGHT ROBIN up to her cheek, nuzzling her like she used to when she was little. Her tears wet Robin's feathers.

Azure tried to comprehend what a life without her friend would be like. How could she possibly go on? What should she do next? How would she ever feel joy again?

She let her thoughts drift back through the years: an image of her and Robin pulling

pranks on Azure's parents sprang to mind. They had tried to make her parents believe that a capybara was talking to them, when it was really just Robin tied to its side with some twine and using the deepest voice she could muster. It hadn't worked, but the laughs were unforgettable.

Another image came to mind. This one a late night in her room, just before Azure was to go on her first ever date. Robin had sat up with her, calming her nerves and giving extremely helpful dating advice.

Azure's mind flitted to another night in her room, when she was crying and completely heartbroken after the passing of her mom. The comfort Robin provided that night and every night since had been invaluable.

A steady thrumming arose in her chest, the low flutter of awakened magic. It was more intense than she had ever felt before. She looked up to find that the world around her had changed. Everything—the sky, the ship, the crew—was much more vibrant, more vivid. It felt like seeing the world the way it really was; as if she had been viewing everything through a veil before.

She looked back down at Robin and she simply *knew* what to do. She channeled a sliver of the boundless magical energy down through her arm and into her fingertips. She held Robin in between the thumb and forefinger of her right hand and let the energy flow into Robin's chest.

Nothing happened, so Azure allowed more energy to pass through. Robin's body convulsed with the force of it. Her talon began to twitch. "Gods!" Robin blurted out, eyes opening. "That was intense!"

ZOTH-AVAREX STRAINED his ears, trying to hear what the voice was saying.

It was so close to being understandable. There was something familiar about it, too, but in his half-dream state, he couldn't put a claw on it.

Then, after a rush of sound like a waterfall, everything became clear.

The voice resonated inside his head.

It was a voice he had grown all-too-used to hearing in the last few days.

"Wake up, jackass," it said.

A RELIEF UNLIKE ANY Azure had ever felt washed over her. The vividness of the world and the thrumming in her chest faded away, but the joy in her heart was in full bloom.

She cried happy tears, and nuzzled Robin to her cheek, again.

Brisa was sitting on the deck, trying to catch her breath. The magic she had used to try to revive Robin had come at a steep cost. Brisa wobbled, then collapsed.

Several marauders rushed to her side. Orok brought her a horn of water and helped her to drink from it.

"Are you alright?" he asked her.

"Yes," Brisa said, her voice weak. "I just need rest, and more water."

"Thank you, Brisa." Azure reached out a hand and gripped Brisa's ankle. She nodded and tried her best to flash a smile.

Orok lifted Brisa and whisked her away to the captain's quarters.

Robin stretched her wings and tilted her head until her neck cracked. She looked up at Azure. "I can't be sure, but I think I was just on the Ring. I went hurtling through this tunnel of the brightest light. And then, somehow, I could see that stupid dragon sinking in—"

Robin's head turned to look behind Azure, her eyes widened, and her beak fell open.

She jumped from Azure's hand and darted past her head.

As if time had been magically slowed down, Azure turned to see Paul Sancti barreling toward her, a gleaming knife held aloft in his right hand.

Robin careened into his face, her wings flapping furiously.

Paul let out a horrific howl. He dropped the knife and clawed at his face, trying in vain to defend himself from Robin's relentless attack.

When he was finally able to brush her away, his left eye had been reduced to a fleshy pulp. Several beak-sized chunks had been taken out of it, and blood ran down his cheek.

Panicked, he spun and ran, but didn't get three steps before colliding with the rail and tumbling overboard.

Azure rushed to the rail and looked down.

Paul's heavy chains were already pulling him under. She watched as his face darkened, then disappeared as he sunk deeper into the sea.

"Yuck!" Robin said, spitting overboard. "I always thought eyes looked so delicious." She spit again. "They're not!"

ZOTH-AVAREX SWAM IN the direction of the barely-visible light with everything he had. His lungs burned and felt as if they could burst at any second. Every move made his midsection flare in tremendous pain, but the panicked need for air overpowered all else.

His peripheral vision began to go black, and he still had so far to go.

He kept his claws and shortened tail thrashing, bringing him toward the sweet, sweet air at a pace that was far too slow.

But then, when he thought he was done for, and his vision had gone almost completely dark, he breached the surface and took in a gasping, lung-filling breath.

He sucked in air and treaded water for several minutes. After getting his breath back, he focused on the overwhelming pain at his waist. He inspected himself the best he could while in the water. Many of his scales had separated from each other, and the skin below was visibly stretched, but he was whole, minus the part of his tail he'd never get back.

The dragon used magic to dull the pain and speed up the healing process, then he leaped from the water and flew to the galleon on the horizon.

Chapter 43 Father and Daughter

Azure's dad approached her, tears welling in his eyes. He obviously wanted to embrace her but stopped himself just short.

"I'm so sorry, Azure," he said, his face scrunching up.

Azure stood, unsure of what to do or say. She wanted to embrace him, too, but didn't.

"You were right. He never cared about any of us."

Azure nodded, still unable to will herself forward.

"I've had a lot of time to think about this since your trial at sea, and this is what I've come up with." He sighed, then started again. "I was so devastated when your mom died." He looked Azure in the eyes. "That despair didn't take long to turn into anger. I needed something, or someone, to blame. I stayed quiet about my feelings for a long time, ashamed of harboring so much rage toward another race. And then Pratt began his run for governor, and suddenly my anger no longer seemed shameful. I had a movement to be a part of. I justified it to myself by identifying with the language he used. It wasn't about oppressing other races; it was just about putting humans first. It was about lifting ourselves up. Now, I realize that was never the case. It was all manipulation. He only ever cared about himself, his own wealth, his own power. Everything he pretended to believe was simply used to whip up anger, just so he could use it for his own gain. And I feel like such a gods-damned fool for falling into it. I nearly lost you because of it. That was something I could not bear.

"When you left the ship, with us having just had that fight... That was the worst moment of my life. Worse than when your mother died. I wanted to go after you, but I thought I had lost you, that you would never speak to me again. And I knew I deserved it." He dropped his face and studied the floor.

Azure opened her mouth to speak, but nothing came out. She closed her eyes, inhaled deep, let it out slow, then looked to her father.

"I love you, Dad."

He broke down, worse than before, but better. When he regained control of himself, he rushed forward and wrapped Azure in his arms, squeezing her tight.

Azure lay her head on his bloody shoulder, squeezing him back, with a genuine smile spread wide across her face.

Chapter 44 Elijah

"**C**an I ever make it up to you?" Azure's dad said when they finally broke the embrace, minutes later.

Azure thought of something she'd heard not too long ago. "You could make it up by climbing Mount Insight with me and helping me find the lost part of the Epiphany."

"Lost part of the Epiphany?" His eyebrows scrunched together.

"Yeah. I mean, maybe it will be there. But I'll tell you all about it later."

"Alright. I'm in for whatever you want to do."

Zoth-Avarex—shrunk back to orc size—alighted on the galleon's deck, wincing with pain. Without a word, he slipped the capybara medallion from off his neck.

"I just wanted to say," he looked down longingly at the glinting gold, "that I have still not changed my mind about this thing. I'm keeping it forever, and that's final."

Azure audibly gasped.

Elijah hung his head.

Anger bubbling up in her, Azure marched over to where the soggy dragon stood.

"You—"

"I'm just kidding." The dragon's laugh was loud enough to hear in Whetstone. "You know, if you'd have seen a millionth of the stuff I've done in my life, you'd be as shocked as I am to hear me say this, but I think I'm done trying to have it all." He shook his head, still smiling. "Gods, that sounds weird coming from me. But seriously, I still love treasure, and I still want a hoard, but it doesn't have to be the biggest ever known." He shrugged his scaly shoulders. "And I don't feel like I have to dominate every being around me, either. It is *so* weird getting old."

Slowly and dramatically, Zoth-Avarex hung the medallion over the edge of the ship. Then, after a gulp of regret, he dropped it.

Everyone rushed to the rail to watch it sink into the sea. Their heads all turned to Elijah, who was still a skeleton.

"It's going to take a while to get to the bottom," Zoth-Avarex said.

"Oh, gods." Elijah put his hands on his head. "What if a shark eats it or something, and it never reaches the bottom?"

"Come on, man." The dragon chuckled. "A shark's not going to eat it. Don't worry. It'll touch bottom in like a half hour or less, I'm sure."

Even though the medallion had long since disappeared, everyone stayed at the rail, alternating between watching the water and Elijah.

"Uh, Azure?" Elijah said.

"Yeah?"

"I've got something I want to say." He rubbed his cervical spine. "To you, that is. I mean, I don't want to say something just for the sake of saying something. The point is, I wanted to say something specific... to you... you see?" He was more awkward than she'd ever seen him.

Azure nodded, wondering what this was.

Elijah's jaw moved up and down as if he were swallowing.

"So I'll just come right out with it."

Silence.

"Alright," Azure said in her most gently prompting tone.

Elijah gulped, again.

"I don't want to sound corny or cliché, but I think I have loved you since the first time I met you." He looked down at the deck, his foot kicking at the air. "It wasn't your looks... er... I mean, you're beautiful, but it wasn't just that. Shit, I'm messing this up already." He rubbed the side of his head with an awkward level of vigor. "It was the way you treated me, like I was an equal." He lifted his head, making eye contact as well as his eyeless skull could. "Every other person I have interacted with since the curse has treated me with varying levels of contempt or pity. You didn't have either. You wanted to help me break the curse, but you didn't look at me like I was less-than because of it."

"Elijah, I—" She didn't know how to finish that sentence. She had grown quite fond of him, as well, but hadn't considered the idea of a romantic relationship with him.

"I understand if this is too weird or if it's too creepy for you. I mean, I am over a hundred years old, technically, even though I was cursed when I was twenty-three."

"It's not weird or creepy. Don't be so hard on yourself."

Robin let out a blurt of laughter, then covered her beak with a wing.

"I—"

Elijah began to glow with a golden light. It built in intensity until it was damn-near blinding. Azure narrowed her eyes but didn't turn her head.

The light completely enveloped him, shimmering in the twilight.

Overhead, Ringfall lit up the night sky like a fireworks display.

Then, as soon as it had started, the light was gone.

Where the skeletal Elijah once stood was now a man about Azure's age. His shoulder-length dark brown hair framed his warm dark eyes.

He smiled at Azure, revealing a dimple in his left cheek.

The smile melted away as he looked down at himself.

Aside from knee-high leather boots, he was completely naked.

Azure couldn't help but admire his toned body as he covered himself and leaped for cover.

Robin whistled.

Mr. Threepbrush, who was awake, now, took off his long coat and wrapped it around Elijah.

Reluctantly, Elijah emerged from his cover.

"Sorry about that," he said. "I should have known... er... thought about that happening." His face was a dark shade of red.

Azure grinned at him.

Zoth-Avarex groaned and rolled his eyes. "Seriously," he said, "this is some real Beauty and the Beast shit right here."

Azure had no idea what he was talking about and couldn't have possibly cared less.

Chapter 45 The Epiphany

Azure and her father had been hiking, seemingly straight up Mount Insight, for hours. Drenched in sweat, thighs burning, she slumped down against a boulder.

"Oh, thank the gods," her dad said, collapsing into a patch of tall grass.

The two of them panted and chugged water while looking up into a clear blue sky.

"So, I've been thinking," John said after his breathing had slowed closer to normal.

"Yeah?"

"Now, hear me out on this." He looked to her with extreme hesitancy written on his face.

"Okay." Azure was nervous already.

"So Pratt had this controlling ring, right? But what if it was just one of many rings? What if there's another ring somewhere that controlled the ring he had? Like one ring to rule them all or something? And what if the Harmony Faction was behind this whole thing?" His hands flew out to his sides. "It makes sense, really, if you think about it. They would want Pratt to be disgraced so they could rise to power. So they constructed this impossibly complicated plan—"

"A plan you have zero proof of."

"Well, I wouldn't say that. The proof is their history of consistently—"

"Dad."

"Yeah?"

"Let's make a pact, right now, that we won't talk politics with each other anymore."

"Why?"

Azure sighed. "Because I'm going to fucking kill you if we don't." She looked at him with the most serious expression she could muster. "I just crossed the sea, awakened a dragon, battled pirates and a leviathan to save you, because I love you, but the politics have got to stop, or I will murder you."

The mountain was silent.

"We can talk about the inn, dragons, sailing, my childhood, your childhood, magic, the weather, music, anything that has to do with our immediate lives, or anything that is just fun to talk about. Anything that doesn't induce murderous rage, really. I will continue to vote and to fight for what I think is right, and I will check you every single time you express anything that is even slightly bigoted. But politics are not something we need to discuss. It's not really living, I don't think. Our lives are happening right now as we climb this mountain together, not in Whetstone. And again, just to reiterate, I will slit your gods-damned throat if you don't learn to shut the fuck up about it. Are we clear?"

"Yes, Az." He shook his head. "I love you."

"I love you too, Dad. You want to finish this climb?"

"Let's do it." His knees creaked as he stood.

After another hour of tough climbing, they were at the peak. They hugged and congratulated each other. Azure gingerly jumped up and down, fists in the air.

After their short celebration, Azure noticed a wooden treasure chest sitting alone on the highest point of the mountain. A glowing blue bubble—the same glow as the Ring above—surrounded the chest.

Her heart, which was already working hard, picked up its pace even more. She no longer felt the burn in her thighs, calves, or shoulders. As she climbed, she hadn't given much credence to the drunk man, Favian, at the bar on Mirth Island. Sure, he had piqued the hell out of her interest, but, if she was being honest with herself, she hadn't been very optimistic about actually finding anything up here.

But here it was. Could there really be an extended version of The Epiphany in that box?

Azure replayed Favian's words in her mind. *If someone deserving of the revelation climbs Mount Insight and simply asks for a new one, the entiiiiiire Epiphany will appear to them.*

A jolt of worry shot through her. What if she wasn't deserving? What made her think she was worthy of the revelation? She wasn't a particularly pious person. She found comfort and truth in the words of Saga, but if she was still being honest, she wasn't sure if those words had come from an actual god, or just some wise, charismatic person. What if absolute faith was a necessary attribute of a "deserving person?"

With these thoughts swirling, she tentatively reached out and touched the blue bubble. A shock coursed through her hand, causing her to jerk it back. It wasn't enough to hurt, just tingle.

"What are you doing over there, Az?" Her dad said, laying on the ground twenty feet away.

"Just a minute..."

They had come this far, might as well ask and find out. The idea of being unworthy frightened Azure. Was it better to not know something like that? She decided it wasn't. The truth was always worth knowing, even if it could potentially hurt.

"Can I have The Epiphany?"

"Huh?" her dad said sleepily.

The glowing bubble around the treasure chest flashed, then disappeared.

Azure opened the lid, revealing a scroll tied with a red ribbon.

Giddy, she picked it up, removed the ribbon, unrolled it, and began to read:

The Words of Epiphany
Spoken by the Physical Manifestation of the King of Gods, Saga, on Mount Insight
(Transcribed by Artemis Consignor)
Yikes. There's a lot of people here.
Alright.
People of the Undering, I have had an epiphany. I have become aware of our—the gods'— mistakes, and I want to correct them.
It was a different time back when the world was new. There was a lot of violence and bloodshed. The world, and we gods, had to go through some growing

pains. That's why fifteen of the thirty-seven gods have to do with strength, vio-lence, war, blame, or death, and yet there is only one goddess of love. I mean, shit, we have eight gods of the different wind directions, but only one goddess of love. Now, after my epiphany, I see we have lost our way, mortals and gods alike. This is not why we created the Undering. We created it for you. And we created you so that you could be happy.

This is kind of like a fresh start for us gods. Things back on the Continent are complicated. The violence and bloodshed is still happening there at an alarming rate. There are more competing gods than you can imagine, and all the infight-ing between our pantheon isn't helping matters. So, I wanted to let the brave peo-ple who sailed through the sea monsters to the other side of the world have a new, simpler start, with clear instructions about how to live as you face new challenges in your new home.

With that in mind, let me get to the nectar of the speech I've prepared.

Basically just don't be shitty to each other and you'll be good.

There isn't much else to it, really.

Azure skimmed through some of the speech, having already read it more times than she could count. She skimmed by all of the mentions of love and its importance, and even the secret teacher part she treasured so much. But when she got to the part about rich people, she had to slow down and read it all, as it amused her every time:

You will literally not get to the Ring if you are rich or you work to harm or oppress others. I'm telling you, as the King of the Gods, don't hoard money and don't harm or oppress others. You will not make it to the Ring if you do. I think few would argue that the most important aspect of this religion is the ac-tual words coming from my actual mouth. Do not twist my teachings into some-thing self-serving or anything which they are not. Because I'm telling you the truth now: a capybara has a better chance of flying than a rich man or an op-pressor has of getting to the Ring.

She kept on reading from this point, because it was almost the end. Her hands were trembling as she unrolled the bottom of the scroll:

I'd also like to tell you about something less important than love, but still pretty cool: magic! We, the gods, have decided to give you human mortals the gift of magic. I mean, humans have accessed the Old Magic back on the Continent, but I already talked about how bad it's going over there. Anyway, this new mag-

ic is pretty easy, but you'll need wands in order to make it work. Oh, and big woe to those who would hoard magic for themselves, just like with the money thing.

This was where The Epiphany that Azure had known her entire life stopped. She had always thought it an abrupt ending, but who had she been to challenge the church?

Heart thumping, she read on:

To make a magic wand, simply carve a stick from a rosewood tree down to about a foot in length and about a half inch wide. To activate its ability to create magic, recite the following incantation: "Oh Magic! Oh Unseen Force Pervading the Multiverse! Please Imbue Yourself Into This Wand I Hold in My Hand! Thank You!"

You can do the same for a conjuring wand, only it can be much smaller and made out of any kind of wood. Use the same incantation but specify "conjuring wand." You can use this to conjure all kinds of fun beings. But please, send them back if they don't want to stay conjured. And use them for good. You got this, right?

The newly appointed Goddess of Magic, Hekana, will give you more specific instructions about using magic when I am done.

All right, thank you for listening. The other gods and I are going to take a break after today. Not for too long. Maybe a few hundred years or so. Maybe a few thousand?

So, be good to each other. See you later.

Hmm... you know, I wanted to end it there, but I just have this nagging feeling that you're gonna screw this up somehow, no offense. So let me be crystal clear; heed the words in this speech over all else. Do not twist them, or edit them, or cherry pick them in order to push your own agendas. Do not use this religion to justify the oppression of anybody, or to justify war, or hate. Do not use it to sow fear into people's hearts and minds.

Oh, and if this speech ever gets lost or burned or stolen, just send someone deserving of the revelation to the top of Mount Insight and have them ask for a new one. Simple as that.

Peace!

"Wands don't have to be made out of gold?" she said to herself, waking up her dad with her elevated voice.

"Huh?"

"The church has been lying to us all along. A wand can be made out of wood!"

"Really?" He yawned.

"And there's a goddess of magic, too. Hekana!" Azure imagined what she must look like. She pictured a beautiful woman with actual fire for hair and glowing blue eyes for some reason.

"How do you know this?"

"I just found the full version of The Epiphany!"

"Oh." Her dad slipped back into sleep, snoring immediately.

Epilogue Several Months Later

Barren came into view as the *Adventure Ship* entered the bay. Azure gazed out from the bow, taking in her hometown, which was quite beautiful from this vantage point.

The Red Dragon Inn sat perched up on the sheer white cliffs, the tendril of smoke from its chimney bending in the breeze. At her angle, the Ring seemed to be coming directly up from the inn, giving it an almost numinous quality.

Behind her, the Marauder King loudly cleared his throat.

When she turned, she found most of the crew had secretly gathered around her.

"The vote is in," the Marauder King said, "and it is my honor to appoint you as my new quartermaster!"

Azure's eyes welled up with tears, but she blinked them away.

"Thank you!" she said to the crew.

Nargol was up front, holding baby Morgak, Orok's massive arm over her shoulder. Syl, Elijah, and Brisa stood smiling beside the new orc family. Mr. Threepbrush—who had changed jobs to sailing master after Mr. Cordingly had left, opening up the position of quartermaster—winked at Azure. Blunderbuss was holding a drink, apparently getting an early start.

Elijah approached Azure and gave her a peck on the lips. He looked at her like he always did, as if she were the only woman in the Undering.

"Congratulations, Az," Robin called from her nest on the mizzenmast. "It probably would have been better to see that from the deck, but, you know, I'm up here sitting on these eggs all day every day." Her voice was thick with disdain.

The Marauder King nudged Nova, who had been staring at the horizon, oblivious. The bird startled, then, at a gesture from the Marauder King, flew up to the nest.

Robin jumped out and perched on Azure's shoulder. "Gods," she said, stretching her wings and legs at the same time. "You know, I realize that Nova isn't a... Well, he isn't the swiftest bird in the sky, but it sure would be nice to get a little more unprompted help out of him. Apparently, all he ever wants to do is dance and...you know."

"How are the eggs doing?" Azure asked, trying to steer the conversation.

"They're fine. But what kind of father is his lazy ass going to be? I'm guessing I'm going to be on worm duty for the foreseeable future." She shook her head. "I'm sorry. This moment is about you. Great job. You deserve it."

"Thank you, Robin."

The Marauder King stepped forward on his shiny new wooden leg. "Hey, Azure, could I have a quick word?"

"Sure."

As she followed him to a secluded part of the ship, she asked, "How is your musical coming along?"

"Good, good," he said, unsure of himself. "That's the smaller part of the reason I wanted to talk to you. I wondered if you might read what I have so far and tell me what you think?"

"Of course."

"It's really just some notes and parts of songs. It's a bit me-centric so far, but I intend to give everyone their due in the story." He was as nervous and awkward as Elijah during the curse.

"I'd love to," Azure said, taking the rumpled collection of notes he handed to her.

"Thank you." He blushed.

Eleanor and Alistair Covington waddled by, prompting Azure and the Marauder King to bow as they passed.

"So, the bigger part of why I wanted to talk to you is that I ran the numbers ya gave me, and I have to say, they look good."

"So you want to do it, then?" Azure tried not to sound too hopeful.

"We'll have to put it to a vote, but I'm in." He patted Azure on the shoulder, then headed back to the crew. "Marauders, we have one more vote to make before we get too drunk up at The Red Dragon. I'll let our new quartermaster explain, as it was her idea." The Marauder King whispered in her ear, "Start 'em off with a joke, if ya got one," then nudged her forward.

Azure gulped. "Well... uh... How many tickles does it take to make an octopus laugh?"

"Eight?" said a marauder from the back.

"No, ten."

No one laughed.

"It takes ten tickles. *Ten*tickles."

Recognition dawned on most of their faces, some of them even chuckled.

"Anyway," she continued, "I sort of drew up a tentative plan for us to become a part-time merchant ship."

There was an audible din, not quite a cacophony, but more of a gentle hubbub.

"Unfortunately, the treasure stores are all gone, so we need a reliable way to make money. We would only need to make about six shipments a year to maintain the lifestyle we've become accustomed to. That would leave plenty of time for treasure hunting, noble quests, Mirth Island, and general marauder fun and adventure."

The Marauder King took a position beside her, leaning against her shoulder as he wasn't completely comfortable on his peg leg yet. "We had considered doing this years ago, but the presence of Captain Roberts made the idea untenable. Because of our Azure, here, that is no longer a problem. He is more afraid of us than we are of him. And it probably doesn't hurt that 'ol Zoth-Avarex likes to leave his hoard on Dragon Island at times to pay us random visits at sea."

Azure and the Marauder King shared a look.

"So, who's in?" the Marauder King said.

Every hand shot up, even baby Morgak with a little help from her mother.

"The *ayes* have it. We'll pick up our first load here in Barren, headed for Ersa Cibosq. Then we should have plenty of time to shoot over to see Mr. Cordingly and his new baby boy, Brighton."

The crew cheered.

"And then," the Marauder King gulped, "I think we might just go to Mirth Island. And I might finally regale my sweet Chastity with tales of our brave deeds!"

An even bigger cheer.

Grinning, Azure took the Marauder King's notes into her quarters to peruse them.

ON THE WALK FROM THE dock to the inn, Azure hoped her hometown wouldn't embarrass her. People poked their heads out from windows and doors, tentatively at first. Then, many actually came out into the streets, some even waving. Most of them were children, and some were admonished for it, but the reception was better than Azure had feared it might be. A ciguapa, a faun, and three orcs showing up in Barren was still relatively unheard of, but, slowly, attitudes were beginning to change in the Isles.

Pratt had been convicted and sentenced to life, and Church leadership had been exposed for their role in keeping magic from everyone. An emergency election was held, and a new governor elected—a relatively mild mannered woman from the Harmony Faction. So with magic now readily accessible, and the divisive rhetoric turned down to a simmer, the League of Islands was already a palpably more peaceful place.

THERE WAS JUST ENOUGH room for the marauders to squeeze into the Red Dragon Inn. Azure's dad greeted every one of them with smiles and handshakes.

Before he could pour the first drink, there was a loud crash as the sea-facing window exploded into shards. Every head in the place turned to see someone crawling up through the window.

Dirty and bleeding, Pratt tumbled in and picked himself off the floor, his movements strange and unnatural.

"Did you really think a jail cell could hold me?" His voice boomed, almost godlike.

Pratt began to laugh. The chilling, terrible laugh filled the inn, making every marauder cringe.

"Look what I have brought this time," Pratt said, more in their heads than anything, while pointing out of the broken window.

Wand in hand, Azure took a step toward the window to get a better view. What she saw made her legs weak.

Just left of the Ring, the sky had been ripped open, revealing a black void. The tranquil sunset had been torn apart as if it were nothing more than a painting.

From out of this surreal opening, a creature emerged. Azure's sanity slipped as she watched a mouth-like orifice, with rows of jagged teeth, encircled by a thousand writhing tentacles spill from the tear and into the Undering. The sheer size of the creature was impossible to believe. It made the leviathan look like a guppy.

Azure raised her wand, hand trembling, but what could she possibly do?

A crash from behind her drew Azure's attention. Every head in the place turned as Zoth-Avarex came cannoning through the front door of the inn with all the subtlety of a tsunami. He stopped and slowly raised his arm. Then, with a mischievous grin on his face, he snapped his claws.

Both Pratt and the otherworldly abomination disappeared. The window was fixed, as good as new.

"You asshole!" Azure rushed forward and punched Zoth-Avarex in the face, stinging the shit out of her hand.

"What?" The dragon chuckled. "It was just a harmless little illusion. No need to go hurting your hand over it."

"You scared the shit out of us." Brisa tried to give him an angry look, but couldn't maintain it.

"I'm sorry. I just couldn't help myself. I mean, everyone likes a good prank, right?"

When he got nothing but blank stares, Zoth-Avarex snapped again and everyone had their favorite drink in their hands.

"I know you guys have limited your drinking to once a week, now, but I'm assuming this is your one night by the goofy grin on Blunderbuss's face."

The crew cheered, and, apparently having quickly forgiven him for his horrifying prank, the Marauder King led a toast to Zoth-Avarex.

"To the scurvy dragon by the name of Zoth-Avarex." He held his drink up high. "Drink up, me hearties!"

"Nice," said the dragon, impressed. "You're really starting to pick up the proper pirate lingo."

John held up a piece of parchment. "You can sign up here if you'd like to sing a song tonight."

Several chairs tipped back as many marauders shot to their feet.

Azure took a swig of her dark ale, hand still throbbing, but unable to wipe the smile from her face.

Acknowledgments

To my family, for a lifetime of love and support.

To Jess and Mandy at Shadow Spark Publishing, for taking a chance on me and a book that doesn't fit neatly into any one mold.

To my friend, Jordan Chaney, who's idea about secret teachers was too good not to borrow.

To Sarah Chorn, for helping me find deeper connections and emotions.

To Susan Floyd for making my writing better.

To Thomas Rey, for the wonderful map.

To Andrew Hutchinson, for the fantastic cover art.

To Sara and Lilly from the Fiction Fans Podcast, for their unwavering, enthusiastic support.

To Barbara Seiders and the Wordherders. I don't show up to as many meetings as I would like to, but I'm glad to be a part of the group.

To all of the people who inspired things in this book: The *Monkey Island* franchise, for inspiring so much of the world and wit (and of course, Mr. Threepbrush), John Connelly, who wrote the song *Fiddler's Green*, and *The Pirates of Penzance*, for inspiring the Marauder King.

To the amazing writing community, including fellow SFF authors, book bloggers, podcasters, YouTubers, and everyone else. I feel very lucky to have found you!

If you enjoyed this book, please give it a quick review. Reviews are everything to indie authors, as they help us find new readers. Thank you very much!

krrlockhaven.com Twitter- @Kyles137

About the Author

K.R.R (Kyle Robert Redundant) Lockhaven writes humorous, fun fantasy books with ever-increasing infusions of heart. He lives in Washington State with his wife and two sons. When not writing or raising kids, he works as a firefighter/paramedic.

He can be found on twitter @Kyles137 or on his website, www.krrlockhaven.com

www.ingramcontent.com/pod-product-compliance
Lightning Source LLC
Chambersburg PA
CBHW051540260626
47170CB00003B/1030